HEAVENFIELD

– A DCI RYAN MYSTERY

LJ Ross

Other books by LJ Ross

Holy Island

Sycamore Gap

Angel

High Force

For James, the love of my life.

"It is my belief, Watson, founded upon my experience, that the lowest and vilest alleys of London do not present a more dreadful record of sin than does the smiling and beautiful countryside."

~ Sir Arthur Conan-Doyle

CHAPTER 1

Sunday, 2nd August—St. Oswald's Tide

He expelled the damp air in short, panting breaths and the harsh sound of it echoed around the walls of the church. His eyes darted across the vaulted ceiling above him and he could smell his own sweat, sickly sweet and cloying.

How poetic that he, of all people, should find himself the victim.

The cold point of a gun prodded his right temple and the taste of fear was bitter and strong, like the bile which flooded his throat. His chest shuddered as he fought to stay calm, though he knew that the end must be near.

"I'm not afraid of you!" he shouted desperately, but there was no answering reply, only an angry shove from the metal aimed at his head.

He trained his gaze straight ahead and brought Anna's face to his mind, imagining her beside him.

How he loved her.

How he *wanted* her.

He heard the soft 'click' of a trigger being pulled back, ready to discharge.

"Just *do* it!" he burst out, tears leaking tracks over the lines of his face.

The sound of the gunshot was like a canon being fired in the confined space. Outside, resting birds squawked their disapproval and fluttered into the night, before settling once again into a silence that was almost religious.

* * *

The air was hushed and reverent as a line of men and women made their way up the gentle incline towards the place known as Heavenfield. A little stone church stood eerie and alone atop the hillside, overlooking the rolling landscape of Northumberland. The sun made its final descent into the horizon at its back, casting deep amber rays over the fields while stars began to pop high in the darkening sky above. Nature was the master here and all around her handiwork bloomed; a patchwork blanket of lush green grass, gorse bush and sprouting purple lavender.

The pilgrims held their lanterns aloft, moving like a fat glow-worm through the empty fields. Their feet made little sound as they moved across the mossy floor, trampling the ground where soldiers had fallen centuries earlier. Now, the only sign that a battle had once waged lay in the simple wooden cross which marked the spot.

The pilgrim leader was surprised to find the heavy oak doors standing ajar. It was true that God's house was always open for business but it was unusual for anybody to make the trip to this deserted spot unless they were part of the pilgrimage trail.

With slight misgivings, he led the crowd into the darkened interior. There was no access to electricity or running water here; only pungent gas lamps, which had not been lit. The glow from the pilgrims' lanterns filtered through the gloom and their excited chatter died abruptly. There was a loud shriek and the leader threw out his arms, urging them back towards the door they had just entered.

A man lay sprawled over the altar at the rear of the church, blood and brains spattered across the floor and the wall at his back. In the sudden silence, they could hear the soft *tap tap* of his life force dripping onto the flagstones. Another man stood over the body, one bloodied hand held out in warning, his tall figure silhouetted against the stained glass window at his back by the last light of day.

"Keep your distance!" he barked.

"You've…you've killed him! Don't come any closer!" The pilgrim leader shouted, his voice wobbling. "I'm going to call the police!"

The man frowned, his dark brows pulling together.

"You don't understand—" he said sharply.

"Keep back!" The pilgrim leader repeated, stumbling as people fled the church, their lanterns swaying dangerously as they took the light with them.

Detective Chief Inspector Ryan watched them leave and wondered how long it would be before two of his colleagues turned up in a squad car. At least it saved him the job of calling it in. He mustered a detachment he didn't entirely feel and looked down at the shell of a man who had once been Doctor Mark Bowers, eminent local historian.

Ryan sighed, his breath clouding despite it being summer outside. The plain lime-washed walls were an effective barrier against the sun and, consequently, the room felt like a fridge.

Or a morgue, he amended, with an eye for the dead man.

He crouched to the floor and took a slow survey of his surroundings, eventually rising again dissatisfied. It was nearly impossible to see the details of the room now that the last of the sun had gone and the light from his mobile phone did little to help. He could still make out the lines of the body in front of him and the skin was warm to the touch; in fact, if he didn't know better, he would have said that Bowers had died only moments before. Blood oozed from the bullet-wound at his skull and was only just beginning to coagulate.

Yet, there was no gun and no other person for miles around.

CHAPTER 2

The *Blue Bamboozle* was a popular drinking hole amongst the men and women of the Northumbria Criminal Investigation Department, being located conveniently less than ten minutes from their headquarters in Ponteland, on the upmarket western edge of Newcastle-upon-Tyne. In deference to its middle-class surrounds, the exterior of the formerly dingy little pub had recently been refurbished in shades of cream and sage, to give the impression of a country manor and not a longstanding den of iniquity.

While its main bar shone with polished brass and smelled of new leather, the function room had yet to receive the same treatment and so, for the time being, it remained a homely space with sticky flooring and red velvet seating arranged around small mahogany tables pock-marked with numerous scratches and scars. At the far end of the room, there was a small raised stage where local bands warbled the angst of their generation.

It was not a bedraggled youth who commanded the stage tonight. Her chin resting on her hand, Detective Inspector Denise MacKenzie watched indulgently as her present beau spun the microphone and threw back his ruddy head, crooning to the accompaniment of Neil Diamond on the karaoke machine.

Her brow arched as she watched him jiggle his denim-clad rear, much to the delight of a group of elderly women seated at the front, who were rounding off a pleasant evening of bingo with an unexpected floorshow. Detective Sergeant Frank Phillips executed an interesting hip wriggle and crooked his finger in her direction, topping it off with a lewd wink which was met with ludicrous giggling from the front of the room.

Denise found her lips curving. One of the greatest facets of Phillips' uncomplicated nature was that he didn't take himself too seriously. The music switched to Glenn Campbell and she rolled her eyes, grateful that there were no rhinestone-studded cowboy boots to hand.

A short while later, Phillips exited the stage to riotous applause and with an apologetic wave to his small army of fans, re-joined their table with a smacking kiss for Denise and a thirsty drink of his pint.

"You've missed your vocation," she smiled, her smooth Irish accent drawing out the words like honey. "It's a singer you should be, not a murder detective."

Phillips affected a modest sigh.

"Aye, it's a shame to deprive the masses of this kind of talent."

"It's a very *rare* talent," she agreed, with a chuckle.

Phillips favoured her with a haughty look, but his response was interrupted by the shrill sound of his mobile phone.

"Bugger," he muttered, eyeing the number flashing on the screen, which belonged to the Control Room. "We're off duty."

"Better answer it," she said, polishing off the last of her wine. "It might be important."

* * *

The room was cramped and smelled of stale urine. The breezeblock walls, which had once been painted an industrial beige, were now yellowed with age and covered in suspect stains. There was a single iron bed, drilled into place with deep bolts to the concrete floor, a metal toilet and a basin. The solitary window was of grimy, reinforced Perspex and boasted a spectacular view of the car park. Since one of the newer detective constables—not a usual member of his team—had deposited him in these glamorous surroundings, Ryan had spent the time alternately pacing or standing motionless as he considered the possible ramifications of a prominent chief inspector finding himself on the receiving end of the law.

"Get out of my way, muppet!"

The gruff voice filtering through the cracks in the metal door had never sounded sweeter. Ryan pushed away from the greasy wall of the holding cell and stretched out his long body in time to greet DS Phillips.

The man in question shrugged off the officious young police constable hovering at his side and barged into the room, planting his stocky frame inside the doorway. He cast a keen eye over Ryan and folded his arms.

"Son, you better have a good explanation for why I've been dragged over here."

Ryan stuck his hands in his pockets.

"I hear that you've killed someone." Phillips raised a single bushy eyebrow.

Ryan nodded briefly.

"Apparently."

Phillips huffed out a breath.

"Unless you've finally lost your marbles and offed that bloke who keeps nicking your parking space, it's a load of bollocks."

"Well, to the best of my knowledge, my marbles are all present and accounted for. Bollocks, too."

"Howay then."

They fell into step down the wide, musty corridor. Ryan was surprised to feel genuine relief as he left the cell behind him and wondered whether it was an emotion felt by all of the men and women he had ever slung inside it. There was a raised eyebrow from the duty sergeant at the desk and a few nudges from junior members of staff as he made his way towards the interview suite, but they were outnumbered by a far greater number of friendly slaps on the back. For too many years, this ugly sixties building had been more of a home to him than his apartment gathering dust on Newcastle's Quayside. Only recently had he begun to appreciate the finer things a home could offer, only since his relationship with Anna.

Anna.

"Crap," he muttered aloud.

Phillips grunted and looked across, a question in his beady brown eyes.

"It's Anna," Ryan explained. "I didn't tell her where I was going. I said I was heading out for a drink—with you, actually."

Phillips cast him a look of stern disapproval.

"I didn't think you'd go in for all that cloak and dagger stuff. She's a nice girl—"

"No," Ryan interjected, before Phillips' imagination could run away with him. "Keep your hair on, Frank, it's not what you're thinking."

Phillips softened marginally.

"She'll need to be told," he concluded.

"I know," Ryan snapped, wondering how he could tell his girlfriend that Mark Bowers, the man she thought of as a surrogate father and had looked up to for most of her life, had been found dead in a deserted hilltop church. Added to which, there was the small matter of him having been arrested on suspicion of the bloke's murder.

"You want me to call her?" Phillips offered, but Ryan shook his head.

"I get a phone call, don't I?" He had to laugh. "I'll talk to her after you've finished the inquisition."

Phillips squirmed. Ryan might have been fifteen years younger, but he was a professional superior. And, after all they had been through together, he was like family. That being the case, it made for an awkward interview scenario whichever way you looked at it.

They made a pit stop for watery, vending machine coffee in polystyrene cups and settled themselves into an interview room.

"Look," Phillips cleared his throat. "We've got to do this properly and have an interview, with two detectives. Best to do things by the book, what with everything else…" he trailed off, lamely.

"No problem," Ryan said, but felt the burn of humiliation. Six weeks ago, he had been unceremoniously stripped of his warrant card and suspended from his duties pending investigation, at the order of Detective Chief Superintendent Arthur Gregson. The inquiry was 'ongoing,' so he was told, but so far there had been little progress. He had hoped to make a triumphant return to CID with his name cleared of all blemishes, but instead he seemed to be racking up further charges.

A couple of long minutes later, the door to the interview room opened and Detective Constable Jack Lowerson bounded into the room. His young face broke into a broad smile when he saw Ryan.

"Sir!" He pulled up a chair and the sturdy brown legs scraped against the carpet tile floor as he took a seat next to Phillips. "Good to have you back."

Ryan raised a sardonic eyebrow.

"Jack, I've been arrested on suspicion of murder. I wouldn't bother organising a party just yet."

Lowerson flushed.

"Thanks, though." Ryan relented.

"Right, let's get on with it then," Phillips began in his 'formal' voice, shuffling some papers, turning on the tape recorder and reciting the standard caution. "You understand your rights?"

"Yes, I understand, and no, I don't need a solicitor."

"You sure?"

Ryan huffed out a laugh.

"Thanks for the vote of confidence."

Phillips gave up on the formality and fixed him with a baffled stare.

"I'm thinking of your best interests. You've got to admit, it looks fishy! Bowers found dead as a doornail, no murder weapon anywhere around and you standing over him with bloody hands…"

"When you put it like that, it does sound damning," Ryan had to agree. "The only problem is, I didn't kill him."

"Well we know that!" Lowerson burst out and then, remembering the tape, snapped his lips shut again.

"Why don't I tell you what happened?" Ryan offered, to make life simple. "At approximately four o'clock this afternoon, I received a text message from a number I didn't recognise. You can check my phone to confirm. The message appeared to be from Mark Bowers, telling me that he needed to meet with me urgently this evening, at Heavenfield Church, at nine o'clock sharp. He said there was something that I needed to see. The message went on to say that Anna would be in danger if she or anyone else knew about the meeting, so I shouldn't tell her.

"Obviously, I thought it sounded like a prank, so I tried calling the number to catch this joker out. There was no answer. I tried calling the visitors' centre on Holy Island, where Bowers worked, but there was no answer there either—probably because it's a Sunday. I called the landline number at his home on the island, but it rang out, and those are the only numbers I have for him. You can trace the calls," he said wearily.

"All things considered, I thought I'd better head up there to see him, just in case he was telling the truth. I expected it to be a wild goose chase."

"Then what?"

Ryan lifted a hand and let it fall again.

"I drove up to Heavenfield on time, arriving just before nine. The place was nearly dark and the door was open. I went inside and saw him straight away. He was already dead."

Phillips nodded.

"How could you tell?" This from Lowerson, who was always keen to know the gory details.

"Aside from the hole in his head? He wasn't breathing," Ryan explained, deadpan.

"Ah."

Phillips ran his tongue over his teeth, preparing for a tricky next question.

"So, after you found his body, why didn't you call an ambulance?"

The ghost of a smile played over the strong planes of Ryan's face and he pitied Phillips his task. Nobody liked to ask difficult questions, especially of a friend.

"I didn't get a chance. I was there only minutes before the others."

"What others? Did you see anyone acting suspiciously?"

Ryan shook his head.

"The place was completely deserted when I arrived, although I could see a bunch of people about a quarter of a mile away, at the foot of the hill leading up to the church. They were carrying lanterns," he added. "Must have been the pilgrims who stumbled in about five minutes later."

"Pilgrims?" Phillips queried.

"Every year there's a pilgrimage from Holy Island to Heavenfield, but there's also a sort of 'mini' pilgrimage from Hexham Abbey to Heavenfield Church on the first Sunday in August—that's today—to commemorate Saint Oswald's famous victory. He's credited with re-introducing Christianity in the region after beating a pagan army off."

"Didn't think you kept up with all that," Phillips observed lightly. Ryan was not a religious man, never had been.

"I don't," Ryan agreed. "But I live with a historical expert, remember?"

Phillips grunted his understanding. Anna Taylor had been a civilian consultant the previous Christmas on Holy Island, when ritual murder had intruded into the quiet lives of that island community. She had paid dearly, losing her sister and nearly losing her own life before the killing spree had seen its end. Perhaps the only saving grace had been the resulting unlikely relationship between a quiet historian and a surly murder detective.

"Still don't know what she sees in you," Phillips joked.

"There's no accounting for taste," Ryan replied easily.

Humour faded and Phillips forced himself back to the matters in hand.

"You don't think one of the pilgrims could have sneaked off earlier, killed Bowers, and re-joined the crowd later on?"

Ryan considered the question, but shook his head.

"The area around the church is remote. It's just a few trees and empty fields until you reach the road. I would have seen someone fleeing the scene. Besides, there were no other cars parked nearby—only mine and Bowers'."

Phillips drummed his fingers against the table, clearly flummoxed.

"The body's been transferred to the mortuary and the pathologist has already given it a quick once-over. He hasn't completed the post mortem yet but he's pretty sure Bowers had been dead less than two hours. Factor in transportation time and that gives us a very tight timescale."

"You're saying that Bowers had only recently died when I found him around nine o'clock? I agree with you," Ryan said simply. "I checked for a pulse, which is how I had blood on my hand. The skin was still warm."

The unspoken question was why he had gone against all of his police training and contaminated a crime scene, but neither Phillips nor Lowerson asked, and Ryan did not volunteer anything further.

There was a humming silence around the table until Phillips let out a long breath and spoke again.

"Faulkner's up there with his team now," he referred to the senior Crime Scene Investigator. "He hasn't found a weapon."

"I couldn't see anything beside the body," Ryan said. Then, for good measure he tagged on, "considering that the church is tiny, without a convenient river nearby for me to dispose of a gun, I hardly think I would have hung around if I had killed the man, do you? Besides, give me some credit for being able to plan and execute something with a little more finesse."

Phillips had to admit that was a fair point.

"So, we've got a recently dead man with a gunshot wound but no perpetrator and no gun."

"In a nutshell."

Phillips sucked in a breath, intending to say something pithy, but was cut short by the entrance of another latecomer. Detective Chief Superintendent Gregson strode into the interview room, recited his name and time for the recording and then signalled for the tape to be stopped. Lowerson obliged, noting that the temperature in the room seemed to have fallen by several degrees. Gregson looked every inch the man in charge, from the top of his steel grey head to the tips of his shiny black shoes. He wore his tailored navy suit with panache and carried an air of dignity to match his expensive aftershave.

"Well," he scoffed. "You just can't keep yourself out of trouble, can you?"

When Ryan replied, his voice was frigid.

"I was the first to find a body. Instead of being treated as a material witness to a crime, I have been arrested by one of your over-zealous cronies on suspicion of murder. If you call that 'trouble,' then yes, I would tend to agree with you." He leaned forward slightly, pinning Gregson with a flinty stare. "You'll find it hard to make any charges stick, considering the utter lack of forensic evidence."

Gregson did not answer, but turned to Phillips, who pasted a neutral expression on his face.

"Control Room say a man was found dead in suspicious circumstances at Heavenfield. Have we identified him?"

Phillips nodded.

"Yes, sir, he was identified at the scene. Doctor Mark Bowers," he thumbed through his notebook. "Aged fifty-three, employed by National Heritage as a senior historian and manager of the visitors' centre on Holy Island. You might remember him from that business on the island last Christmas."

Gregson stood very still and said nothing until he could trust his own voice.

"You're sure it's him?"

Phillips frowned slightly, while Ryan watched the exchange with interest.

"Positive, sir."

Gregson recovered himself quickly.

"I want MacKenzie handling it," he commanded, overriding the automatic objection on Phillips' lips. There was little Frank could argue against, in any case. DI Denise MacKenzie was an excellent detective; sharp-witted and fair, with good instincts for sniffing out criminal behaviour. She was a higher-ranking officer, but the fact that she happened to be his girlfriend didn't hurt, either, Phillips thought wickedly.

"MacKenzie will be grand for the job," was all he said.

"And," Gregson purred, "I am sure I can rely on her professionalism. If I so much as get a *whiff* of any protocols being breached, she'll be straight up to my office on disciplinary charges, with you straight after."

Satisfied that his threat had hit the mark, he took another glance at Ryan, who was seated comfortably in an uncomfortable plastic tub chair, one long leg crossed indolently over the other. He looked supremely confident, Gregson thought uneasily, for a man being questioned on suspicion of murder.

What did he know?

Gregson thought back to that night six weeks ago, when he had suspended Ryan. He had felt liberated, happier than he had been in months, perhaps years. He could take charge of his life again and get his house in order without Ryan's constant hawk-like presence watching his every move with distrust. In the early days, he had treated Ryan like a protégé, a man with a talent for the job and instincts that were second to none. He had nurtured him and promoted him accordingly.

That was then.

Now, Ryan had become a serious threat, one that needed to be neutralised by fair means or foul. It should have been a simple matter to trump up some disciplinary charges and have the suspension upgraded to dismissal. Unfortunately, things weren't going to plan and the Chief Constable was threatening to muscle her way into the inquiry, which would make things even more difficult.

For all these troubles, Gregson had just been given the greatest news he could have hoped for.

Mark Bowers was dead, and he was free at long last.

CHAPTER 3

Monday 3rd August

Doctor Anna Taylor looked fragile and forlorn as she perched on the very edge of one of the broken visitors' chairs in the foyer at CID Headquarters. Her dark hair fell in a long wavy curtain over one shoulder and she had thrown on some slim blue jeans and a baggy wool jumper. In her hands, she jiggled car keys while she waited. She had taken a call from Ryan just after ten-thirty in the evening asking her to come and pick him up from the police station; it was now nearly one o'clock in the morning and she had been watching people—mostly drunk—coming and going for the past two hours. At one point, Denise MacKenzie had swung through the main doors but hadn't stopped to chat before hurrying towards lock-up and the duties awaiting her there. Consequently, Anna was no further forward in understanding what had happened to call her out here. All manner of dreadful scenarios played out in her mind.

Finally, the security door buzzed and she jolted out of her seat. She watched as Ryan was escorted out of the secured area, a tall, absurdly good-looking man with a mop of black hair and a curiously unhurried gait, regardless of the circumstance. In his present predicament, it would have been gratifying to see him hurry across to her, to hear some effusive apologies and quick explanations about why she had worried herself sick for, apparently, no good reason. Therefore, she was disinclined to feel sympathetic and she stood up, jabbing a finger at the air in his direction.

"You lied to me."

She might have looked fragile, but looks could be deceptive.

"Wait a minute," Ryan said, holding both hands out in mute appeal.

"Don't tell me to *wait,*" she snarled. "I could write the book on it!"

"Now, just calm down—"

That clinched it.

"*Calm down?* Do you have any idea how long I've been sitting here worrying about you? I didn't know what had happened, you didn't give any details over the phone and nobody has told me a thing," she flicked an accusatory look towards the duty sergeant. "What are you doing here, anyway? I thought you were supposed to be having a drink with Frank but now I find you're happy to lie to me without batting an eyelid. I won't have it—"

"I didn't want to lie," he said quietly, bringing her up short.

"Explain, please."

He cast a glance around the empty foyer and then towards the duty sergeant who was sitting behind his safety glass window wearing a studiously disinterested expression as he thumbed through a glossy magazine.

"Can't we get out of here?"

She said nothing, but continued to regard him with stormy eyes. He ran an agitated hand over the back of his neck then shoved both hands in the pockets of his jeans.

"Fine. You want to do this here, that's fine." He met her eyes, cool grey clashing with warm brown. "I found Mark Bowers dead up at Heavenfield Church. A couple of rookie PCs joined me shortly afterwards and assumed I must have killed him. I didn't."

The hard lines of anger fell from Anna's face, leaving it slack and strangely empty of emotion. Mark was dead? No, it was not possible. There must have been some mistake.

"It can't have been Mark," she said slowly.

Ryan often had the unenviable task of imparting bad news to the families of the dead. It was the worst part of the job: worse than picking over the remains of a body like a scavenger or feigning detachment at the mortuary. The abject grief of those who still lived, and must learn to live with their loss, was always harder to bear.

"I'm sorry," he murmured, kicking himself for blurting out the awful news without a basic level of tact. He led her back towards a chair. Pliant and shocked, she followed him.

"I don't understand," she shook her head.

"He sent me a text," Ryan explained. "It said explicitly that if I told you that we were meeting, you would be in danger. I had to make a judgement call, but I'm sorry that I couldn't be open with you."

"He—how?"

Ryan took one of her cold hands and held it between his own, hoping to warm it.

"He was shot."

She thought of Mark, the man who had been more of a father to her than her own flesh and blood. Now, they were both dead and she had no family left. The sense of loss was so acute, so keen, that it stole her breath away. Memories flooded in, of weekends spent on the island digging up treasures from the past, of his tanned hands with their calloused fingertips, of his soft blue eyes looking on with pride at graduation ceremonies. He had been to every one.

She swiped at tears with the cuff of her jumper in the absence of anything better, and then turned back to the man who sat quietly beside her waiting for the storm to pass.

"You said that they think it was *you?* They can't be serious."

Even in the throes of grief she offered her support, without a trace of doubt that he could ever have killed in cold blood. It was humbling. Ryan squeezed her fingers and said simply, "thank you."

Anna mustered a wry smile.

"You may be many things," she observed. "But a murderer isn't one of them."

* * *

It had taken the combined forces of MacKenzie, Phillips and Lowerson to convince their unyielding superintendent that Ryan should be released without charge, rather than suffering a chilly night in the cells. Tempting though it had been to insist that Ryan remain there, Gregson was a pragmatic man and had eventually acknowledged that he presented no flight risk. However, he refused to dismiss Ryan as a suspect until a thorough forensic investigation had been completed and he could be unequivocally ruled out. He had taken pains to point out that Bowers had been a regular feature in Ryan's life thanks to his connection with Anna Taylor, which presented all manner of questions as to motive. Had Ryan felt threatened by Bowers' longstanding relationship with Anna? Was there some hitherto undiscovered vendetta? Furthermore, Ryan's story about having received a text from the dead man sounded somewhat far-fetched. He had rounded off his speech by saying that, unless evidence could be brought to light, Ryan remained the prime suspect in his eyes and he didn't give a damn that he was one of their own.

On that note, Gregson had swept out of the incident room in the direction of his own office, intending to place a call to the Chief Constable weighted heavily in favour of Ryan's guilt.

The three who remained loyal released Ryan into Anna's care with apologetic eyes, reminding him that he should return to CID Headquarters to answer further questions if required.

* * *

Later that morning, while forensic specialists combed through the debris on the floor of Heavenfield Church and the pathologist lifted what was left of Mark Bowers' brain out of his broken skull, Ryan paced the walls of Anna's tiny cottage.

"Why don't you go out for a walk?" she suggested, putting the finishing touches to her make-up in an attempt to conceal the ravages of a broken night's sleep. She had wept for her friend until morning had finally broken, washing away the tears with its bright reminder that life must go on; she could not help Mark by hiding under the covers, wallowing in her grief.

Apparently, Ryan agreed with her.

"I should be out there doing something, not sitting around here getting fat," he muttered irritably, coming to a brief standstill in front of one of the pretty picture windows overlooking the river.

Glancing at his reflection in the mirror above the dresser, she knew that he wasn't appreciating the view. Outside, the sun shone down on the city of Durham, glittering diamond-bright over the water, but Ryan's eyes were stony and unseeing, his mouth flat and unsmiling.

"It won't help to prowl around the house," she said.

"I can't just sit around doing nothing," he ground out. "I need an occupation, for God's sake."

Anna cocked her head at him.

"I don't think self-pity suits you."

He spun around, eyes blazing.

"I'm telling you they've cut me out; *Gregson* has cut me out."

Anna shrugged a shoulder.

"Yes, he has, and wouldn't he be delighted to see how much it's affecting you?" She paused, waiting for her words to sink in. "You need to find another way to fight him."

Ryan felt his throat go dry. Damn it, she was right.

"Pretty smart, aren't you?"

Anna turned back to the mirror.

"I've heard it said."

"Mm hmm," he murmured, moving away from the window to stand behind her, tugging her back against his body until the top of her head tucked snugly beneath his chin. "I can think of other ways to fill my time."

"Oh?" She made a show of checking her mascara. "Are you planning to take up a hobby?"

She felt the low chuckle rumble through his chest and watched his dark head in the mirror as it lowered to nuzzle her neck. Her mascara wand paused mid-air while her head fell to one side, to allow him better access.

Just for this moment, she savoured the present and the simple joy of being alive.

CHAPTER 4

Detective Chief Superintendent Arthur Gregson checked his watch again and fidgeted beside the display of curtains in the home furnishings department of Fenwicks, the famous local department store in the centre of Newcastle-upon-Tyne. Discreet lighting illuminated the handiwork and he fingered some fabric, picked up a few picture frames and sniffed at scented candles for a further five minutes while he waited with resentful impatience for the other half of his meeting to arrive.

Finally, he saw her weave through the stands of expensive vases and display bowls, looking very much at home beside the glinting china and polished glass. Professor Jane Freeman was, as always, dressed impeccably in tailored trousers and a cream silk shirt. Blonde, carefully highlighted hair framed her face in an attractive halo and she looked much younger than her forty-three years.

She came to a standstill beside him and her glacier blue eyes swept over his greying figure with ill-concealed contempt. Her lip curled at the display of roman blinds and she let out a quiet laugh.

"Thinking of redecorating, Arthur?"

Gregson turned a slow shade of red, as much in anger as embarrassment at his choice of meeting place.

"Nobody is likely to recognise us here," he said, defensively.

Freeman spared a smile for the hovering sales assistant but shook her elegant head to ward off any assistance.

"We're just browsing," she explained in friendly tones, which died on her lips when she turned back to Gregson. He was starting to crumble, she thought idly. Sweat pearled on his pallid skin and the spotlighting overhead made him look old, highlighting the deep wrinkles on his forehead and the crow's feet beside his eyes.

He scanned the room nervously.

"Spit it out, Arthur," she kept her voice low, but it cracked against him like a whip. "You've brought me here, now tell me what's bothering you. Getting cold feet? It's a little late for that."

"Cold feet? No, I wanted to thank you."

Freeman's face remained impassive and she waited for him to elaborate.

"I suspected…I thought you would do something. But I didn't know for sure. I wanted you to know you have my full support."

Freeman said nothing and moved away to look at another display, not bothering to check that he was following. Of course he would follow. With a subtle glance, she made sure there were no CCTV cameras to capture their discussion.

"I take it Bowers has been found," she said carefully. She was always a careful woman.

"Yesterday evening," Gregson affirmed. "Ryan found him."

That brought a smile to Freeman's painted lips and, to the casual observer, her face was transformed suddenly into something beautiful.

"Did he, indeed?" She laughed huskily. "I never knew he had such a sense of humour."

"Bowers? You think that he told Ryan about us—?"

Freeman shrugged her slim shoulders in a gesture of extreme indifference.

"What does it matter, now? I presume you have Ryan in custody, as your prime suspect."

It was a statement, not a question.

"I had to release him. We didn't have enough to hold him."

Neither her stance nor her eyes wavered from their cool inspection of his face.

"That's disappointing, Arthur," was all she said.

"I've made my position clear," he hurried on. "I've spoken to the Chief Constable and to the other members of the disciplinary committee. If he isn't charged with murder, he'll be dismissed from his post. I'm sure of it."

"Good. That's good," she murmured, running her fingers over a china bowl in the shape of a conch. "I can rely on you to ensure that things progress as we discussed?"

Gregson swallowed a sudden panic. In his haste to celebrate the removal of one threat, had he overlooked the creation of an even greater one?

Too late to think about that now.

"I'll do what I can."

Freeman fixed him with another unblinking stare.

"You will do whatever is *necessary*. You've been given a great deal of latitude in recent times, considering your complete ineptitude," she didn't bother to mince her words.

He nodded dumbly.

"The Circle needs a new Priest," she continued, her eyes glittering. "This time, we will have a Priestess. I'll see you tonight, Arthur."

Gregson watched her turn away from him. He continued to watch until the top of her shiny head disappeared on the escalator to the ground floor and then he sank for a moment into one of the display chairs, releasing the pent-up air in his lungs in one long, shaky breath.

* * *

DI Denise MacKenzie stood on the threshold of St. Oswald's Church at Heavenfield watching the dust motes dancing on the air. Sunlight beamed through the windows and there was a light breeze from the fields outside which freshened the dank smell of the evening before. It would have been a prosaic, unthreatening scene inside the little church on the hill, were it not for the presence of Faulkner's team of CSIs in their white paper suits to remind them that a man had died there only hours before.

Beside her, DC Lowerson stood poised and ready to serve as acting sergeant. Phillips had been deemed 'too close' to the investigation and was not listed as part of its task force in case he should bias the outcome, whatever that might be. MacKenzie knew that she, too, had been on the borderline. But, the regulations required a person of sufficient rank to act as Senior Investigating Officer in a murder investigation. If Gregson vetoed every man and woman in CID on the basis of their friendship or respect for DCI Ryan, there would be very few options left to choose from.

So, for now, MacKenzie remained in charge of proceedings.

"Faulkner?"

He looked up from where he had been swabbing an area around the altar and raised a nitrile-gloved hand in greeting, gesturing that it was safe to enter in their plastic-covered shoes.

MacKenzie and Lowerson walked slowly along the main aisle of the church, past the rows of plain wooden pews, their eyes tracking the details of the room. She had lost count of the times she had seen Ryan silently observing a crime scene, eyes sharp, his senses consciously heightened as he committed it to memory and she followed his example.

The church itself was a boxy piece of nineteenth century architecture partly obscured by a few trees and a small boundary wall. It was certainly not the kind of ancient masterpiece one might have expected to find in an area famed for its historic buildings. Inside, there were no fancy touches. Spirituality without artifice, MacKenzie thought, as she noted the basic pews and functional font, the cork board displaying everyday, run-of-the-mill notices for those who happened to visit. She saw a glossy leaflet advertising the annual pilgrimage to the spot and wondered if their intake would be lower or higher next year, after this year's excitement. That would be an interesting observation on human nature.

"Every detail, Jack," she murmured to Lowerson, who stood a few inches behind her right shoulder. "Let's try to get a feel for the place. You never know what might be important."

"Yes, sir," he replied, then corrected himself hastily. "Ma'am."

MacKenzie smiled inwardly. There weren't many senior female detectives in Northumbria CID, certainly not under Gregson's leadership, but times were changing. She thought briefly of her progression, which she owed largely to Ryan having noted her abilities during several early cases. Unlike some of the other inspectors who belonged to an earlier generation of middle-aged men who enjoyed bawdy humour and cups of tea made by their female colleagues, Ryan had seen past her face and figure to the brain beneath. He made sure that she had the experience to support an application for promotion and had given her the confidence to reach for it. She remembered asking him why he had bothered.

"I don't give a damn what you look like, so long as you do a good job."

She smiled at the memory.

"Hello Denise," Faulkner's suit rustled as he moved from his crouched position. "Jack, good to see you fit and well again."

"Thanks," Lowerson replied automatically, but pushed the memories of weeks spent in hospital to the back of his mind. "What can you tell us?"

Faulkner moved his mask to one side and scratched an itch on the side of his unremarkable face. Tufts of mid-brown hair sprung out at the edge of his paper cap and his glasses stayed on his nose with the help of a long elastic band wrapped around his ears and the back of his head. MacKenzie wondered why he didn't try contact lenses.

"Do you want the good news or the bad news?"

"I'll take the good news," she replied, with a sinking heart.

"Well, the church is small, which means that there's less ground to cover. We're making good progress," he waved a hand vaguely in the direction of his staff, who worked painstakingly to cover every inch of ground. "It'll take a while longer to go over the pathway outside and the track from here to the road, not to mention Bowers' car, his house and all that."

"And the bad news?"

"We've got nothing," Faulkner replied, succinctly. "I should say, we've got nothing that won't turn out to be DNA belonging to Joe Bloggs who popped in to say a prayer and sneezed beside the altar. There are a few old hair samples and clothing fibres strewn across the pews and dug into the cracks in the stonework, over the floor…you name it. Separating them and distinguishing old from new will take days if not weeks, and that's just for starters. In the immediate vicinity we've got fairly large scale blood loss, but that'll be Bowers' blood or I'll eat my paper hat."

"Anything else around the body?"

Faulkner huffed out a breath and his myopic eyes were filled with regret.

"One or two clothing fibres found on Bowers," he said. "Looks like dark grey or black wool."

MacKenzie took his meaning straight away. The dead man had been wearing a thin raincoat over cream chinos and a polo shirt, whereas DCI Ryan had entered the holding cells wearing a thin grey jumper and jeans.

"Surely, that's to be expected," she said, a bit desperately. "Ryan found the body and took the man's pulse. A bit of wool might have come off as he leaned across in the dark, don't you think?"

Faulkner pulled a face.

"No question that we both want that to be the case. There isn't a murdering bone in Ryan's body, even if he is an irritable sod most of the time," Faulkner surprised himself by saying. "But the fact of the matter is, I have to record what was found. How that's interpreted is up to others to decide."

MacKenzie nodded. She wouldn't ask him to betray his integrity by leaving it off the inventory, just as she wouldn't ask it of herself.

"Alright, anything else found roundabouts?" she asked hopefully.

"That's a little odd," Faulkner reflected. "The place was practically spotless—and I mean spotless—except for two things. An empty crisp packet, which we found near the entrance, and half of a broken ice lolly stick."

"The little wooden ones? Where did you find it?" Lowerson piped up.

"It was lying a few metres away from the altar, in the middle of the floor over there," Faulkner pointed to the relevant yellow marker.

"Only half the stick? Where was the other half?"

"Who knows?" Faulkner shrugged inside his overalls. "For all we know, it could be weeks or months old. We swabbed the area and there was no sugary residue to indicate that the corresponding lolly had melted away beside it. The stick looks old and it's bone dry, but we've sent it in for analysis along with the crisp packet and the fibres."

"OK, I guess that's all we can do for now," MacKenzie agreed. "What about the weapon?"

"Um, well. We recovered a lead ball from the floor beside the wall on the eastern side," Faulkner pointed to his left, where a scattering of yellow markers showed the estimated trajectory of the little round ball. It had passed through Bowers' skull, flown for a little way until it ricocheted off the wall a few metres behind him and then fallen to the floor. An inanimate object briefly animated to kill a man.

"Lead ball? You mean a bullet?"

Faulkner shook his scruffy head.

"No, it looks much older than a modern bullet. It's just a lead ball, no metal casing or anything like that."

"We're looking for an older weapon, then?"

"I would say so."

"Alright," MacKenzie murmured, tracing the path of the leaden ball from the altar to the wall directly behind where Bowers' head had lain.

"We found traces of fine black powder covering the altar and the floor around it. There was some on Bowers before they moved him," Faulkner continued. "That says to me that our perp fired a single shot into Bowers' head at close range and a bit of the powder was discharged along with the lead ball. I've sent the samples over to ballistics—"

"Put a rush on it," MacKenzie interjected.

Faulkner nodded his approval and then cleared his throat.

"Already done, Mac. Hope you don't mind, I thought you'd approve the resources."

"I will. Carry on, Tom."

"Well, it doesn't necessarily help Mark Bowers right now, but it gives me a great deal of pleasure to point out that there is no way this came from a Glock, or any modern service revolver."

Lowerson asked the necessary question.

"Glock?"

"Glock 17," MacKenzie answered shortly. "It's the semi-automatic pistol of choice for Authorised Firearms Officers."

"Ryan's authorised," Lowerson said. "And I'm guessing he has a Glock 17."

"Not any more he doesn't," MacKenzie corrected him. "It was confiscated when he was suspended from duty. In the circumstances, that's a very good thing."

"It certainly wouldn't have helped his case," Faulkner agreed. "But, as I say, we're looking at something much older, maybe even an antique piece since we've found traces of powder. The lead ball was about yea big."

He used thumb and forefinger to sketch out the size.

"Much larger than the usual," MacKenzie agreed. "Looks like it should belong to a rifle, except that wouldn't match the injuries."

Faulkner shook his head.

"There would have been nothing left of his head, if a rifle had been used at close range. No," he shook his head again. "You're looking for some kind of pistol, but you'll have to wait until ballistics come back with their report because this is way out of my league."

They stepped outside into the morning light and allowed themselves a moment to settle their nerves. The church was just a building, but the dark red stains sullying its walls were a poignant reminder that they hadn't driven out into Hadrian's Wall country to appreciate the scenery. Slowly, they walked around to the back of the church, getting the lay of the land.

"Couldn't have been suicide, then," Lowerson broke the silence, tucking his hands into the pockets of his pristine, tailored grey suit. "If the weapon is missing, I mean."

MacKenzie stopped to gaze over the undulating hills towards the north and west, enjoying the feel of the breeze ruffling her hair and cooling her skin. The view was panoramic, a sweeping vista towards the Scottish borders. A group of inquisitive sheep congregated on the edge of the graveyard, as if they knew it would be sacrilegious to venture further, then scattered as the two detectives continued their tour of the church grounds.

"It seems that way, at first glance," MacKenzie answered. "But a weapon is a commodity, Jack. Who's to say that an unknown person didn't stumble upon Bowers a few minutes before Ryan entered? He or she could have pocketed the gun, thinking they could hock it later on for a bit of cash in hand, especially if Faulkner's right and it was an antique weapon. On the plus side, antique weaponry tends to leave a decent paper trail."

"I hadn't thought of that," Lowerson admitted.

"Not everybody is as upstanding as you, boyo," she smiled over at him. The sunlight lit up her hair so that it shone a blazing red around her face. It was so tranquil here, they might have been the only two people around. Just them and the unprepossessing church which looked as if God himself had dropped it accidentally in this incongruous spot.

Lowerson blushed, feeling young and ridiculous.

"We'll need to speak to the pathologist," MacKenzie was saying. "He'll be able to tell us whether there was any residue on Bowers' hands that might indicate that he discharged a weapon himself. But first, let's track down the caretaker and see what he can tell us."

With a final look out across the hills, she turned and headed down the incline towards the main road.

CHAPTER 5

"We shouldn't be here."

It was a rare thing for DCI Ryan to feel uncomfortable. For the most part, he was a man unmoved by the opinions of society, preferring to follow his own path in all things. Right now, he felt distinctly uncomfortable.

In fact, he felt naughty.

"We definitely shouldn't be here," he repeated. "I'm going expressly against every regulation there is."

"Oh, don't be such a scaredy-cat."

Rendered momentarily speechless by a description he hadn't heard since prep school, he found himself following Anna's lead into the well-tended stone cottage.

Inside, they were met with a musty silence and overtones of aromatic spice, suggestive of wax polish or potpourri. The hallway was dark and covered in framed photographs, cataloguing the life of a man who liked to remember the past. There were images of Mark Bowers as he had been in life, decked out in his ubiquitous chinos and shirt against backdrops of castles and archaeological excavations. Ryan peered closely at the pictures to try to gauge the man's character from what he had chosen to immortalise in print, but all they could tell him was that Bowers had been passionate about his work. Every picture showcased a new excavation site, arranged chronologically, by the looks of it. The oldest print was positioned on one side of the front door and showed a fresh-faced Bowers standing amid a group of university students, perhaps from his history days at Oxford. The newest wrapped all the way around the hallway to the other side of the front door and showed a much older Bowers posing in front of Bamburgh Castle, beside a small group of people Ryan presumed to be members of his excavation team.

Ryan scrutinized the people in the photographs, committing faces to memory on the off chance that one of these smiling academics had taken it upon themselves to put a bullet in their friend's brain.

Anna disappeared into the first room on the left, which she knew to be the epicentre of Bowers' home. His study was exactly as she remembered it: floor to ceiling bookshelves crammed full of books, many of them old and cracked with age. This had been a working library, she recalled, for a man who read every volume and didn't care for books that hadn't earned their place on the shelf.

"It looks just the same," she murmured.

"It's been less than twenty-four hours," Ryan replied from the doorway, his voice unaccountably loud.

"I know, but..." she trailed off. "I don't know. I expected it to feel different, somehow. Empty, maybe. Instead, it feels like he could walk through the door at any moment."

Ryan heard tears clogging her throat, so he brought her sharply back to the present.

"He may not walk in, but Faulkner and his team might. Let's get moving, we're on borrowed time, as it is."

"I just want to see if there's anything which might help," Anna said, obstinately. "You didn't have to come."

"Oh, yeah right. I'd just sit at home with a cuppa and a digestive while you sneak around here looking for clues, no doubt getting yourself arrested for perverting the course of justice."

"There's no need to be facetious." She didn't bother to point out that, of the two of them, he was the only one who had been arrested lately. There was a time and a place for everything and she doubted that he was ready to find humour in his situation.

Ryan dipped his head back into the hallway to listen for the sound of any imminent arrivals.

"Let's save the chitchat for later," he muttered. "Take a look around but don't touch anything."

Anna glanced at the grandfather clock in the corner of the room, which ticked methodically.

Ten-forty. Definitely time to get moving.

"We're looking for connections," Ryan said, running his eye over the books and smiling slightly at the complete works of Conan-

Doyle. They had shared a love of detective fiction, he thought with a brief smile, which froze on his lips as he noticed a small, pocket-sized volume of Milton's *Paradise Lost* propped against one of the shelves.

Connections, he had said, and here was a connection.

His fingers itched to pull the book from the shelf and rifle through its pages, to look for handwritten footnotes or hidden pockets. Good sense prevailed and he kept his hands to himself while his mind raced. On shelves stuffed with classics, it was not unusual to find Milton amongst their number, was it? It was important to remain logical. And yet, there had been a volume on the shelves of a murderer's home six weeks ago, and scribbled quotes amongst the notes kept on each woman he had killed. Ryan had read *Paradise Lost* cover to cover in his attempt to understand what had motivated Doctor Patrick Donovan to kill. Had his warped mind led him to believe that Milton's words gave him carte blanche to take lives? There was plenty of fodder in that evocative piece of poetry to inspire a madman to put his thoughts into action.

Very slowly, Ryan took a pair of nitrile gloves from the pocket of his jacket and drew them on. Logic had its place, he thought, but it was a foolish man who ignored his instinct.

Gently, he removed the book from its shelf and it came away easily. He dropped it into a transparent evidence bag, then into his coat pocket where he felt the guilty weight of it pressing against him.

Oblivious to the theft, Anna made a beeline for the large walnut desk beside the window and peered at the paperwork strewn across it, angling herself awkwardly so as not to disturb anything. Ryan turned a full circle in the room. He found himself facing a decorative fireplace cluttered with knick-knacks, overshadowed by a large, ornate sword hanging above it. The thin blade was highly polished and still looked sharp, which was unusual for a display piece. The hilt was finely welded with what appeared to be a blend of gold and silver, twisted to look like flames licking along the handle. Leaning closer, Ryan read a small inscription:

For Dr Mark Bowers, with grateful thanks for his dedication to the history of Northumberland, from his friends at National Heritage. February 2012.

"Ryan!" Anna broke his reverie and he spun around, instantly alert. "I think I heard somebody at the front door!"

Galvanised, they made for the back of the cottage, which led to a small garden and then onto a narrow street where Anna had parked her car out of sight from the main road.

The back door clicked softly shut behind them.

"I think we got away with it," Anna said, a bit breathlessly, as they made for the creaking gate at the end of the garden.

"Don't speak too soon," he returned.

Following the direction of his gaze, she came to a shuddering standstill. Leaning idly against the side of Anna's car stood DS Frank Phillips, puffing on an e-cigarette while he waited for them to join him.

"Well, fancy meeting you here," he boomed, tucking the white stick back into his breast pocket. "You folks lost your way?"

"Phillips, listen—"

"Son," Phillips held up a hand in warning. "Don't insult my intelligence. Do I have 'MUG' written on my forehead?" He jerked a thumb at the forehead in question, which was deeply grooved.

"Alright, I won't," Ryan agreed, deciding to brazen it out.

"So," Phillips took his time rubbing the side of his jaw. "I s'pose I don't need to tell you how stupid that was?"

Anna and Ryan exchanged a glance but didn't contradict him.

"With Gregson ready and waiting to pounce on any little infraction, you decide to break into a dead man's home—"

"I had a key," Anna said, weakly, but subsided at one look of patriarchal disapproval.

"—to break into his home," Phillips continued, "and contaminate the scene."

"I—" Anna opened her mouth again and then thought better of it.

"Gregson will have a field day with this," Phillips concluded.

Ryan remained silent, ready to accept Phillips' judgment, whatever it might be. He deserved to be reported for blind idiocy, if nothing else. Then, a thought struck him.

"How did you know we'd be here?"

Phillips favoured him with a knowing look.

"It's my sixth sense as a policeman, that's what it is."

"Sixth sense, my arse," Ryan replied. "You were planning to do the same thing yourself."

Phillips pursed his lips and had the grace to look abashed.

"You—"

"Language, lad, think of your language in front of the lady," Phillips said swiftly.

"You sly old fox," Anna breathed.

Phillips barked out a laugh and then grew serious, his voice lowering to a stage whisper. "A little birdie tells me that Faulkner's lot are still going over the church and will take the rest of the morning, at least."

"Does this little birdie have red hair?"

Phillips tapped the side of his bulbous nose.

"She's got Lowerson with her and he's a good lad, but Gregson is breathing down her neck, watching everything she does."

"He's involved."

There was a short silence following Ryan's bald statement. There was an unspoken taboo discouraging overt accusations against your colleagues, but they were long past feeling any loyalty towards their superintendent.

"Aye, I know it," Phillips cleared a sudden constriction in his throat and wished he could spit it out. "All these years—"

"Mean nothing, if he's dirty," Ryan finished flatly.

Phillips crossed his arms across his chest and clasped his elbows.

"Got to do this right," he said. "We're already taking too many risks."

"Agreed," Ryan let out a breath and looked up and down the street, partly to ensure there were no idle pedestrians to overhear them and partly to give himself a moment to think.

"The disciplinary hearing has been brought forward," he said. "If Gregson gets his wish and I'm out, then it'll be up to you, Frank, along with MacKenzie and Lowerson."

"It won't happen," Phillips said quickly. "The brass would have to be out of their minds to let you go."

"We have to plan for every eventuality," Ryan kept his voice level, while the thought of being dismissed from the work he loved and that he had been born to do, burned a hole in his heart.

"Who'll be chairing the disciplinary hearing?"

Anna's calm voice broke through the tension and they were all grateful for it.

"I made some demands myself," Ryan admitted. "I've requested that the Chief Constable chairs the hearing. She's a fair woman."

"Gregson's been yapping at her heels," Phillips warned. "Trying to win her over. Lost count of the amount of dinners, phone calls and whatnot."

"I expected that."

"All the same, he's got the gift of the gab, that one."

"Then, we'll have to see how the cards fall," Ryan said, with finality. "I can have a representative with me if I want one, probably some snivelling union bloke who spends two hours out of every day being a policeman and the other seven writing policies. I'm better off going in alone."

"I can come."

Ryan looked over at Anna, into her steady brown eyes. He was caught off guard by the offer; shocked to need another person's help when he had managed for so long without it.

"I—you don't have to."

"If you want me there, I'll be there."

Phillips looked on with approval. She might have looked like a gust of wind could carry her off, but underneath all that soft hair and soft skin, there was a will of iron.

"That's a good idea," he fixed Ryan with a beady stare. "It'd do you good to have somebody beside you, to keep things even. I'd be there myself, except—"

"I know. You're required to give a statement. Look, I don't need anyone to hold my hand," Ryan began belligerently, then stopped himself and tried a more moderate tone.

"Thanks, Anna, that'd be great."

Before he could change his mind, Phillips clapped his hands together.

"Right! Now that's sorted, let's get back to it. Did you touch anything while you were in there?" He butted his chin in the direction of Bowers' cottage.

"We were careful," Ryan kept his voice low. "But if Faulkner finds anything, we were here for dinner the other night. That should cover any prints, or whatever."

Phillips nodded.

"I reckon I'll leave you two to finish the job, then. I'll tap on the door if you need to get moving. We can spare half an hour, then we'd better make like a tree."

Ryan pulled a face.

"Make like a *what?*"

Phillips regarded Ryan with deep pity.

"Your ignorance of classic filmmaking never ceases to amaze me."

CHAPTER 6

Keith Thorbridge was a meticulous man in his early sixties. After a dubious background in petty crime and peddling drugs during his formative years, he had subsequently seen the light, turned his back on the past and devoted himself to a life of regular worship and the serious business of keeping the church of St. Oswald's clean and tidy.

Indeed, as the years passed, he began to feel that the little church at Heavenfield was more home to him than the poky ex-miner's cottage he rented in Wall, which was the closest village and had been named unimaginatively after the Roman wall which cut through the fields nearby, all the way from the North Sea to Cumbria.

Seven days a week, Keith parked his ancient Volkswagen by the side of the Military Road and lumbered a hundred yards up the hill to spend a few hours polishing the stained glass, scrubbing the floors and waxing the wooden pews. The diocese of Hexham only paid him for one morning per week, but he didn't mind working the rest of the time for free. It was the least he could do, to repay the deity who had spared him from an early grave, considering the amount of ale he had been in the habit of drinking.

He missed the taste of it; the wonderful, bitter, foul-smelling taste of it warming his belly and numbing his senses.

Clean and tidy, he would say to himself, forcing his weak mind away from temptation. *Clean and tidy.*

DI MacKenzie found him muttering while he tended the tiny patch of garden at the front of his cottage, greying shirtsleeves rolled up against the midday sun which beat down upon the perfect bald circle on top of his head.

"Mr Thorbridge?"

Keith surveyed the glamorous woman with bright red hair. A young man stood beside her, his face cleanly shaven and his hair gelled, reminding him of one of those limp-wristed posers who worked down at the estate agents in the village.

"Aye," he replied sourly. "What're y'after?"

MacKenzie pulled out her warrant card and made the introductions.

"DI MacKenzie and DC Lowerson, from Northumbria CID," she said. "We're sorry to disturb you, Mr Thorbridge, but we need to ask you some questions concerning a death at Heavenfield Church."

Keith had already heard about the business up at the church. Nothing happened at Heavenfield without him knowing about it.

He grunted and dug his spade into the soil he had freshly turned.

"A man was found dead up there, late last night," MacKenzie expanded.

"Aye," he said again.

"Can you tell us when you were last at the church?"

"Saturday night."

"I see," Denise tried a friendly smile, which usually had the desired effect of softening up a male witness, but seemed to be having little impact. *Tough nut,* she thought. "Do you remember what time you arrived and what time you left?"

"I go up at five, come back at ten."

Five hours? MacKenzie wondered how much cleaning could be accomplished in the tiny church in that time and concluded that it would be quite a lot.

"In the morning?"

"Evening," he answered shortly.

"Do you go every Saturday?"

Realising that conversation was unavoidable, Thorbridge set the spade to one side and tucked his thumbs into the belt loops of his muddy trousers.

"Weekdays, I go up at seven in the morn', come back at eleven. Saturdays I go at night, so as the church will be ready for a Sunday service next day."

"I see," MacKenzie nodded, but thought of her brief research on the journey here. She tapped the tip of her biro against the small notepad she held. "I understood that there aren't many regular services at the church."

"Aye, but you never know when folk might visit," he replied, aggressively. "Might not get the same crowd as some, but we still have special services, weddings and that."

"So, you like to keep the place spick and span just in case," MacKenzie said, in friendly tones.

He nodded, just once, and calmed down.

"Getting back to Saturday night, then, can you tell me whether you noticed anything unusual?"

"The place was the same as it always is."

MacKenzie pursed her lips.

"Were you alone, Mr Thorbridge?"

"Aye," he nodded. "Get a rare few people up at that hour."

"I understand that you're only contracted to work on a Monday morning," she prodded. "What motivates you to work the extra hours, Keith?"

His mouth flattened into a cat's arse of lines, the price he paid for a forty-year smoking habit. Small price, considering.

"*Gratitude,* that's what." He tugged at his ear and shuffled his feet a bit, unsure of how to express himself. "I had nowt before the church gave me a chance. Got me off the booze, gave me something to do with my hands." He held both hands up, gnarled with age and toil.

"You know what I used to be," he said simply, correctly assuming that they had done a standard run on his background and had seen the list of convictions for possession, drunk and disorderly behaviour and theft. "That's behind me now. Mayn't seem like much to you, but looking after the church, looking after this garden, it keeps me straight."

"I understand," MacKenzie said quietly. "You care about your work."

He nodded again.

"I'll bet nobody knows that church as well as you," she continued, conspiratorially.

"Could say that," he was softening, just a bit.

"How did you leave the place?"

"Sparkling," he said with pride.

"I'm sure. Do you think people might have wandered around it sometime on Sunday? Only, some of our team found a bit of debris on the floor. A bit of a lolly stick and an empty crisp packet."

Thorbridge bristled and shuffled his feet again, this time in irritation.

"There's a bin right outside," he said angrily. "Don't know why folk can't just put their rubbish in there. Doesn't take a bloody genius, does it?"

Lowerson stifled a laugh but recovered himself after one telling look from his superior.

"I'm telling you, the place was clean when I left it. Didn't know there was any service planned for Sunday morning, but the pilgrims were up there on Sunday night, like every year."

"You didn't choose to join them?"

Thorbridge seemed to withdraw, suddenly, his face taking on a shuttered expression.

"No, I didn't."

* * *

Back inside MacKenzie's Fiesta with the air conditioning blasting, Lowerson turned to her.

"What did you make of him?"

"Dedicated, reclusive…weird," she admitted. "But he seems adamant that there was no rubbish when he left the place on Saturday night. There could have been visitors during the day on Sunday, but the place isn't exactly a revolving door."

"Maybe Thorbridge isn't telling us everything."

"Quite possibly."

There was a slight pause.

"Why do we always get the dodgy old blokes?" Lowerson complained. "I keep hoping for a young, female killer who left behind a modelling career for a life of crime. Naturally, she would have been forced to kill under extreme duress."

"Oh, really?" Amused, MacKenzie slanted him a look. "And what if she decided to make you her next victim?"

Lowerson made a sound a bit like a raspberry and flashed his best smile.

"One look at this angelic face and she'd change her ways."

* * *

The three conspirators left Bowers' cottage as silently as they had arrived and did not choose to linger, preferring to quit the island before attracting any unwanted attention. The few hundred people residing on Holy Island had been rocked to the core, their peaceful solitude disturbed only months before by two killers who had lived amongst them. Anna had grown up on the island and was moved each time she visited by its atmospheric beauty, but could not bring herself to feel at home. Too much had happened, too many heartaches prevented her from enjoying the harmony of wind and sea. Yet, as she steered her car along the winding road leading from the island to the causeway, she felt a momentary lift in spirits. She could appreciate the natural grandeur of the windswept water, which lapped against the road and granted access to the mainland for a short time each day before the waves washed over it again.

"It's still spectacular," Ryan said quietly, taking in the view. "Despite everything, the place looks as if it could stand another thousand years, come what may."

Anna accelerated over the causeway, feeling the wind buffeting against the sides of the car and slipped on a pair of sunglasses to shade the bright sunshine reflecting off the water.

"Yes, it's still lovely," she agreed, but she felt a shiver of remembrance.

Ryan didn't miss much.

"It's over," he murmured. "He'll never try to hurt you again."

She glanced across and wasn't sure whether he referred to her father, who was long-dead, or more recent encounters. Either way, she hoped he was right.

"Did you find anything interesting at Mark's house?"

Ryan shifted mental gears, happy to accept a change of subject.

"Couple of interesting items," he said vaguely. "Nothing concrete. Bowers was liked and respected. It'll take a while to work through the full list of people in his immediate circle, without any helpful indications from forensics to guide us."

"Mm," she chewed on her lip as they reached the mainland and headed towards the main road. "I suppose MacKenzie will be in touch?"

Ryan watched a seagull swoop and dive into the sea, rising again to soar into the sky.

"I would be, if I were running the investigation. It's likely they'll inform next of kin, speak to any material witnesses and then work up to close friends and acquaintances."

Anna smiled to herself.

"Oh, stop pussyfooting around. I know you're dying to ask me some questions."

Ryan grinned at his reflection in the passenger window and relaxed into his seat.

"Did I ever tell you, you're a wonderful woman?"

"Not often enough."

"Well, I'm saying it now. First question is, who would be Bowers' next of kin?"

Best to start nice and easy.

"His sister," Anna replied. "She lives somewhere down in County Durham, although I've never actually met her."

"Were they on good terms?"

It was on the tip of her tongue to answer in the affirmative but she gave the question deeper consideration.

"He didn't talk about her very often, come to think of it. Now and then, he mentioned a family dinner. I suppose it's unusual that, in all the years I've known him, I never met her."

Ryan made a mental note to dig into Bowers' family history.

"We can keep it in mind," he said. "You can never jump to conclusions when it comes to family relationships."

"Speaking of which, you owe your mother a phone call," Anna interjected, as smooth as you like.

He scowled across at her, but she kept her profile towards the road ahead, forcing him to agree that a telephone call was a few days overdue.

"Sorry to drag us back to the point," he said caustically, "but I have a few more questions for you. I knew Bowers to be an intelligent, academic bachelor who liked living alone and fiddling about with old relics."

She had to laugh at his description of the work of a talented archaeologist.

"He was polite and a bit reserved," Ryan continued. "But, he hardly knew me. He took on the role of father figure and treated me as the man you brought home for tea. I expected him to be a bit standoffish, and he was."

Anna nodded her understanding. Mark had taken her under his wing, in more ways than one.

"What can you tell me about the man? You've known him since you were a child."

Unexpectedly, tears filmed her eyes and the thin sunglasses did little to disguise them. Ryan stifled a sigh. He hated himself for this, for doing what needed to be done. Whilst MacKenzie and Lowerson would do a stellar job, he felt a personal duty to clear his own name, to give Anna some answers and help to bring justice to the dead. He couldn't do any of that without raking over painful ground but he was sorry for it all the same.

Anna thought of Mark and all that he had meant to her. As a child, he had known about the kind of home life she had grown accustomed to: domestic spats, violent episodes from a father who liked to drink too much and periods of emotional absence from a mother who shut herself off from the world. Yes, Mark had known, as the village and consequently the entire island had known about what happened in Andy Taylor's house.

There had been whispered gossip about her mother and another man, until they found Sara Taylor crumpled at the bottom of a flight of stairs, her lovely neck broken.

The whispers continued and there were many who believed Andy had pushed his wife in a jealous rage, regardless of his own indiscretions, believing that Sara was his property. The village had grown frightened, for themselves and for the two little girls who no longer had a mother to fend off the blows.

Until, one day, Andy Taylor's body had been found, half-eaten by the fish and washed to shore by a merciless tide.

The violence might have stopped, but the whispers didn't. Had Andy jumped, unable to live with what he had done, or had he been pushed?

Through it all, Mark had offered Anna shelter, an alternative reality where she could learn about the history of Northumberland. She spent weekends at the Heritage Centre, listening to him giving tours and bringing the past to life. She learned how to treat the relics with care, how to sweep the ground for artefacts and log her finds. Eventually, he helped her find a place at university in Durham and now she was a recognised authority herself. Yes, she owed much to Mark and his quiet, undemanding presence in her life.

"Mark is…*was,*" she said after a long moment, "a kind and generous man. I loved him, in a way I wish I could have loved my own father."

Ryan said nothing, but waited for more.

"Our family was notorious," she murmured. "In every town or village, you've got that one family who are renowned in the area. Well, we were that family."

"I'm sorry," he said, inadequately.

Anna shook her head, not needing sympathy, not any more.

"What I can't understand is how my father never came in for more trouble with the law, or with social services. They came to our house once, then never again."

She didn't bother to add that she and her sister had kept their mouths firmly shut about what really happened behind closed doors, and Ryan didn't push for answers. He didn't need to: in his line of work, he'd seen plenty of other cases just like hers.

"I remember Mark had words with my father, at least once that I know of," Anna remarked. "I'd forgotten all about it, but I remember now. It was after my mother died and Mark walked me home after a shift at the visitors' centre. He said it was because it was getting dark, but back then, nothing sinister ever happened on the island. People walked home by themselves all the time."

"He wanted to speak with your father?"

"Yes. I remember he met us on the doorstep and told me to go to my room, but I snuck into the dining room where you could hear the conversation outside from the open window there."

"What did they say?"

"I don't remember everything—it was ten years ago, or more. But, I do remember Mark telling my father that he should save his anger for those who could fight back. He said something like, '*You should channel your anger into the real fight, which is out there and not in here. You've lost her, take it as a warning—you're drawing too much attention.*' "

"That's an odd thing to say."

Anna nodded, reflectively.

"I suppose he meant that people were talking and that he'd have the police around, if he wasn't more careful. Well, whatever Mark said to him worked pretty well, because my father left us alone after that."

Ryan filed the information away and moved on to the next point.

"Let's skip ahead to recent times. We had dinner with Mark on Friday night at his place, and as far as I remember it was all social chitchat and spaghetti bolognese. Nothing noteworthy. Am I right?"

"Sounds right," Anna agreed.

"OK. When was the last time you saw him, prior to that?"

Anna waited until she had overtaken a large lorry before speaking again.

"I met him for lunch in town, last Monday," she replied. "We took a stroll along the river and stopped for a bite to eat."

"How did he seem? Was he concerned about anything?"

"No, not concerned. Distracted, perhaps," she mused.

"About what?"

"He didn't say. I was thinking of his demeanour. He seemed short-tempered, which isn't like him."

"Tell me about it," Ryan advised.

Anna tried to arrange her thoughts, aware of how important any minor detail could be in finding whoever had killed her friend.

"I met Mark outside the station at around eleven-thirty. He seemed happy to see me. We walked along Dean Street towards the Quayside, along past your apartment building," she paused, retracing her steps. "We doubled back towards the courthouse because we wanted to go to that little gastro place beside it. Honestly, I can hardly remember what we talked about. Nothing important, nothing that stands out."

"All right," Ryan soothed, sensing that she was berating herself for not being more useful. "This is all helpful. It gives us a better idea of his movements, so we can piece together a timeline."

Anna nodded.

"We sat down to lunch and his manner changed. Suddenly, he seemed a bit snappish with me."

"What triggered it, do you think?"

Anna shifted in her seat, feeling disloyal.

"I told him that I'm thinking of starting a new project at work which would revisit some of the conclusions drawn by another historian. You remember her from the investigation at Sycamore Gap—Professor Jane Freeman?"

"How could I forget?" Ryan answered, thinking of a sleek woman with a tendency to micromanage and interfere in police work.

"Yes, well, I found some of her old publications when you asked me to look into her background and credentials. She and Mark were at Durham together. In fact, he signed off her doctoral paper a few years ago. Since then, she's had a lot of success in her field."

Ryan watched the passing scenery with unseeing grey eyes, while his mind scrolled back in time.

"I also remember you telling me there had been talk, at the university, about Freeman having been awarded her doctorate. There was some suggestion that her work hadn't been up to standard, but Bowers passed it anyway."

"Yes, that's right," Anna confirmed, unhappily. "But, Mark was such a straightforward man. He was so honest, Ryan, I can't believe it of him."

Ryan shook his head.

"You never truly know what people are capable of," he argued, thinking of all the quiet, mild-mannered men who had killed, or raped, or kidnapped. He'd put many of them behind bars. "Believe me, Anna, it's the quiet ones you want to watch. Was there anything romantic between Bowers and Freeman, which might lead him to forget his principles?"

She thought of Mark and tried to see him objectively, as a woman and not as the girl she had been, or the daughter she had tried to be. She supposed he had been handsome, in an older, outdoorsy sort of way. He had been intelligent and—it was a stretch to imagine it—but perhaps he had been charismatic. Yes, he had been, she admitted.

"Maybe you're right," she said, eventually. "It's still hard to see him with Jane Freeman. They're such different people."

"So are we," Ryan rebutted, with a smile. "Freeman is an attractive, successful woman. Maybe they had something going on."

Anna's face twisted.

"You could be right, but she's so…so…" she lifted a hand from the wheel and made a turning motion in the air as she searched for the right word, without being unkind. Ryan took pity on her.

"Go ahead, just say it," he grinned.

"Alright, then, I think she's like a shark dressed as a fancy poodle. I can't imagine the two of them getting along."

"Miaow," Ryan said, earning himself a shove in the ribs. "What was Mark's reaction, when you mentioned the project you're thinking of starting?"

"He was angry. He told me to leave well alone and that a good historian doesn't need to fly on the coattails of someone else's work. He said that if I was so desperate for a project I should stick to teaching. It was a hurtful thing to say, considering that the body of academic history is made up of people taking pot shots at other people's research, using polite language of course."

"He didn't want you touching Freeman's publication, picking holes in it?"

"I suppose not."

Ryan stretched his legs in the cramped space of her Mini and looked across at Anna, who was driving strictly at the speed limit. Safety first, and all that.

"I think it's about time I took more of an interest in local history, don't you think?" he said, with a roguish smile.

"Wonders never cease," came the dry reply.

CHAPTER 7

MacKenzie could almost hear Lowerson's stomach churning as they walked along the long corridor in the basement of the Royal Victoria Infirmary towards the mortuary. She was mildly embarrassed to admit that she, too, found the sight of death arranged clinically on a metal gurney infinitely more disturbing than if it were stuffed in a dumpster, or bloated from the river. Somehow, the detachment of the morgue, with its white walls and its squeaky clean floors was more dehumanising than the violent act itself.

"Y'alright there, Jack?"

He cleared his throat manfully and affected a cheerful expression.

"All part of the job, isn't it?"

MacKenzie nodded wisely and hid a smile. He was looking green around the gills.

"All the same, it's been a while for both of us. If you feel like you're going to throw up—"

"I won't."

Lowerson wore an affronted expression and she was sorry to have wounded his pride, but the last thing any of them needed was projectile vomit over the cadaverous remains of their victim.

They gathered themselves together as they approached the double doors, which led to an open-plan examination room flanked by rows of metal drawers. A unique scent assailed their nostrils: an indescribable mix of chemicals and natural gases, which could only be associated with death. Lowerson's stomach did a small somersault, but he followed MacKenzie into the airy room and began to tug on a lab coat, adding a squirt of hand sanitizer, for good measure.

"This way," she made directly for the other side of the room towards the office housing the senior pathologist attached to Northumbria CID. After a peremptory knock, there came a brief call beckoning them to enter.

"Jeff?"

Doctor Jeffrey Pinter rose from his swivel chair with a broad smile and an outstretched hand, which he withdrew again after realising that he still wore gloves bearing the human debris from his most recent examination, in gleeful disregard of the bright yellow biohazard bins dotted around the mortuary.

"Sorry," he chuckled, removing them in exchange for a fresh pair. "Jack? Good to see you, too. You're looking well."

"Thanks," Lowerson replied, laconically. Would people ever forget?

"You're here to talk about Mark Bowers? Follow me."

They followed his tall, spare figure into a separate examination room and Lowerson came to a hasty stop inside the doorway. Ahead, their victim lay underneath a paper sheet and a tag dangled from the protruding big toe of his left foot, which was grey and beginning to distend as his body began the process of putrefaction.

"Here's your man," Pinter began gaily, whipping back the sheet to reveal Bowers' lifeless face then stepping back to clutch at the lapels of his lab coat in the manner of a forties schoolmaster. Lowerson gulped and looked away, counting the wall tiles to distract himself from the wave of nausea which rocked over him.

"What can you tell us?" MacKenzie's voice was level, even if her gut wasn't.

"First and most obviously, you can see that we've got a case of serious perforating head trauma—"

"We picked up on that one ourselves," MacKenzie remarked.

Pinter chuckled, a bit nervously. Denise MacKenzie had that effect on him.

"Um. Well. The lead ball passed through the cranium at the sphenoid bone here," he indicated the hole in Bowers' right temple. "It went cleanly through the skull, breaking through the parietal bone on the posterior side—"

"Give us the Idiot's Guide, will you?"

"You've been spending too much time around Phillips," he said and then cackled at his own joke while MacKenzie and Lowerson looked on with straight faces. He subsided quickly.

"Put simply, the ball went in at the right temple and then passed through the left hand side at the back of his head. The entrance wound is fairly small, as you can see, with a bit of scorching around the skin," he pointed to the area in question. "Whereas the exit wound is somewhat larger and shaped a bit like a plug, which would suggest that the bullet was fired at close range—or rather, the lead ball.

"Unfortunately, it did a hell of a lot of damage on its way," Pinter continued in a slightly condescending tone, as if Bowers could somehow have prevented it. "It burned straight through the cerebral hemisphere, passing through the ventricles in the brain causing extensive lacerations—it would have killed him instantly."

"We're waiting for the ballistics report but, from your experience, what kind of weapon are we looking for?" MacKenzie asked.

Pinter tugged at his lower lip while he thought about it, which was a pointless display considering he had already spent considerable time pondering the question.

"I haven't seen anything like this before," he said gravely, drawing out each word for dramatic effect. "In usual cases of bullet wounds, particularly to the head, I'd expect to see damage consistent with a bullet fired from a semi-automatic, a rifle, or some kind of hybrid, home-made variety you can pick up if you know the right people."

"But?"

"The damage to the brain tissue and to the entrance and exit wounds is much more widespread than usual. The diameter of tissue damage is perhaps twenty times the size of the lead ball. Factor in the black powder which was found on his skin and it suggests that we are looking for a model not in general circulation."

"Something rare, you mean?"

"I would say so."

"What about signs of restraint? Was he tied down, or immobilised?"

"I'm waiting for the toxicology report to come back," Pinter replied. "There could have been something swimming around his system but on the face of it, no, there was no sign that he was restrained. No friction burns on the wrists, no pressure marks or bruising elsewhere and I haven't found any puncture wounds. There are some very minor burns on his face," Pinter raised a bony finger to indicate the singed skin, almost invisible to the naked eye. "These might be consistent with an older weapon. Perhaps something with a spark?"

"OK," MacKenzie moved to the next question, one that might be a game-changer for all of them. "Any indication that the wound was self-inflicted?"

Pinter looked between the two of them, his twinkling brown eyes savouring the moment to its fullest before answering.

"None whatsoever. I found traces of black, powdery residue on his face and neck, but there was no residue on his hands or forearms and we already know he was not found wearing gloves." He paused, then reached for a clipboard. "There were small traces of some other waxy residue, which looks like glue of some kind. I've sent the samples for analysis."

So, MacKenzie thought, *that ruled out one possibility.* Unfortunately, it did not assist their friend.

"But…"

She snapped to attention again as Pinter tacked on a final thought.

"There is one little thing which might have, ah, played on his mind, if you'll pardon the pun. Our friend Bowers had a tumour the size of a quail's egg nestling beside his medulla oblongata."

* * *

An hour later, MacKenzie skirted around a large flowerbed whose wilting begonias spelled out the name 'Fair View Nursing Home' and headed directly for the entranceway to the squat, stone-clad building beyond. Lowerson was manning the desk back at CID, combing through the statements given by the pilgrims. Each had consented to their fingerprints being taken, as well as a swab, which did not suggest that any of their godly number had something to hide but you could never tell.

With that sombre thought, MacKenzie pressed the outside bell and stated her name, waiting for the electronic doors to buzz open. Stepping through them, she found herself in a foyer fashioned in the style of a suburban home from the late eighties or early nineties. Low-pile, mint green carpet covered the floor. An ornamental fireplace in stained pine provided a focal point to the room and, instead of a grate, there stood a large arrangement of dried flowers in a chunky vase. A carriage clock and a couple of porcelain animals rested on its mantel and a brass-framed Monet print hung above that.

A cheerful woman in grey slacks and a frilly white shirt greeted MacKenzie from behind an overloaded desk housing an old-model computer and grubby keyboard, numerous framed pictures of what MacKenzie assumed to be the woman's children, a mug filled with an assortment of biros and, perhaps most disturbing, a calendar devoted entirely to hamsters in sunglasses and miniature bikinis.

"Hello! Welcome to Fair View. Are you here to visit a relative?"

MacKenzie took out her warrant card.

"I've been trying to reach Judith Bowers. I understand she's a resident here?"

The woman inspected the warrant card before answering.

"Yes, Miss Bowers has been with us for a few months now. She had a nasty accident and hasn't been the same since, poor lamb."

"Oh? Was it a car accident?"

"No, no, she was attacked. They never found who did it. Terrible thing. And that's where our taxes go, on so-called public services, when there's people like me caring for the sick and the elderly and getting paid a pittance. Disgraceful—"

The woman broke off from what was clearly a well-rehearsed routine when she realised that she didn't have the most receptive audience.

"Why do you need to see Judith?"

MacKenzie smiled politely. She had, of course, already looked into the circumstances that had brought Judith Bowers to Fair View Nursing Home. An assailant had beaten her to within an inch of her life and then left her for dead, on her way home from an evening at the cinema. Now, she required round-the-clock personal care at the age of forty-nine.

"I'm afraid I'm not at liberty to discuss those details just yet. Where can I find Miss Bowers?"

"Alright, if you want to be like *that,*" the receptionist sniffed. "She's in Room 23, in the Rose Wing. On the right hand side, door code is 2552. Sign here," she tapped an iridescent pink fingernail on the guest book and then returned to her online chatroom.

MacKenzie scrawled a signature in the book and cast her eye over the list of recent visitors, none of whom she recognised, then let herself into the secure Rose Wing. Upon entering, she became instantly aware of her own mortality. The men and women roamed the corridors around her like zombies, she thought, watching them shuffle vaguely in the direction of the security door she had just entered and, presumably, towards freedom. There was a lemony smell of detergent pervading the atmosphere, alongside the hint of a custard-based pudding wafting from the kitchens. Beneath that, she smelled *old people.*

MacKenzie tapped on the window to the nursing station and was met by a man with cropped grey hair and a tidy paunch beneath his uniform. His badge declared him to be the senior nurse in charge.

"Judith?" The man called Paul shook his head sadly and tried not to stare at the attractive policewoman with the serious green eyes. "I don't know if you'll have any joy there. She hasn't had many good days, recently."

"That's a pity," MacKenzie sympathised. "Can you tell me a little more about her condition?"

"I can't discuss her medical details unless you've got the proper warrant, but no harm in saying that Judith is mostly unresponsive after what happened to her—she's a selective mute and she's blind in one eye. You can see that for yourself."

MacKenzie clucked her tongue.

"Terrible thing," she said. "They say she was attacked?"

"Aye," Paul leaned against the doorframe, getting comfortable. "She came to us after a couple of months in hospital. Your mates still don't seem to know much about what happened to her."

MacKenzie smiled sadly. The detective in charge of Judith Bowers' investigation had already written off any hope of finding a perpetrator and was looking forward to his summer holiday in Greece.

"Did her brother help her to move into Fair View?"

Paul scratched the top of his head and dislodged a small snowfall of dandruff, which settled on his rounded shoulders.

"Tall feller, tanned?"

"Could be." MacKenzie fished out a pocket-sized photograph of Mark Bowers, one that had been taken by Anna and showed him looking healthy and happy on a windy beach.

The nurse peered at the photograph and nodded decisively.

"Aye, that was him. He signed the papers on the first day and hasn't been back since, at least not that I've seen."

MacKenzie affected a look of surprise.

"Perhaps he's been busy," she suggested.

The nurse snorted, meaningfully.

"Aye, they're always *busy,*" he muttered, pushing away from the wall. "C'mon, I'll take you along and you can see for yourself why he can't be arsed to visit."

MacKenzie didn't bother to enlighten him that Mark Bowers was not in any fit state to visit anyone; it didn't seem fair to interrupt the man's righteous tirade.

Judith Bowers was sitting placidly in a navy blue wing chair facing the window of her room, which had been wallpapered in a cream print covered with tiny rosebuds. A small television set blared in the corner, which she was either unaware of, or deliberately ignored. Her dark hair was streaked with silver and had been cut into a short, manageable style, leaving much of her face bare. It was impossible not to notice the dislodged bones beneath the papery white skin.

"Miss Bowers?"

There was no reaction, but MacKenzie persevered.

"My name is Detective Inspector Denise MacKenzie. I'm from Northumbria CID."

MacKenzie waited, but still no response. Sighing, she moved forward to perch on the edge of the windowsill. In the harsh light, she could see the myriad scars criss-crossing the woman's face, inflicted by repeated blows from a blunt instrument. MacKenzie swallowed her pity and forced herself to look again. The woman could still hear and was known to talk when the mood struck her.

Nobody had mentioned Judith Bowers having lost any of her mental faculties.

"Judith? I know that you have good days and bad days. If you aren't feeling up to talking to me right now, I'll understand, but it's important that you listen to what I have to tell you."

The woman blinked and then resumed her fixed, partially-sighted view of the courtyard garden outside her window.

"I'm sorry to tell you that your brother, Mark, was found dead late last night."

Slowly, the woman's head turned from the window, eyes clouded but still searching, darting this way and that. Her good eye came to rest on MacKenzie.

"Can I get you some water? Would you like me to call a nurse?"

Judith began to laugh. Rusty with disuse, her voice sang with mirth and a moment later the nurse stuck his head around the doorway.

"Is she alright? What happened?"

MacKenzie shrugged helplessly.

"I've just informed her that her brother is dead."

They watched as the woman continued to cackle, tears rolling down her hollowed cheeks.

"Is this a normal reaction, for her?" MacKenzie queried, thinking that people handled grief in different ways. Severe shock could cause laughter, tears and all manner of hysterical behaviour.

The nurse shook his head firmly.

"I've never seen her like this. She barely speaks, nowadays. It's…well, it's amazing."

"Yes," MacKenzie agreed, watching Mark's sister rejoice at the news of her brother's death. "That's one word for it."

* * *

Ryan waited until Anna had taken herself off for a bath upstairs before he drew the little plastic-covered book out of his jacket pocket. He was not a fan of deliberate subterfuge and, ordinarily, he preferred to be up front with Anna in all things. However, he did not believe in heaping bad news onto an already brimming pile. She had recently seen enough grief to last a lifetime and he would not be the one to cause further upset, unless it was unavoidable. With that in mind, he resolved to make completely sure that his present suspicions were correct before burdening her with their weight.

He glanced upwards at the sound of water running and settled himself on the edge of the sofa, where he laid out some paper on the coffee table and drew on his nitrile gloves once again. Only then did he retrieve the gilt-edged copy of *Paradise Lost* from its transparent evidence bag and set it on the paper-covered surface.

Using the extreme edge of the book cover, he opened the first page.

On the inside cover, there was a list of eight names and dates, written in fountain pen ink in varying shades of intensity depending upon the date.

Ryan could feel his heart begin to thunder against his chest as he noted the most recent additions to the list:

Andrew David Taylor, 1984 – 1997

Steven Anthony Walker, 1997 – 2015

Mark Oliver Bowers, 2015 –

There were five more names written inside that little book, dating back to the late nineteenth century. A quick check told Ryan that the earliest date roughly corresponded with the print edition of the book and it didn't take much for him to conclude that it had probably been purchased as a gift to the first man whose name was scrawled at the top of the list, dated 1877. It was not difficult to determine that the book had passed to each of the names listed on the inside cover, in date order.

Given the manner in which Bowers died, it was clear that nobody had been given an opportunity to update the list, nor to pass the book to a new owner.

There, in the quiet living room, Ryan knew that he had stumbled across an important piece of information. When he had first seen Bowers' name amongst the others, he had felt a stab of anger. He had nourished the hope that his instincts had been wrong on this occasion; that he might never have to tell Anna that her beloved friend was not the man she had thought he was. Now, that hope died a quiet death and was replaced with the cold resolution that he must find who had become Bowers' successor. Whose name should have been added to this seemingly innocuous list of men, amongst whom Anna's father was named alongside a known serial killer?

Ryan heard footsteps upstairs, indicating that she had finished her bath. With economic movements, he slipped the book back inside its plastic bag and returned it to its hiding place.

He stood for a moment longer, staring at the outline against his jacket pocket and wondered whether somebody would be looking for it. If so, they probably knew by now that it was missing from Bowers' shelf and might have come to their own conclusions about who had taken it.

* * *

The Circle was in full attendance later that night. Those from the island and the mainland met on consecrated ground to elect their new leader, a High Priest who would be their Master's representative on earth.

More than fifty men and women stood in a circle around a large bonfire. They left their ordinary lives behind them, shedding jeans and jackets for long dark cloaks to swathe their naked skin. The most coveted cloak of all—a long robe of pure animal pelt—rested on the ground in front of the fire, awaiting a new owner. Nestled amongst its folds was a small, double-edged *athame* dagger with an ornate handle.

The faces were anonymous in the darkness, only shadowed masks lit up by the glare of the fire, but in daylight they belonged to well-known local businessmen and women, people who had risen in their professions with a little help from their friends. Among them, DCS Arthur Gregson stood, his bare feet curling into the grass. He watched as a red velvet bag made its way around the circle and, for once, he was not so eager to partake of the little seeds which would fuzzy his brain and mellow his conscience. There were others who took greedy handfuls, shoving the hallucinogenic drug into their mouths with gusto. It was all part of the fun.

Beside him, Jane Freeman stood tall and proud, her slim body just visible through the gap in her robe and her hair a pale shimmer behind the mask she wore to hide her face. He was an ordinary man and he admitted that, over the years, women had been a weakness. Still, he felt no stirrings of desire.

All he felt was fear, more potent and more penetrating than any desire he could ever have imagined.

Eventually, once the group was silent and sedated, he stepped forward.

"Brothers! Sisters!" he called out, and the Circle fell silent, but they did not kneel. That was a mark of respect afforded only to their leader and he had never been that.

"We gather here this evening to mourn the loss of our High Priest, and to call upon the Master to choose a successor."

In truth, a successor had already been chosen. Gregson acted as Chief Whip, making sure that each member was prepared and ready to bend the knee to the woman who stood a little inside the circle, quivering in anticipation of the moment she would be called forward.

"Our Master rewards loyalty," he continued, in a pleasing baritone which had fared him well over the years. "Though each of us is loyal, there can be few who have given so much in recent times as our sister, Jane."

Freeman took a step further into the firelight and felt masked heads turn towards her.

"Our sister has been with us many years, recognising early on which side of the battle lines she belonged. There are few who can claim the same."

There were murmurs of agreement and admiration.

"There have been disappointments these last few years, setbacks borne from poor leadership. There have been some who have forgotten the true reason for our circle. The Master grants us rewards, but he does not wish us to be distracted from our purpose," Gregson said. "It is time for change, for a return to our true path. There is only one who can steer us towards it."

He gestured to Freeman, who bridged the remaining distance. She looked down at the long animal pelt lying on the ground beside her feet. A simple cloak, she thought, but it could wield so much power.

Gregson raised his voice over the crackle of the bonfire.

"Do any amongst you contest the Master's choice?"

The Circle remained silent and with a heavy heart Gregson lifted the long animal pelt and held it out to the woman beside him. Freeman shed her black cloak and kicked it away with one narrow foot, meaningless to her now that something better had presented itself. She accepted the pelt and enjoyed the feel of it against her skin. Around her, the Circle fell to the ground, compliant and ready to serve. Suddenly, she felt intoxicated; her head swam with endless possibilities and pleasures. The fur seemed to vibrate, as if it were a living thing once more, pulsating around her. She thought of all the men who had worn it over the years, all of whom had died. They deserved their fate, she thought. Fat-headed men who had grown pompous and arrogant. This time, the Circle would have a Priestess whose reign would be long and fruitful.

She raised the dagger above her head and sketched the shape of an inverted pentagram in the air, with deep, slashing strokes. Her voice rang out into the night and with the fire at her back, she became something ethereal.

Emperor Lucifer, master of all the rebel spirits,

We beg you to favour us in the call that we make to you.

O, Count Astarot!

Be favourable to us and make it so that this night you appear to us in human form.

Accord to us, by the pact that we make with you, all the riches we need.

Ave Satani!

Gregson looked up at her from his position at her feet, his joints stiffening and his mind racing. A new age had begun and he was more terrified than ever before.

CHAPTER 8

Tuesday 4th August

The Chief Constable of the Northumbria Police Constabulary was a short woman with hair the texture of straw and strong features not enhanced by the tightly fitting dress suit, which was necessary apparel on formal occasions such as disciplinary hearings. Beneath the fuzzy hair and pronounced overbite, Sandra Morrison had a mind as sharp as a tack and a shrewd idea that something was seriously amiss in this cop shop.

She was seated at the centre of a long, boardroom table, flanked on either side by two mousy chief inspectors drafted in from the neighbouring Tyne and Wear division. The fourth member of the panel was a woman called Daphne, who worked in Human Resources and was nearing retirement. She had agreed to act as note-taker.

"Full name and rank," Morrison began quietly, without looking up from her inspection of the paperwork stacked neatly in front of her.

"Detective Inspector Denise Mary MacKenzie."

"You're Irish?"

"Yes, ma'am."

"I had an Irish grandmother," Morrison pronounced.

MacKenzie didn't know how to respond to that and an awkward silence descended. If the admission was intended to be an icebreaker, then it had fallen flat. Thankfully, the Chief Constable dived straight into her list of questions and rendered further small talk unnecessary.

"On Wednesday 24th June this year, you were involved in an unauthorised sting operation. Correct?"

"Partially correct, ma'am. On that date, I was involved in a sting operation properly authorised by my superior officer, DCI Ryan, who is of sufficient rank."

Morrison steepled her fingers together and raised her eyes to meet MacKenzie's indignant glare.

"To your knowledge, was your commanding officer informed of the sting?"

"DCI Ryan was my commanding officer."

Morrison sighed.

"Denise, we can make this process as easy or as hard as you like. You know that I was referring to Detective Chief Superintendent Gregson."

MacKenzie took a breath and acknowledged that Morrison was right. Losing her temper would only make things worse.

"Given the gravity of Donovan's crimes, the very real time pressure before he killed again and our strong suspicion that Donovan was gleaning information from DCS Gregson on the basis of his former relationship with Northumbria CID, it was best to keep the operation under wraps."

Morrison's gaze did not waver.

"You are referring to Patrick Donovan's association with the department as an occupational psychiatrist?"

"Yes, ma'am. He was the department's preferred clinician for a number of years."

"Did you agree with the determination that DCS Gregson should not be informed?"

"Yes, I did," MacKenzie replied, without hesitation.

Morrison tapped the tips of her forefingers together, while the other two inspectors continued their silent observation.

"Why? You said something about 'gleaning information.' What did you mean by that?"

MacKenzie treaded carefully, now.

"Gregson and Donovan were friends. I believe it would have been understandable if certain facts—"

"DCS Gregson is aware of the meaning of 'confidentiality,' surely?" Morrison interrupted, in the same gentle voice.

MacKenzie licked dry lips.

"I simply meant that it would not have been beyond the realms of possibility for Donovan to have used his inside knowledge, perhaps from private clinical discussions as well as friendly chats, against us."

"Do you believe DCS Gregson was aware of Donovan's…extracurricular behaviour?"

There was a tiny pause, hardly noticeable, but Morrison caught it.

"Of course not, ma'am. I'm sure that DCS Gregson was as surprised as we all were."

"I see."

There was a tense silence and MacKenzie crossed and then re-crossed her legs before instructing herself not to fidget. She glanced up at the clock, which told her that she had been inside the room for less than ten minutes, but the air was stuffy and the collar of her blouse was strangling her.

"Moving on to the details of the operation itself, it has been alleged that you were placed in a highly dangerous scenario by DCI Ryan, which might have been avoidable. Do you agree with this assertion?"

MacKenzie thought back to her role in capturing Patrick Donovan. Yes, it had been frightening, it had been risky, but there had been no other way.

"No, ma'am, I disagree that the situation was avoidable. Donovan was escalating his activities and had evaded capture for over ten years. We are still in the process of uncovering his many victims, based upon the detailed notes we uncovered at his home. It is highly unlikely that we would ever have found this evidence or secured a partial confession from him, without taking positive action. He was planning to kill another woman that night and, without our interception, he might have been successful."

"I understand what you are saying, Denise. Although you feel that the operation was necessary to bring him in, did you feel that it was executed in a manner which adequately safeguarded your own life and the lives of others involved in the operation?"

MacKenzie's lips firmed.

"I wore a wire and my partner, DC Lowerson, was in a car outside the property at all times. DCI Ryan and DS Phillips, accompanied by a team of armed support staff, moved into position quickly afterwards and surrounded Donovan's home. I knew that these plans were in place. Likewise, we knew his preferred method of immobilising his victims: Donovan used a potent sedative which enabled him to move his victims to his kill site—"

"Which was where?"

"We don't know the answer to that question yet," MacKenzie answered, honestly.

"Alright, carry on please."

"He used a sedative, the effects of which could be reversed or at least reduced by its antidote, a drug called Flumazenil. We were prepared for this eventuality and I was administered a safe dose before entering Donovan's home."

"Who administered the drug?"

"Doctor Jeffrey Pinter."

"He's a pathologist," Morrison said, sharply.

"Yes, and he's also a trained medical doctor, trusted by the department. I consented."

Morrison's fingers began to tap again.

"What else?"

"Aside from these precautions, I have extensive training in self-defence and had prepared myself for physical combat, if necessary."

"This is all very neat, Denise."

MacKenzie smiled slightly.

"Thank you, ma'am. I'm glad that you agree."

* * *

"Full name and rank," Morrison repeated, in a carefully measured voice.

DS Phillips fiddled with the knot of his tie, which was a sedate number in tasteful blue. No patterns, no silly design; just blue, the same colour as the sky. He was a man who understood propriety and that there was a place for all things; now was not the moment to unveil piano keys or pineapples in woven silk. That, he would save for later.

"Detective Sergeant Frank Henry Phillips."

"Thank you for joining us," Morrison began, smiling in a sisterly fashion. Phillips was a popular character throughout CID and beyond. They were of a similar age and had joined CID around the same time, she going on to carve out a political career within the constabulary, he to focus on legwork, which was what he loved best. She remembered him as a younger man, full of the blarney and with plenty of charm to go around. It seemed that not much had changed.

"Frank, I know this will be difficult for you, but I want to say outright that I need you to set aside your personal feelings towards Ryan. Try to answer my questions honestly and objectively."

Phillips grunted, but said nothing. Morrison set her teeth and carried on regardless.

"How would you describe your working relationship with DCI Ryan?"

Phillips pulled an expressive face.

"Professional, friendly…it's smooth," he lifted a blunt-fingered hand and held it flat. "He's a safe pair of hands."

"I know that you may feel a fatherly affection—"

"Aye," he overrode her, with ease. "I do. But I'm not a blithering fool who follows any old pied piper. Like I said, he's a safe pair of hands."

"Would you say he is sometimes cold—ruthless, perhaps?"

Phillips huffed out an irritated sigh. The woman had a way of twisting things.

"We can all be cold when we have to, but he's not an unfeeling bastard."

Daphne stopped her careful note and flashed him a look of matronly disapproval.

"Excuse my language, Daff," he muttered.

"Moving on, then," Morrison continued, firmly. "To 24th June. Were you confident that DCI Ryan's planning, execution and oversight of the sting operation to entrap Patrick Donovan included adequate safeguards?"

"Yes."

Phillips did not elaborate. Sometimes simplicity was best.

"I understand that you are involved in a romantic relationship with DI MacKenzie?"

"What of it?"

"You did not, at any time, feel worried for her safety?"

"'Course I did! What do you take me for? Anyone would have felt nervous, but the fact of the matter is that Denise knew what she was doing and so did Ryan. That's what being a team means, *ma'am*. You trust one another to keep their end up."

Morrison chose to ignore the insubordinate undertone and continued in the same, monotonous tone which she had found to be highly effective in wearing people down.

"Individual members of the team may very well have kept their end up, as you put it," she said. "But there must always be an adequate safety net to cover unexpected variables. What if, for example, Donovan had chosen to kill Denise on the spot?"

"The operation was a calculated risk," Phillips argued. "All of them are."

Morrison and Phillips waged a silent battle over the breadth of the table, eyes locked, neither willing to budge an inch from their position. Eventually, it was she who cracked.

"Patrick Donovan was later found dead in his cell, in the early hours after his arrest. Correct?"

Phillips crossed his arms over his chest and prepared himself for the next part. There was a lot he could say about the circumstances surrounding Donovan's 'suicide,' about the whitewashing of the entire situation by Gregson and his cronies, but he didn't have any hard evidence.

"Aye, that's right. He hanged himself."

"I understand that you accompanied him into Holding?"

"No," Phillips shook his head. "Ryan and me, we made the arrest, then handed him over to a couple of DCs and a medic." Phillips rattled off their names, for the record. "Medics said he was fit and able and the last I saw of him, he was getting into a squad car shouting blue bloody murder at all of us."

"He didn't seem depressed?"

Phillips barked out a laugh.

"He was full of himself. Shouting about how we'd regret it, how nobody held him back, never had and never would. Started mumbling in tongues, or something."

"Tongues?"

"Aye," Phillips frowned, thinking back. "Couldn't make it out, thought he was muttering obscenities, or something."

"Alright. So, you last saw him getting into a squad car. Then?"

"I checked that he'd been booked in, which he had. Duty sergeant took care of all that and offered him the usual amenities. He refused a legal rep, which was fine by us. It was getting late, so we made the call to leave it until the next morning to begin questioning."

"We?"

Phillips scowled at her.

"Alright, you want to be pedantic, Ryan made the call. I agreed with him. We were all worn out, needing a night's sleep, Donovan included. He was tucked up in his cell, all the formalities were seen to and so we went home to clear our heads."

"Yet, sometime during the night, Donovan managed to construct a makeshift noose and hang himself."

"That's a fact," Phillips agreed.

"Who was responsible for checking him, through the night?"

"There was a PC who had sentry duty. Claims he fell asleep on his watch."

"You don't believe him?" Morrison's eyes bored into him.

"If he says he fell asleep, that must be what happened," Phillips dodged the question with aplomb.

"To your mind, then, Donovan had been through the proper motions, presented no apparent suicide risk and the fact that he wound up dead was a case of bad luck and the oversight of a humble PC?"

"Seems to be the long and short of it."

Morrison set aside her black biro and leaned back in her chair, suddenly weary. There were undercurrents here, she thought, which made her neck tingle.

"One final thing concerns Detective Constable Jack Lowerson. He was attacked in the course of his duties last Christmas on Holy Island. He sustained severe head injuries and was in a coma for six months."

Phillips nodded soberly. They had all worried over Lowerson. He and Ryan had visited his unresponsive body as it had lain in a hospital bed. They had chatted to him about football match fixtures, gossip and cases they had worked on, for nearly six months before he had eventually awoken. The lad still couldn't remember who had done it to him but they had their suspicions.

"Only days after DC Lowerson emerged from his coma, he was taken from hospital by DCI Ryan before being granted medical release, to assist in a pivotal role in the aforementioned sting operation. Correct?"

Phillips didn't bother overmuch with formality at the best of times, and now all pretence flew gaily out of the window.

"Now, just wait a minute," he began, in a deceptively calm voice, which was infinitely more threatening than his usual lyrical twang. Morrison's brows lowered, ominously.

"I don't like your tone, Frank."

"I couldn't give a stuff, love. I won't have you suggesting that Ryan barged into the hospital without a second thought about Lowerson's wellbeing. Firstly," he tapped one stubby finger, as he began to list his arguments. "The doctors told us Jack was physically fit and well. The only thing they were scratching their heads over was his amnesia. Well, he wasn't remembering anything sitting in bed all day, was he? Secondly, he was bored stiff and was desperate to get back on the horse, he told us himself. Thirdly," Phillips leaned forward, butting out his chin to emphasise the point, "Ryan came with me every Saturday—*every* Saturday, mind—to see the lad. Just sat beside him, talking to him and all that. So don't give me any twaddle about him not caring."

Morrison spent a moment or two considering whether it was worth writing him up for insubordination but concluded that she must be growing soft in her old age, because looking at Phillips' jowly face, she couldn't bring herself to do it.

"Alright, Frank. You've made your point."

* * *

Ryan studied the mud brown carpet tiles on the floor of the hallway outside, forearms resting on his knees, hands clasped together. Anna was seated beside him, one shapely leg crossed over the other, clad in expensive hosiery. If he wasn't so distracted, he would have had a greater appreciation of the picture she made, dressed to kill in a tailored black dress and heels, long hair swept away from the fine bones of her face. Slender fingers flicked the pages of the Northumbria Constabulary's monthly newsletter.

Her fingers stilled and his head jerked upwards as the door to the conference room swung open and Phillips trundled out, looking harassed. Ryan searched his face for clues, for any indication of what had happened beyond the scuffed doorway marked 'MEETING IN PROGRESS.'

Phillips took a furtive glance in either direction before snaking his way over to where they had congregated beside a bank of visitors' chairs.

"Morning," he nodded to both of them, noting the signs of strain. "Won't be long now. It's almost over."

Ryan wouldn't ask what had been said, it wasn't his way. But then, Phillips had just told him all he needed to know and the warmth of his greeting spoke volumes.

"Thanks, Frank," Ryan said, meaningfully.

"Don't mention it," came the easy rejoinder.

* * *

Arthur Gregson could think of many things he would rather be doing at the present moment than driving across town through lunchtime traffic to meet his wife. After a disappointing morning where he had seen his diplomatic efforts of the past six weeks go up in a billowing cloud of smoke, he was not disposed to find humour in the fact that Cathy Gregson had locked herself out of their extensive, five-bedroomed home.

Damn woman was going senile, he grumbled, pressing hard on the accelerator to edge past a learner driver.

There had been three text messages waiting for him, each more hysterical than the last. Why on earth she couldn't have gone shopping, or had a coffee with one of her dull friends, he didn't know. All he knew was that it wasn't worth the argument, not at his time of life, so here he was crawling along the streets of Newcastle towards the upmarket cul-de-sac where they lived.

He fiddled with the radio, swearing loudly when the local dance station blared out some kind of shouty, electronic crap. He gave up and switched it off altogether, turning his mind to the problem of Maxwell Ryan.

The man just wouldn't go away. Like a bad smell, Ryan plagued his life. Sleepless nights and indigestion abounded at the thought of him finding out about half of the things Arthur had taken great pains to conceal. Ryan loved nothing more than hunting out vice and violence, shining a light on the shaded underbelly of their little northern town and the countryside around it. How admirable, Gregson thought, with a prick of conscience. Had he ever aspired to the same?

No, he was honest with himself, in the privacy of his luxury car. But then, Ryan had been blessed with all the things that Arthur Gregson had never had. A comfortable, upper-middle-class background, where doors opened without you ever needing to ask. Brains, which ensured that those doors stayed open. Looks, which meant he was never short of women throwing themselves at him if he crooked a finger. Easy to have high ideals, if you've never known what it was to *need* something, to *want* something so badly, without the means to get it. *Easy to lord it over the rest of us mere mortals,* Gregson thought waspishly, *when you'd been blessed with every worldly advantage by an accident of birth.*

Gregson remembered all too clearly his own evolution from a stuttering, introverted loner. The Circle had changed his life, giving him all that he had dreamed of. After a while, the stutter had disappeared, replaced by a tone of command. He couldn't make himself taller or change his face, but he made himself stronger and fitter. He learned how to exude charm and exert influence, which was just as good.

There was one thing that the Circle had never been able to change; he had never been a father. At one time, it had bothered him, the lack of an heir to continue his name. There had been an atavistic desire to procreate but it hadn't happened. After a few years, it became obvious that he might be the one to blame. After all, it wasn't just his wife who had failed to conceive; none of his other women had fallen pregnant either.

He hadn't taken a test. He didn't need some know-it-all doctor telling him that he was a failure. He'd spent his life making sure that nobody ever made him feel a failure ever again. Cathy had gently suggested that they adopt but the idea was anathema to him and he'd given her a couple of good slaps, just to be clear on the subject.

But every now and then, he remembered that he would have liked to be a father.

Gregson shook himself and made the turn to the west of the city.

CHAPTER 9

MacKenzie stood at the front of the incident room pinning a photograph of Mark Bowers in the centre of the display wall. Tables were arranged in a rough semicircle facing it, partially occupied by a measly gathering of indifferent detective constables assigned to Bowers' murder inquiry. Lowerson provided a welcome relief from the sea of unfamiliar faces and he had seated himself at a table in the front row so that he could listen attentively to her briefing.

MacKenzie knew that there was a giant elephant sitting in the corner of the room and his name was 'Ryan.' Usually, it was he who headed these meetings, prowling the front of the room like a jungle cat while he laid out his plans. His restless energy was infectious, demanding that they approached their task with the same dynamic fervour that he did. Instead, it was she who stood at the front, her hair pulled back into a loose ponytail and a pencil stuffed into the back of it. Five pairs of eyes watched her, waiting for her to begin.

She squared her shoulders.

"Look, before I get started, I just want to say that I know this feels different. We all want to help Ryan the best way that we can, and that's by doing our jobs."

Lowerson nodded encouragingly.

"Alright, I guess we'll get started."

Before she could, the door opened and several more members of CID piled into the room, chattering like magpies. They raised a hand in greeting and settled themselves on the scattered chairs. MacKenzie watched in surprise as the canteen staff poked their heads around the door, meandered into the room and huddled together in a corner. Staff from every corner of CID were making themselves at home—a motley crew ranging from the lowliest caretaker to several higher-ranking inspectors.

MacKenzie was about to say something when she saw Phillips amble towards her. She gestured him to one side.

"Frank, you can't be in here. In fact, none of these people can, I'm in the middle of a briefing. What the hell is going on?"

"Didn't you check your e-mails?"

"In the past ten minutes? No, Frank, I've been trying to investigate a murder."

"Now, now," he polished off the last of his cheese and onion pasty and crumpled the greasy brown paper in one hand, while he fished out a paper napkin with the other. "I didn't know you were about to start a briefing."

MacKenzie massaged the tension at the back of her neck.

"Whatever you have planned, is it going to take long?"

Just then, a sudden hush fell amongst the gathering and they both turned to see Ryan enter the room wearing a disgruntled, slightly confused expression on his face. He stopped dead as he surveyed the gathering of people and sent a swift 'what the fuck?' at Phillips, who shrugged blithely.

They never knew afterwards who started it, but people started to clap. One-by-one, they rose from their chairs and clapped, strong and hard. There were a few playful wolf whistles too.

Ryan stood on the threshold of the dingy conference room and felt his throat burn. They were clapping for him, he realised, while his heart hammered. They were clapping because they had heard he had been cleared by the disciplinary panel. Slowly, he looked at the faces of those around him who smiled their approval that the wheels of justice had turned in his favour.

Overwhelmed, honoured, he took a step forward, then another until he stood amongst them once again. The sound of applause dimmed, allowing him to speak.

"I don't go in for speeches," he began, and emotion made his voice harder than he intended. "But let me say thank you. Thanks to all of you who kept a bit of faith these last few weeks, and for shirking off to come and give me a warm welcome. Now, get back to work!"

There was laughter, as he had intended.

There was more back-slapping, firm handshaking and murmured words of encouragement as they filed out again, back to their day jobs as if nothing had happened.

He moved across to clasp Phillips by the hand and plant a grateful kiss on MacKenzie.

"Better not make that a habit," Phillips grumbled, good-naturedly.

"Have to take the opportunity when I can. Jack? What the hell are you doing lurking over there? Get over here so I can slobber all over you, too."

Lowerson practically skipped across the room and ignored the outstretched hand, enveloping Ryan in a rib-cracking hug instead.

"Alright," Ryan tapped Lowerson's back. "Alright."

Releasing him, Lowerson grinned.

"Looks like the Chief Constable made the right decision then?"

"She said the accusations appeared to be unfounded and that Donovan's death was an unfortunate circumstance which would be handled in a separate inquiry. It will, she suspects, lead to recommendations that internal procedures be updated and CCTV cameras replaced, which is what usually happens. 'Lessons learned,' or something like that."

"Where does that leave you?" Phillips asked.

Ryan shrugged.

"I'm back on the job," he answered.

MacKenzie turned away and started to gather up the paperwork relating to Bowers' death, until a gentle hand stilled her arm.

"This is still your baby," Ryan assured her, though he would have liked to see the reports. "The Chief Constable wants me back to full duty but not working on this, for obvious reasons. I'm too involved and I knew the man before he died. Aside from the fact you can't clear me from your list—"

"Ryan, I—" MacKenzie started to protest but he shook his head.

"Mac, I don't want to hear any apologies from you. You're doing your job and that's precisely what I want you to do. I don't want anybody to say there was a stitch up. Clear me through the proper process."

MacKenzie just nodded and let the papers fall back onto the desk.

"Besides," Ryan continued. "I'm sure that the usual roster of manslaughter and rape will keep Phillips and me occupied for the time being."

MacKenzie nodded, searching his impassive face but finding it unreadable.

"You don't want to, ah, *discuss* anything?"

Ryan's eyes twinkled.

"That would be against the rules, Mac, and I'm nothing if not a stickler for the letter of the law."

* * *

Gregson pulled his car onto the driveway beside his wife's silver Audi and turned off the engine. He couldn't see her anywhere around the front of their impressive home, with its creeping ivy and faux Tudor façade. She was probably hiding beside the patio doors at the back of the house, he reasoned, since it would be less likely that the neighbours would catch a glimpse of her there. Avoiding social embarrassment was of paramount importance in Cathy Gregson's insular world.

He paused for a moment longer to stare at the cushioned leather steering wheel as he thought of his wife. Perhaps if she hadn't been so uptight, so damn *proper*…

Arthur sighed deeply. There was no use trying to lie to himself. To others, maybe, but never to himself. Cathy had been a vibrant young woman when her father had introduced her to a young Arthur Gregson. She wasn't to know that the meeting had been carefully engineered, or that her family fed him titbits so that he would be better equipped to woo her from the start. She had fallen for the sweetly romantic Arthur, with the shy smile and vulnerable exterior. He made her believe that, in marrying him, she was rebelling against her family's cocoon.

How wrong Cathy had been, he thought, to trust him all those years ago.

To his surprise, he had fallen in love with her—after a fashion. She had been bubbly and pretty as a picture, not to mention a catch for a man from the rough end of Newcastle. He had been proud to have her on his arm. *Look,* people would remark, *isn't that Teddy*

Smyth's daughter, married to that young policeman? It made people stand up and take notice of him.

Over the years, things had slipped. There came promotion after promotion, while Cathy took care of the social side of life. The barbeques, the parties, the events with local people of influence and standing had come in quick succession and she had smiled and laughed at each of them. That was breeding, he supposed.

Arthur wasn't moulded the same way. He liked a wife at home, with all the airs and graces, but he also liked a little something on the side to remind him of where he had come from. He liked a bit of attention from the kind of woman to appreciate his success, not the kind of woman he had at home, who expected it. Those side dishes had come a little too frequently for Cathy's liking and her love had frozen into a kind of cynical acceptance. They'd discussed it, of course, calmly over dinner. He knew that she had wept afterwards, in the privacy of her own room, but she had still come down to breakfast the next morning and carried on just as before.

Now, they found themselves stranded in a kind of seventies time warp, she with her ladies and he with his work; *both* kinds of work. If Cathy presumed that he was visiting a woman for long hours into the night, rather than imagining him atop windy hillsides surrounded by people in dark cloaks, perhaps it was better that way. It was often true.

He sighed again and heaved himself out of the car. He was still in shape, thanks to regular tennis matches and a careful diet, but he couldn't prevent the march of time leaving its mark on his thickening middle or from turning his dark hair to grey. He felt it, as his knees creaked out of the car and he stretched out the aches in his legs.

One of the neighbours waved to him from across the road and they agreed to a round of golf the following weekend.

He had always hated golf. Damn boring game, wandering around hitting a ball with a stick. But his neighbour owned a chain of successful restaurants in the North-East and if he wanted a table in any of them, he had better toe the line.

Gregson headed around to the back of the house and was mildly surprised not to find Cathy sitting on one of the outdoor trestle chairs, tapping her toe in agitation. The patio was empty. Everything was quiet, except for the sprinklers fanning the rear lawn with a gentle spray so that the grass didn't dry out over the summer months. Another ridiculous notion, he mused, given that summertime in the North of England hardly equated to the baking heat of the African desert.

He tried the patio doors and found them unlocked. Rage, quickly suppressed, washed over him. Was this a ruse to try to control him, to curb his movements and bring him to heel? Obviously, she was not locked out of the house. Why, then, tell him to come home in the middle of the working day, except to frustrate him?

Stepping through the patio doors, he could hear the sound of the radio in the kitchen. Some chatty drivel, he thought with misogynist peeve, designed for bored housewives. He trailed across the pristine rose-coloured carpet in the lounge, eyeing the china figurines with disgust as he made his way to the kitchen.

"Cathy?" he called out, angrily. "Cathy!"

The call died on his lips as he approached the kitchen and he drew a strangled breath, sucking air into his lungs like a dying man.

Cathy hadn't heard him. She hadn't been capable of hearing anything, not since earlier that morning.

She lay crumpled on the expensive Mediterranean tile floor, pooled in her own blood. The brassy smell of it filled the air, oozing from the deep knife wound running across her belly. There was a smaller cut on her chin, where she must have banged her head on the edge of the sink as she fell. Her eyes were wide and staring, glazed over and empty. One of the silly velvet pink slippers she liked to wear had fallen from her foot and lay a short distance away, its material stained and beginning to crust with blood from the floor.

Tears fell but he didn't feel them. Motionless, he stood there, his body shaking.

Cathy, he thought.

A sob escaped him, guttural and fierce. This was not part of the agreement, he thought wildly. He had made vows and he accepted the consequences of betrayal, but Cathy had not. She hadn't drunk the blood of a baby goat and howled at the moon. She had stayed at home, watching *Strictly Come Dancing.*

Anger warred with panic. Was this a punishment? Was it a message from the Circle? He didn't have long to find out. His trained eye could see that she had already been lying there for hours and, on a hot day, he couldn't leave her much longer. There was no use trying to drive away and pretend that he hadn't found her, since he had already spoken with his neighbour and others might have seen him.

Gregson raised wide, frightened eyes to the countertop and caught sight of a cheap mobile phone that did not belong to his wife. His heart plummeted to the floor and his stomach rolled at the certain knowledge that the pay-as-you-go mobile was one of his own, which he used for Circle business. He wanted to grab it up, to destroy it, but there was a river of blood between the countertop and where he stood. He could not risk leaving prints on the floor—things were sticky enough already.

He turned away and started to fumble for his other mobile when a thought struck him. The previous day, Ryan claimed to have received a text message from an unknown number claiming to be Bowers, leading him to Heavenfield Church. It was too much of a coincidence.

Sick and afraid, he knew that it was only a matter of time before MacKenzie's team triangulated the source of the text messages sent to Ryan. They could only trace an unregistered to within a certain radius but they would connect the dots and make a permanent connection between him and Bowers. After that, they would delve into his private life, uncovering all manner of things not intended for public consumption.

He needed to think fast.

CHAPTER 10

Miles away, Ryan took a hefty bite of prime beef burger and washed it down with a slug of *Irn Bru.* Beside him, Phillips flipped his tie over one shoulder and dug into fish and chips caked in salt and vinegar, while Anna looked on in despair.

"Given this healthy lifestyle, I don't know how you've managed to dodge a heart attack, or diabetes," she remarked, watching as Ryan loaded his burger with extra sauce.

"It's all those hours chasing down the bad guys," he supplied, taking another bite.

"I'm naturally athletic," Phillips said, laughing in the face of his growing belly and sagging chin. "No use in being jealous," he added, with a wink.

Anna couldn't help but giggle. They made a fine pair, the two of them.

"It's wonderful that you don't have the inquiry hanging over your head any more," she turned to more serious matters. "But what happens now? Do you carry on as if nothing has happened? Surely Gregson will come in for some flak?"

Ryan licked ketchup from the side of his mouth and pushed his empty plate aside.

"The fact is that we need something concrete against him. At the minute, we're rolling on instinct, and the Crown Prosecution Service doesn't give too much weight to that."

"It's like he's got the bloody eye of Sauron all over you," Phillips muttered and then looked up into the ensuing silence. "What? Haven't you ever read Tolkien? You know, the baddie with the black eye who wants his ring of power back…"

There was a short pause.

"Anyway," Ryan continued blandly, shaking his head, "since I don't have a ring of power to tempt him out of hiding, I'm going to have to rely on normal methods of investigation. I want to know more about Gregson's private business. Let's start with his finances. If he's dirty, there'll be money changing hands somewhere."

"Need a warrant for that," Phillips commented.

"Usually, yes."

Phillips tutted.

"That's another risk, lad. If you go poking into his private affairs without the proper paperwork, anything you find won't be admissible. Added to which, it'd be illegal. Added to which, if you get caught, you'd lose your job."

"It might throw up some useful lines of enquiry," Ryan said. "Besides, I won't get caught."

"Oh, you're a technological whiz now?"

Ryan just smiled.

"Well, don't say I didn't warn you."

"Has there been any progress finding Mark's killer?" Anna said it lightly but her voice trembled. For her, it was their number one priority.

"MacKenzie has it in hand," Phillips said reassuringly. "She's got our best people looking into it. Pinter, Faulkner…they're working their socks off."

"I know, you're right."

"It always feels like forever," Ryan added, pinning her with smoky grey eyes that were both sympathetic and uncompromising. "But it's only been a couple of days. These things can take time."

"I want to help."

"You are helping," he said firmly. "Everything you tell us about his past is invaluable information."

Phillips coughed in the manner of one about to impart information he shouldn't.

"I had another chat with that little birdie I was telling you about," he said, voice lowered beneath the chatter of the restaurant. "And the pathologist found something out of the ordinary. It seems that Bowers had a brain tumour."

Anna nearly dropped her fork but instead placed it back onto her plate with extreme care while she processed this latest shock.

"He never told me."

"Aye lass, I guessed that," Phillips scratched at his ear.

"They're thinking suicide?" As usual, Ryan sliced through the emotional mire.

"That's just it. They don't know what to think, because there's nothing else which points to him having blown his own brains out—"

Phillips cut himself off with a grimaced apology for Anna.

"Sorry, love. I meant to say, they can't understand where the weapon has gone and there were no signs of Bowers having pulled the trigger himself."

"Which means," Ryan said, "Gregson will be swinging his evil eye back in my direction."

"Surely, they must know by now there's no evidence against you?" Anna turned worried eyes to Phillips and he said another prayer to the God of Police to be forgiven for the confidential breach he was about to make.

"There's nothing but a bit of wool off your jumper, as far as they've found. Still waiting for the telephone company to triangulate the source of that text message you got from Bowers. He wasn't found with a phone."

"Nothing in his house—his car?"

Phillips gave one brief shake of his head and took a lazy glance around their immediate vicinity.

"No phone or wallet, nothing except his car keys which were in his trouser pocket when they found him. No mobile phone at his house, either. They're going over his computer now."

"No weapon, no phone, no wallet. Interesting that he managed to send me a message without access to a mobile phone, don't you think?"

"One last thing, while I'm burning all my bridges," Phillips said, eyeing up the banana split making its way across to a neighbouring table. "The bullet they've found is from an old weapon, something much older than anything in general circulation at the moment, even on the black market. In fact, it wasn't even a bullet. It was a lead ball and some black powder. They're trying to trace the source."

"Mark didn't own anything like that," Anna said. "He had a decorative sword, which was a gift, but he didn't own any other weapons that I know of."

"That you know of," Ryan repeated and then gestured for their bill.

* * *

Jane Freeman sipped daintily at a chai latte while she waited for the phone to ring. He was later than expected but perhaps Gregson was caught in the throes of matrimonial grief and needed time to gather his wits before he came running for help with his latest catastrophe.

She chuckled to herself and rose from the leather-backed chair to walk to the large window of her office. Outside, the sun was high in the sky and beamed ladders through the blanket of fluffy white clouds. *Jacob's ladders,* they called them. The masses did enjoy spinning their yarns about God and his kingdom.

That kingdom was changing, she thought maliciously, pressing a slim hand to the window to block out the rays.

Finally, the telephone rang.

"Freeman."

"Jane! Thank God," Gregson's urgent voice came down the line. "Something's happened. It's terrible. I don't know who—who—"

"Arthur, the last person you ought to be thanking is *God,*" she remarked silkily, in tones of quiet reprimand.

"I—Yes, yes, I'm sorry. I wasn't thinking."

"There's a surprise," she muttered, flicking lint from the material of her expensive skirt. "Come to the point."

"It's—it's Cathy. She's dead."

Freeman waited a beat.

"That was careless," she said.

"What? No, no! You don't understand," Gregson said, feverishly. "I came home and I found her. Somebody—somebody's killed her."

"My condolences," Freeman replied.

"I need help! There's a pay-as-you-go phone on the countertop beside her and—and I think it was used to text Ryan. They'll think it was me!"

"How vexing. I presume it belongs to the unknown perpetrator, which will therefore mean this is all a dreadful coincidence."

At the other end of the line, Gregson's eyes closed against what he was about to admit.

"It's mine. I—I misplaced it the other day and—and now there it is, on the countertop."

Freeman bit her lip to stop the bubble of laughter.

"You mean to tell me that you have compromised the Circle once again?" Her voice was sharp as a razor. "You have the audacity to telephone me—I presume using a non-regulation telephone—endangering me with exposure as well as yourself?"

"I—I panicked. I need help!"

Freeman relished the next part.

"It's over, Arthur. As of this moment, you are no longer our brother. You will relinquish or destroy all artefacts pertaining to the Circle on pain of retribution. You will not contact us directly again."

"No! No, please!"

"Goodbye, Arthur."

Freeman pressed a button to end the call and began to deconstruct the phone into parts. She would throw them in the river later.

* * *

Gregson remained seated on the armchair in his living room, staring at the blank screen of their new television. It stared back at him, an empty black void mirroring his life.

His hands trembled and he was shivering despite the mild weather, his mind succumbing to the shock. Part of him realised that he was a cold bastard. What kind of a man was more upset to find himself ostracised than to find his wife lying dead on the kitchen floor?

But then, it wasn't as if he'd just been kicked out of the tennis club and was no longer able to attend socials at the clubhouse. For over thirty years, the Circle had been his family; it had given him more purpose than he might have felt in a hundred years spent as a policeman.

Now, it was over. The cord had been cut and he was floating, falling, unable to grasp a lifeline.

He didn't know who had killed his wife but he didn't really care. It might have been Jane Freeman; she was not a woman who liked competition. Yet, he had never coveted her position. He had always been happy as the fixer, the one who took care of the details.

Gregson's chin lifted.

That's right, he thought. He could take care of the details.

* * *

It had been a while since Jimmy 'The Manc' Moffa had made a house call. Semi-legitimate business interests allowed him to lead a comfortable, cleaner existence than had previously been the case. But now and then, the engine needed oiling. Hands required shaking and, in this case, bodies required disposal. Every good turn deserved another, so they said, and Arthur Gregson had rubber-stamped plenty of business ventures in recent years. True, he had skimmed a healthy retainer off the top, but he still had enough leverage to be able to call Jimmy at short notice to help with his dirty work.

Moffa exchanged his £3,000 hand-made suit and cushy office in central Newcastle for a pair of greasy overalls and a nondescript white van. His bodyguard donned a similar get-up and, not long after receiving the call, they pulled up in front of Gregson's house in the suburbs of the city. They reversed onto the driveway, so that the back doors of the van were flush to the garage door, which had been left open as instructed.

Nice house, Jimmy thought with a sneer. *So, he had offed his old woman, had he?* Now, he would be the one to pay. After today, Jimmy would be writing his own ticket, thanks very much.

He cast an astute, watery blue eye over the quiet street and was content. One broken CCTV camera—they had already taken care of that on the way in. A few flickering curtains but no passers-by to complicate matters. That was good.

They walked around to the back of the house and found Gregson hovering around the patio doors waiting for them. He held a hand out, which Moffa ignored.

"Where is she?"

Gregson swallowed and let his hand fall away.

"In the kitchen," he jerked his head. "Through the lounge, on the left."

Moffa pinned him with a stare.

"After this, you'll owe me. Understand?"

Gregson looked at the young man with the strangely old eyes seasoned by the things he had seen and done. Moffa looked equally at home in a Michelin-starred restaurant as in a boxing ring, scrapping for fun. He liked to think he was a chameleon, able to blend into any level of society, that was his gift. Beside him stood a heavyset man with a reddened face, riddled with broken veins. Small eyes sunk into cheeks that were puffy from too many steroids and both ears were cauliflowered to the sides of his head. Gregson knew him as 'Ludo,' which derived from his love of Quaaludes and other recreational drugs in his younger years and also explained why he wore a perpetually unfocussed expression on his gorilla-like face.

"I understand."

"Step aside until we're finished."

"You need to get rid of everything," Gregson swallowed again and rubbed a nervous hand over his face. "There's a black mobile phone on the kitchen counter. I need that back."

Moffa laughed in his face.

"Piss off, old man."

Gregson opened his mouth and then closed it again. There was really nothing more to say. He turned away, slumping into one of the bistro chairs on the patio and Moffa laughed under his breath.

"Don't you want to know what we're going to do with her?"

Gregson looked away, deliberately.

"Tosser," Jimmy said, matter-of-factly, to which Ludo grunted his agreement.

Moffa pulled out some heavy protective gear from the sports bag Ludo carried. Suitable against chemical and toxic waste, it covered them from head to toe.

Sweating inside the thick overalls, they began the task of removing all traces of Cathy Gregson. Fresh plastic sheeting was taped to the floor, a makeshift path leading from the kitchen through the garage to the van, another from the patio doors to the kitchen. Once complete, they turned their minds to the mess on the kitchen floor. There, on the Mediterranean tiles she had chosen herself, Cathy was wrapped in plastic sheeting and then rolled up in an old carpet, ready for transportation to one of Jimmy's warehouses where she would be dissolved in acid before nightfall. The kitchen was cleaned and scrubbed, layered with bleach from top to bottom until the colour of the tiles turned a half-shade lighter. Jimmy cracked the windows to minimise the smell but that was Gregson's lookout. He was a copper, so he should know that you could never really get rid of all blood traces. If he was lucky, he'd have twenty-four hours before his bum chums at CID would be along to sniff around the house.

Either way, he couldn't give a shit. Nobody would pin this on him because he wasn't fool enough to kill anybody in his own home or leave a mobile phone hanging around like a gigantic map with 'x' marking the spot.

Prat.

Jimmy palmed the black phone he found on the countertop and decided to keep it as insurance, careful to remove the plastic SIM card.

They spent another twenty minutes messing up the house, pocketing jewellery and cash. That's how Gregson wanted to play it. Burglars entered the house and Cathy surprised them. Anybody looking would see a white van with fake licence plates, parked sometime in the afternoon. At worst, they'd see a couple of workmen loading a roll of old carpet into a van. When they heard the bad news, they'd tell themselves that was the van that had kidnapped poor Cathy Gregson. As for her husband, he's just a hardworking officer of the law who stumbled into a crime scene. Poor old Arthur, what a tragedy.

Afterwards, Moffa joined Gregson on the patio and saw that he was shaking badly from head to toe. He rolled his eyes and gave the signal to Ludo, who stomped across and heaved him out of the chair.

"W-wait," Gregson muttered. "I've changed my mind—"

"Too fucking late."

Ludo propelled Gregson away from him so that he stumbled across the patio, as if fleeing for his life. Inevitably, he fell, and Ludo didn't hesitate to administer a couple of good blows to the back of his head—enough to concuss, to see some serious damage, but not enough to kill.

Of course, there was always a margin of error.

Moffa pulled the garage door shut and climbed behind the wheel of the van. Beside him, Ludo was breathing a bit heavily.

"You're getting soft," he bit out, then gunned the engine.

CHAPTER 11

"It looks like I'm going to have to eat my paper hat after all," Faulkner said.

At the other end of the telephone, MacKenzie pulled a face.

"Sorry Tom, I'm not following you."

"It's the blood samples we took from the altar at Heavenfield," Faulkner supplied. "I was wrong. It wasn't just Bowers' blood that we've found—there was plenty of his, for sure, but we've also found seven new samples, maybe more to come. They're being analysed as we speak."

"How much more blood?" MacKenzie told herself to stay calm.

"We're talking about very significant blood loss, Mac. I had the boys go over the site again with luminol spray and the place is covered in old stains, particularly on the floor around the altar. Some of that will be the bleach, of course."

MacKenzie gave into the urge to rest her head on her hand, propping her elbow on the edge of her ancient desk chair while she did.

"Bleach?"

"Yeah. Bleach reacts with luminol in the same way as blood, which is why it's a good option if you're planning to cover up a murder," he laughed shortly. "It can give us a false positive in terms of testing for blood samples and obviously causes confusion, although finding bleach in widespread quantities would be suspicious in itself."

MacKenzie massaged her temple.

"Are you telling me that you can't be sure if it's blood or bleach that you've found?"

"No, we've got positive blood samples, like I say. Haven't run them through the database yet—"

"Make it a priority and call me if you find a match."

MacKenzie ended the call and met Lowerson's curious eyes, wondering what awaited them just around the corner.

* * *

Dusk was only just beginning to fall when Ryan and Phillips received the order to attend the scene at 17 Haslemere Gardens, in an area of Newcastle known as Gosforth. Well-heeled families resided in that part of the city, a mix of old and new money who enjoyed being closer to the bustling centre. Communities stayed close and *Neighbourhood Watch* was more than an organised group of safety-conscious citizens; it was a state of mind. Right on cue, curtains flickered and the more audacious amongst them stood outside their houses to watch the comings and goings. Twenty minutes ago, they knew, a police car had pulled up outside Arthur and Cathy's house, followed by an ambulance and two paramedics who had transferred Arthur on a stretcher and driven away, presumably to hospital. Yet there had been no sign of Cathy and wasn't *that* interesting? The police were probably inside the house questioning her right now.

Cathy must have attacked Arthur. That was the only *possible* explanation, they twittered.

Of course, it could have been a stroke.

Or a heart attack.

Or, heaven forbid, one of those youth gangs might have broken in and attacked both of them. They had seen something similar on *Crimestoppers* only last week.

They watched with widened eyes as a sleek, dark grey Mercedes pulled into the cul-de-sac and parked on one of the grass verges.

They tutted and thought immediately of making a complaint.

A tall, dark-haired man unfolded himself from the driver's side and moved around to the boot to retrieve a small bag. Another man hefted himself from the passenger side, inches shorter and thicker all round, but the two made their way towards Number 17 with single-minded purpose.

"Bit like Stepford, eh?" Phillips commented, taking in the manicured borders.

"More like my idea of hell," Ryan muttered, feeling the force of at least ten pairs of eyes boring into the back of his shirt. "I don't know how people can stand to live like this, with everyone knowing their business every second of the day."

"Not all of us are as antisocial as you," Phillips was forced to observe. "Some of us actually *like* people."

"I like people," Ryan argued half-heartedly but let it drop as they approached the PC manning the front door. He took their names for the log book, recording their warrant card numbers with the kind of painstaking detail only to be found in a newly qualified constable.

Formalities complete, Ryan cornered the other PC hovering beside them.

"PC Yates?" Ryan snapped out, so the young woman was forced to face him. "You were the first on the scene?"

"Yes, sir." Yates drew herself up to her full height, feeling hot and bothered under his scrutiny. DCI Ryan was known to have that effect on people.

"I'll have your report, please." Silently, he offered her a bottle of water, which she accepted with surprise.

She took a few sips to steady herself.

"Control Room received a call at twenty past six, from the next door neighbour on that side," she pointed to the house at their left. "Mrs Anjuli Sisodia. She reported that she and her husband were due to have dinner with the Gregsons this evening at six-fifteen. She tried calling their house several times during the day to confirm, but the number rang out. She says she tried knocking on the front door around five o'clock after seeing a white van leaving the premises, but there was no answer. She was becoming concerned since she could see both cars on the driveway but decided to try again later in case Mr and Mrs Gregson were…um, *busy*." Yates wiggled her sandy blonde eyebrows expressively and Ryan's lips quirked at the thought.

Risible, if it wasn't so nauseating.

"Mrs Sisodia and her husband came back to the house at six-fifteen on the dot but found it in darkness. They were worried, so they tried around the back and stumbled across DCS Gregson, who was lying face down on the patio in what appeared to be a critical condition. They rang for an ambulance immediately and the call was referred through to us."

Ryan nodded.

"What time did you arrive?"

Yates gestured to her partner, who continued to man the door as if it were Buckingham Palace, standing rigidly to attention.

"PC Wickham and me, we got here at six-thirty, maybe six-thirty-five."

Ryan glanced at his watch. *Fifteen minutes ago.*

"We made our way around to the back of the property as the paramedics had already arrived. I directed Mr and Mrs Sisodia to remain inside their house for the present, until a statement could be taken from them."

"Good," Ryan approved.

Yates' heart rate accelerated under the praise. She was only human.

"Some of the other neighbours were congregating on the driveway, so we moved them on."

Ryan's eyebrow flicked upwards, since he could still see several people milling around on their front lawns. Yates shrugged.

"Well, we did our best," she qualified.

"Just a minute," Ryan strode into the middle of the street, where he raised his voice so that he could be heard. "I'm DCI Ryan, from Northumbria CID. We will be paying each of you a visit to take down a statement but for the present you've all been asked to remain inside your own homes. I see that you have chosen to ignore that instruction, so I'm going to ask you once again to return to your homes or risk receiving a police caution. That goes on record," he added, darkly.

Sure enough, they scurried back into their houses.

"Aye, and now there'll be some busybody making a complaint about police brutality, no doubt," Phillips said.

"Give me strength," Ryan muttered, then turned back to PC Yates.

"Tell us what happened to Gregson."

"Well, sir, the paramedics were worried about moving him since he had head injuries—"

"What kind of injuries?" Phillips asked, starting to pull on paper overalls.

"He was attacked, sergeant. The back of his head was covered in blood and the paramedics were concerned about clotting in his brain. His body was also in deep shock; he had been lying out there for hours."

"Did you find a weapon, an implement of any kind?"

Yates shook her head.

"No, sir. We haven't made a full search the property, I—we—felt it would be best to preserve the scene."

Ryan raised his eyes from the task of zipping up his own overalls.

"No sign of Mrs Gregson?"

Yates understood him immediately.

"No sir, there's been no sign of her, but her car is still on the driveway."

Ryan noted the silver Audi parked a short distance away, beside Gregson's larger saloon. At that moment, he also caught sight of Faulkner's less impressive vehicle pulling into the quiet street and the corresponding flicker of curtains in several windows. He was taking no chances with forensics. Whatever the Powers That Be would have him believe, Ryan was convinced that whatever incident had put Gregson in hospital, whatever they would find had happened to his wife, was nothing to do with bad timing or bad luck. That being the case, he wanted his best CSI on the job.

He turned back.

"Thanks, Yates. Continue to man the entrance here, we'll call you if we need anything."

Ryan let his eyes linger on the other PC, who had been silent throughout the exchange, and made a mental note of his name and identification number.

"Got anything to add to that, constable?"

The man's eyes blinked but he shook his head.

"No, sir. PC Yates has covered it all."

Ryan wondered why the man was avoiding eye contact but he decided to shelve it for now, as Faulkner ambled towards them dragging a small wheelie-bag filled with what Ryan assumed to be forensic gadgetry.

"Where's the fire? I'm up to my neck working on the Bowers case," he began.

"I know, Tom. I appreciate you coming over. I'm not sure what we're dealing with yet but Gregson was attacked and they've taken him to the RVI," he referred to one of the larger hospitals in the city. "There's been no word from his wife, so your guess is as good as mine on that score. As far as the Chief Constable is concerned, DCS Gregson deserves our best efforts, so that's what we'll give him."

Faulkner looked towards the house.

"You're thinking she might be somewhere inside?"

"Only one way to find out."

* * *

Anna shed the dark dress she had worn earlier in the day for more comfortable attire—jeans and a faded t-shirt emblazoned with an old *Guns 'n' Roses* motif. She was ensconced in the smallest bedroom in her cottage, which had been converted into a comprehensive home office. Her computer had long since reverted to 'stand by' mode, owing to a period of inactivity where she had done nothing more than stare at the screen.

She couldn't stop thinking about Mark.

What had happened? How could a man with so many friends and the esteem of his colleagues wind up dead at a church in the middle of nowhere? Why hadn't he confided in her about his tumour—unless, he hadn't known it existed.

Ryan had warned her to leave it to the professionals. In kind but firm tones, he had asked her not to begin her own amateur sleuthing. In his view, she was too close to the victim to remain objective, besides the fact that she was a civilian.

Try telling that to her dead friend.

Ryan, MacKenzie, all of them were hindered by the Police and Criminal Evidence Act, which came with a list of rules and regulations as long as your arm. People could be reticent to speak to the police, whereas if Anna did a little gentle prodding around the university, spoke to Mark's family and followed a few leads of her own, perhaps she might find out something that could help.

First, she needed to understand where Mark had been found.

With renewed energy, she packed up her papers and made a grab for her coat.

* * *

Night had fallen by the time Anna reached Heavenfield Church. The roads had been empty for the past fifteen miles, the fields silent as her car motored from the city limits towards relative wilderness. She imagined her friend making this journey, alone and defenceless against the calamity that would eventually befall him. Her lip trembled, thinking of Mark's final moments. Who had pulled the trigger? Whose face had loomed above him as he died?

She parked in the lay-by nearest the church, almost precisely where Mark's car had rested two days before, then sat for a few minutes with her hands resting on the steering wheel. Ahead of her, the night sky was ablaze with stars. For an instant, she was transported back in time, through her imagination, to this place centuries before. Had Oswald's army looked overhead into the mystical cosmos, as she had done? Had they prayed for victory to a God she had never believed in?

Anna shook herself and slammed out of the car, the sound echoing into the quiet night. Her torch flickered on, shining a comforting pathway ahead. She could see the church on the hill, spotlighted by the white light of the moon overhead. It was the stuff of old-fashioned horror movies. There ought to be bats flying out of the bell tower and zombies rising from the graveyard to complete the picture. She half expected to see Peter Cushing's ghost emerge from behind a gravestone.

It was nothing more than light and shadow, she told herself. Uneasiness came from the knowledge that Mark had died here, but that was all.

Resolutely, she walked towards the church, her boots squelching into what smelled like sheep dung or a cattle pat as she traversed the gentle incline.

Lovely.

She marvelled at her own predictable nature, recognising the signs of heightened stress as her mind and body responded to the darkness and the unnerving outline of the church looming above her.

Approaching the entrance, she could see police tape stretched across the doorway barring entry. Despite it, she was startled to find that a dim light shone through the small diamond-shaped windows, suggesting that she was not alone. Somebody had disregarded the barrier and let themselves in.

Her torch swung back around, its light seeking the outline of her car at the foot of the hill but finding only a thick blanket of darkness as opaque as any fog she had ever known.

With a shiver, Anna tugged the door open and stepped inside.

CHAPTER 12

The church smelled of mildew and something faintly sulphuric. Two of the gas lamps were alight and fizzed away, giving off a thin yellow light which softened the unrelenting darkness. Somewhere, a rodent scuttled.

The church was empty but Anna could have sworn that the walls were alive. The room seemed to watch her and the night breeze whistled through the mullioned windows like a banshee.

Get a grip, she thought, taking a firm handle on herself.

She used her torch as a guide, taking a couple of steps further inside before she remembered the yellow forensic markers still tacked to the floor. The idea was to come and go clandestinely, not like a bull rampaging inside a china shop.

She stepped carefully to one side and traced the perimeter of the room, keeping her eyes on the thick wooden slab which served as an altar at the back of the church. She was overcome by sadness at the thought of Mark lying there, alone, his body violated. Anger followed quickly and she forced herself to take in the details. The placement of the pews, the number of windows. She took out her phone and snapped a few images for reference. Carefully, she skirted the edge of the wall and captured different angles, her heart in her throat each time she was forced to step deeper into the shadows.

All of a sudden, she knew that she was not alone.

She heard no sound; she saw no flash of a shrouded figure. She *felt* it, as an animal feels that it has become prey to a hunter, her skin tingling with awareness.

Anna slunk back into the shadows, extinguished the light of her torch with shaking fingers and waited.

Sure enough, another person crept into sight. She saw them crouch to the floor as if searching for something. She heard their agitated breath as they fanned the floor near the altar, growing ever closer to where Anna stood, her body plastered to the damp stone wall.

It rose again and Anna tried to note identifying features; anything which could help her to describe what she had seen, but in the gloomy light all she could make out was a person dressed in dark clothing, of average build. She would have thought male, but something about the movement of the arms, the posture, told her that she could be wrong.

The figure continued to search, its movements hurried but thorough, then it rose again and seemed to study a patch of stonework at the rear of the altar. Anna frowned, trying to make out what had captured its attention, but as far as she could tell it was nothing more than a bare wall.

The figure turned, suddenly, scenting the presence of another and a scream welled up inside her throat.

* * *

In the city, Faulkner stood beside the patio at the rear of 17 Haslemere Gardens snapping pictures with an expensive-looking camera. Lowering the zoom lens, he let his studious gaze travel over the scene, illuminated by a bright safety light which responded to movement. Every now and then, Phillips waved a hand to keep its garish light shining.

"Well?"

Faulkner continued to scan the ground, noting the direction of the blood spatter and the overturned bistro chair a few feet away from it. He retrieved a fresh stack of yellow flags and stepped forward to mark the blood where Gregson had been found spread-eagled on the tiles.

Eventually, he shook his head in the manner of one trying to solve *The Times* cryptic crossword.

"It's a pity nobody took a photo of Gregson in situ when they found him. At the moment, Yates' description tells us that the direction of his body was angled away from the house. That would suggest he was fleeing from the direction of those patio doors," he pointed towards the French-style veranda doors that were standing wide open. "If and when Gregson wakes up, I suppose he'll be able to give us a clearer picture."

Ryan held off making any caustic response to that.

"The blood spatter is consistent with a hard blow to the back of the head," Faulkner continued, directing their attention to a patch of drying blood on the floor. "There are a couple of prints leading away from the house, which suggests that our perpetrator either used his boot, or trod in some blood on his way out. There's just one thing."

"What's that?"

"The chair, over there," Faulkner replied. "It's lying as if somebody overturned it, in a rush to get up. But, looking at the scene as a whole, it's nowhere near the spot Gregson was found and doesn't match the direction he was heading."

"Somebody else might have been sitting there," Phillips offered. "Mrs Gregson, perhaps?"

"Could be," Faulkner's brow cleared at the thought. "Yes, that might make sense."

His brow furrowed again.

"I suppose if she had been sitting outside and saw her husband fleeing…but that doesn't match what we know about her movements, does it?"

"Nope," Ryan agreed, roundly. "Cathy Gregson was supposed to be at home today. Gregson was at work, or should have been. It would make more sense to imagine him coming back home for some reason and finding her in distress."

"She could be the aggressor," Phillips pointed out. "He might have been running away from her."

"It's possible," Ryan said, fairly. "And some might say he had it coming."

Faulkner and Phillips exchanged a telling glance.

"I think it's time we took another look inside the house," Faulkner said swiftly.

They had taken no more than a few steps inside before they smelled the bleach. The scent was overpowering, assailing their nostrils with its noxious odour.

"It's funny," Faulkner said softly. "Earlier today, I was talking to MacKenzie about bleach being the disinfectant of choice for a killer trying to cover up widespread blood loss."

"Somebody's used a vat of it in here," Ryan observed, taking in the smart living room with its new widescreen television. "It's coming from the kitchen," he added, following his nose.

The kitchen was gleaming, every surface shining. The windows stood open in a pathetic attempt to clear the stench of disinfectant.

"Either Cathy Gregson believes that cleanliness is next to godliness, or somebody died in here," Phillips concluded.

"And, before you say it," Ryan warned, "I agree that Gregson's injuries weren't self-inflicted, so it's more than likely that we're looking for a third party. The angle made it impossible, for one thing, and for another it would take a seriously fucked up person to smash their own skull in order to provide themselves with a defence."

"No weapon lying around, either," Faulkner said, letting out a tired breath. His mid-brown eyes were glassy with fatigue. "I'll snap some pictures while I'm here, but I'm going to have to hand this one over, Ryan. I can't be in two places at once."

Ryan made his own quick assessment and nodded briefly.

"Understood, Tom. The Bowers investigation should be your first priority. All we've got here is a hell of a lot of suspicions but no facts. I'll do my job and start getting those facts. Maybe, by the time I do, some of the legwork on Bowers will have been completed."

Faulkner nodded.

"You've spoken to the Chief Constable?"

"Yeah. Let's just say, we're on the same page. For the moment," he tagged on. Turning, he met Phillips' placid eyes beneath his paper cap. "Let's start by getting chatty with those neighbours."

Phillips pointed a broad finger at Ryan's chest.

"You're not throwing me to the wolves, lad. If I've got to sit around drinking herbal tea and listening to neighbourhood gossip, then I'm taking you down with me."

Ryan grinned.

"Privilege of rank," he explained breezily, chuckling as Phillips' brows fell into an ominous line.

* * *

MacKenzie rubbed at her eyes, which were itchy and sore after three hours spent trawling through digital files. She heard the faithful, monosyllabic tap of Lowerson's fingers against the keyboard at his desk across the incident room. Sensing her inspection of him, he paused to look up.

"Any news, Mac?"

She had been forced to issue a strict command that he no longer call her 'Sir, I mean…Ma'am.' It was embarrassing for them both.

"The lab came back with the data on those blood samples. There was some cross-contamination, so they've been working to separate the blood types. They've managed to analyse four of the samples for DNA. I've been searching the Missing Persons DNA Database to see if I can find a match."

"Any luck?"

MacKenzie leaned back and wondered whether luck had played a part, then set questions of philosophy to one side.

"Well, the DNA Database has only been up and running since 2010, so that limits the scope of potential matches, but actually we hit lucky on two of them. Both missing women, one aged eighteen and the other twenty-three, dark-haired. We've seen their faces before."

Lowerson turned his whole body towards her.

"Donovan?"

"And the prize goes to…" MacKenzie affected a drum roll on the edge of her desk, "DC Lowerson! Bang on, Jack. The samples match two of the women listed in Donovan's private notes. He wrote a detailed summary about how he had killed them but never told us where. Officially, they're still listed as missing. One back in 2011, another in 2013." She sighed. "We can inform next of kin tomorrow."

"They're still excavating the site around Hadrian's Wall," Lowerson said, hopefully. "We might uncover their bodies."

"Anything's possible," MacKenzie said, dubiously. "It's time those girls were brought home."

"Do I get a bonus prize if I guess the dates they went missing?"

MacKenzie smiled without any humour.

"That would be too easy. We're back around to the Circle again, Jack. I didn't need a database to tell me that those girls went missing on or around 21st June."

"Summer solstice," Lowerson said.

"Here's the *really* scary part," MacKenzie continued. "We've got a bunch of girls confirmed missing around the summer solstice over the past ten years, but what about the winter solstice? Three people died around the winter solstice on Holy Island, but we haven't even thought about how many others might have gone missing before that."

Lowerson just looked at her, his jaw drooping at the thought of more dead women, more pointless waste of life.

"We should speak to Ryan," he said firmly.

MacKenzie massaged an ache between her eyes.

"I know that, Jack. For what it's worth, I agree with you. There's just this little thing called 'police misconduct.' "

"Ryan didn't kill Bowers."

MacKenzie rolled her eyes and told herself to be patient. Lowerson looked up to Ryan as some kind of demigod.

"Christ's sake, I know he didn't kill him, Jack. That's not the point. We need to be able to record it in black and white, without any improper conduct or mishandling of the evidence. That includes bringing him in to consult on the case, at least until we can strike him off our list as a suspect. It's a big help that no powder traces were found on his clothing but we're still waiting for those phone records to come back to confirm his version of events."

Lowerson jiggled one leg petulantly but he did not contradict her.

"Tell me what I can do," he flicked a disgusted glance at his computer, a clear sign that he would rather be out in the field than sitting behind a desk.

MacKenzie fixed him with a stony green-eyed stare.

"I don't need any fucking tantrums from you, boyo," she ground out. The shock of it had him shrinking back in his chair. "You knew what this gig involved when you signed up. It's not all car chases and fist fighting. Go and be a stunt man, if that's the life you want."

"I don't—" he swallowed.

"Good, because the way we hunt a killer is through trial and error. We follow the dots and we use our heads. And we wait. Yeah, sometimes the waiting is a bitch," she acknowledged dryly, "but it pays off. Thanks to the lab team, we might be able to give some grieving families an answer to where their daughters went. Thanks to the fact that we are investigating one man's death, we can look into others..."

She trailed off, as the import of her words hit home.

"And...that's no coincidence," she said finally.

"You mean Donovan?" Jack Lowerson's attention was rekindled as the conversation changed track. "He's dead, Mac. Even if he killed those women up at Heavenfield, Donovan couldn't have killed Bowers. He's six feet under, himself."

"Yeah...yeah," MacKenzie said distractedly, turning to stare at the board. "But a good friend of ours is always saying that he doesn't believe in coincidences."

They both smiled, thinking of Ryan's regular tag line.

"Come to think of it, neither do I," she said. "Whoever killed Bowers up at Heavenfield wanted us to find that site. The church is too obscure for it to be otherwise."

Lowerson ran his fingers through his hair, then rubbed them absently against his trousers to get rid of the crusted gel.

"So you're saying that whoever killed Bowers knew about Donovan?"

"Yeah, that's what I'm saying. I've got no evidence yet," MacKenzie laughed shortly, "But that's what I'm saying."

"Which also means that whoever knew about Donovan might also know about the Circle?"

There was a pause, while MacKenzie thought of all the possible connectors, including those involved in their last two major cases. It was a gigantic thread to pull, but they were about to start tugging on it.

"Yes, we have to assume that the dates were significant to Donovan, as they were in the ritual murders on Holy Island. Whoever knew about Donovan's habits must have guessed the reason for them, must have known he was part of the Circle. It's fairly safe to assume that Donovan was a rogue member, considering the amount of attention he drew to himself.

"I'm asking myself why this person doesn't just come and tell us all about it. Walk right up to the station and knock on my door."

"They might be too scared," Lowerson said quietly, but MacKenzie didn't hear him.

"Why kill Bowers?" she continued. "It seems like overkill, if the point was to draw our attention to Heavenfield as a site of importance."

Lowerson shrugged.

"Could have had another reason to pop him off."

MacKenzie rose from the chair to pace a few steps and then turned back.

"Jack? Get Ryan on the phone."

"Wha—? But you just said…"

"Forget what I said," she snapped, and then took a deep, calming breath. It wasn't every day that you went against your training. The law was there for good reason; at least that was what she had always believed.

She watched Lowerson retrieve his personal mobile rather than using the office desk phone, with a self-deprecating shrug at his own sneaky methods. He was learning.

MacKenzie watched him reflectively. Over the last year, the detectives of CID had begun to feel a presence in their lives. Interference from a negative force, one which had engulfed three men and convinced them to kill, which had convinced other men and women to assist them as accessories. It wasn't like any of the other murders she had dealt with over the years, and MacKenzie had seen plenty. She had seen men, women and children violated so that her heart wept for them. It was a question of violence, control and mental illness, sometimes. Other times, it was a case of plain and simple bloody-mindedness. Warped animal instinct, whatever you wanted to call it.

This was different.

This was indoctrination, a fever in the minds of weak people. Some, like Patrick Donovan, were wired to kill. They liked it; they *enjoyed* doing it. But the Circle had given them a code, lending a specious legitimacy to their actions.

MacKenzie knew almost nothing about the Circle's organisation, its structure or even how it came to be about. How did people join? Were they selected?

It was past time they found out.

CHAPTER 13

Ryan drove the short distance from Gregson's home through the centre of Newcastle to the neighbouring city of Durham. He let himself into Anna's cottage, which was nestled in a scenic spot beside the river in sight of the fairy tale outline of the cathedral. Conscious of the fact it was past ten, he was careful to close the door quietly behind him. There was no sound in the cosy sitting room, no sign that she had stayed up except the light burning in the hallway. He couldn't blame her. Anna had hardly slept since finding out about Mark's death and it had been an emotional few days coming to terms with it.

He padded through the house towards the kitchen, intending to forage for some kind of snack. He stooped to avoid the low beams in the higgledy-piggledy house, congratulating himself on his foresight, and flicked on the light.

Then, nearly squealed. Only ingrained manliness prevented him.

"Anna? What the hell are you doing lurking about in the dark? You nearly gave me a heart attack."

She stood leaning against the sink, her face in profile as she sipped at a glass of water. Receiving no response from her, Ryan took a closer look. Her hand was shaking against the glass tumbler and she still had her coat on, despite the warmth inside the house.

Slowly, he ran a hand over her back and felt the automatic shiver run through her.

"Darling, what's happened?"

"Nothing," she said automatically, continuing to sip at the water.

Ryan looked away briefly and wished for a troubleshooting manual he could consult in moments like these.

"Ah," he rubbed his hands along the sides of her arms while he thought of what he might have done wrong. "Sorry I'm back so late. We caught a big one, Phillips and me. It concerns Gregson."

"No problem," Anna replied tonelessly.

Something was definitely wrong, he thought worriedly. Normally, she was the first to chew his ear off about work, particularly where DCS Gregson was concerned.

"Anna," he said gently, "please tell me what I've done."

She looked up at that.

"Done? You haven't done anything. I'm sorry…I…I'm just feeling under the weather."

Most men would have taken that at face value, perhaps presuming that she was struggling with grief. Maybe they would offer to make her a cup of tea and tuck her up in bed with some aspirin.

Ryan was not 'most men.'

"Yeah, nice try, sweetheart." Abruptly, he set her away from him and crossed his arms. "You don't like secrets between us? Well, neither do I, so start talking."

"I—"

Her voice faltered, so she took another sip of water.

"I had a bit of a fright, that's all."

"What?" Ryan was instantly on guard, his body braced to search the cottage for intruders. "Was somebody in the house?"

Anna's lip twitched.

"Stand down, soldier. Nobody has been in the house, apart from us." She began to shrug out of her coat and, ever the gentleman, he leaned forward to help her.

"Thanks," she murmured, finally meeting his eyes. "Look, don't be angry."

Ryan's jaw set.

"That depends on what I'm not supposed to be angry about."

To his chagrin, small-minded worries popped into his mind. Visions of Anna with another man, of her telling him that life with a policeman was not what she wanted after all. He waited for her to speak, heart thundering in his chest, blood pumping in his ears. Fear grabbed him by the balls and held on like a vice.

"I realise now that it was a bad idea, but…well, I drove up to Heavenfield."

The torrent abated and his heart rate slowly returned to normal. Before he could think better of it, he snatched her up and pulled her against him in a crushing embrace.

"I thought you'd be mad," came her muffled voice against the hard wall of his chest.

He closed his eyes and then slowly released her.

"I am. Of course, I am," he said, more firmly, distracting himself by filling the kettle. The ordinary task steadied his schoolboy nerves and, when he turned back, his face was impassive. "You're not with CID, Anna. You're a historian, and a very good one."

Anna got the message.

"Look, Mark was my friend. Nothing seems to be happening and I wanted to help, rather than sitting around growing old."

"I understand that," his voice was level. "And I can empathise."

Of course he could, she realised. His own sister had died. He knew what it felt like to wait for long hours beside the phone.

"Sorry, I forgot," she murmured. "I just wanted to help."

Ryan flashed a lightning-quick smile.

"Since when have I been able to stop you interfering in police matters? The day that you actually follow my advice will be one for the record books." He thought of their excursion to Mark Bowers' home, the quick and nimble way she had searched the man's belongings and concluded not for the first time that she would have made a good detective. "Why don't you tell me what you found?"

He went about making coffee for both of them.

"Shouldn't we have decaf? It's getting late…" she broke off at one look of affronted disgust from the man in her life.

"If you're a coffee drinker, you have to *commit* to it," he said, then took a long and satisfying gulp from his own mug. All was right with the world again.

Anna warmed her hands on the cup he handed to her and began to regale him with her adventures of the evening.

"Let me get this straight," Ryan held up a hand. "You drove out into the middle of nowhere, as darkness was falling, to a site where a man was recently murdered."

"Yep."

"You proceeded to breach the police 'do not cross' line and walked into a crime scene."

"Correct."

Ryan just stared at her.

"Haven't I told you that murderers often return to the scene of their crime? You could have been hurt."

Anna shivered violently and set the cup aside.

"I think I might have seen him…or her."

Ryan's face transformed into a neutral mask, an expressionless palette he wore so well.

"Tell me everything you can remember."

* * *

Three men and a woman sat in the visitors' car park at the foot of Bamburgh Castle, a towering edifice built into the craggy hillside overlooking the North Sea. Long ago, the first kings of England had looked out over its battlements, over the grey-blue water towards Holy Island, which was just visible eight miles further north. To the west, the village of Bamburgh huddled at the foot of the castle, quaint and postcard pretty with its tearooms and gift shops.

Night cloaked the car in darkness, protecting its occupants from any wandering eyes, but in any event the residents of Bamburgh would be home in their beds at this hour, doors closed to the chilly evening air.

"We couldn't find the book anywhere in his house," one of the men was saying. "And it's not on the inventory or with forensics."

"It's missing," another man said. "I've asked around and Bowers didn't give it to anybody else for safekeeping."

Jane Freeman felt indignant. Bowers dared to deprive her of her *right?* She wanted to see her name beside all the others, written in pen and ink as the first woman ever to act as their Master's vessel on Earth. She needed to see it, to satisfy her own pride.

Where had he put the damn book?

A sudden thought struck her, as she looked through the windscreen at the enormous shadowed castle. Perhaps somebody else had taken it, somebody who was not part of their circle. There could only be a limited number of people who would have the means to do that and they were all part of DCI Ryan's team. Her mind ran through the list of possibilities, starting with Ryan's milky-faced girlfriend, she thought bitchily. Anna Taylor had been Bowers' only weakness and it seemed that the woman had a talent for winding certain men around her skinny little finger.

Freeman might have admired her for it, if she didn't already hate her so much.

Yes, she thought. It was possible that Bowers had given Anna access to his home, like the weak-minded idiot he had always been.

"I want all the loose ends tied up," she said decisively. "It's incredible that Ryan is still alive and kicking. He could ruin things for all of us."

"He hasn't said anything so far," one man said, equably.

Freeman turned her head and the whites of her eyes shone in the reflected green light of her dashboard.

"The Master demands it."

The man's lips trembled shut. He knew better than to argue with the wishes of his Master.

"*Ave satani,*" Freeman breathed.

* * *

Keith Thorbridge brooded into the empty silence of his miner's cottage from the discomfort of an understuffed armchair that badly needed re-upholstering. The living room was plain, sparse of furniture except for a boxy old television on a plastic stand and a cheap foam sofa he had bought third-hand from a thrift shop. There was an electric fire in the centre of the room that he never used, even in the winter when Northumberland grew bitterly cold. He would rather wear another layer of clothing than pour cash into the hands of those fat cat utility companies.

At his feet, a fawn-coloured whippet sat with her head on his knees.

Thorbridge thought about the woman while his fingers stroked rhythmic circles against the downy fur.

"Shh," he soothed.

What had she done?

The church was his solace. It was more than a building; it was his salvation, his penance to the deity that had shown him another life. He would do anything to protect its walls from taint, from misuse.

He had known about the doctor. He had watched him, driving like a madman in the dead of night, lighting the gas lamps. That's how Keith had known, at first, that somebody was using the church late at night. He had left the lamps burning, running down the gas supply.

That, and the bloodstains, of course.

Did that fool of a doctor think that he would not have noticed? He knew every grain of wood in that place.

Now, the man was dead and buried. Apparently, after pulling a noose around his own neck in the police cells.

Rest in peace, Thorbridge thought with a snort, taking a long swig from the glass of ale resting loosely in his other hand.

His thoughts circled back around to the woman and his fingers dug into the dog's fur until the animal yelped.

CHAPTER 14

Wednesday, 5th August

Ryan was up with the larks, leaving Anna to catch up on some sleep while he donned a pair of old trainers and warmed his muscles with a jog around the cobbled streets of Durham. He followed his usual route, keeping to the western bank of the River Wear. The route took him past the shopping centre and dipped underneath Milburngate Bridge, away from the grandeur of the oldest part of the city towards the industrial quagmire of government buildings and abandoned warehouses.

He passed one or two others who puffed out their exertion and passed him with a brief glance of recognition for a fellow morning jogger. If he had looked properly, Ryan might have recognised one of them from the pool of constables in CID.

But he didn't.

His feet pounded the pavement, echoing against the concrete surrounds until he crossed the river again and made his way through the town. He counted off the college buildings as he followed the loop back around the underside of the city. Eventually, he came full circle and the Cathedral, which dominated the landscape like a beacon, told him that he was almost home.

Home.

The thought of making a home with another person, someone who understood the vagaries of his life and could handle his shifting, mercurial moods, had been little more than a pipe dream. Until, under the most unlikely circumstances, he had met Anna.

She, with her deceptively quiet temperament that made a man think of silky garments and mood music, had stormed into his life with the force of a typhoon, sweeping away any silly notions he might have had about protecting her from the darker sides to life.

She needed no advice from him about how to handle herself.

And wasn't that a breath of fresh air?

For the first time in many months, he recalled the only other relationship he could reasonably describe as such. A girl six…no, *dear God,* eight years ago. A woman he'd met in police training and spent a couple of years casually dating while he was working at the Met. Emma, he remembered, thinking that it seemed like a lifetime ago and he felt like a different person.

A better one, he hoped.

He sprinted the rest of the distance back to their front door and let himself be enveloped by the distinctive scent of fresh coffee and something meaty. Bacon, he thought, while his mouth watered.

He found her in the little breakfast nook off the kitchen, sitting at the fairy-sized table with copper pots and pans hanging precariously around her. She was bundled into an oversized tartan dressing gown and her long legs were bare, one foot swaying in time to the morning radio while she read a broadsheet paper.

She turned and met the look in his eyes.

"Ready for breakfast?"

"It can wait."

* * *

The time was still shy of seven-thirty when their visitors began to arrive. Lowerson was early, true to form, followed by Phillips and MacKenzie. Phillips' choice of tie was an embroidered masterpiece in shades of purple, reflecting his own unique interpretation of professional attire.

"Welcome to New Scotland Yard," Ryan quipped, as they divested themselves of their coats.

"It's a lot more comfortable," Phillips replied, topping off a mug of steaming coffee. "Do we get code names?" His button-brown eyes lit up at the thought. "I already know what mine would be."

"Oh, and what's that?"

"Golden Eagle," Phillips supplied.

Ryan rubbed a hand across his chin to hide his smile.

"I was thinking more along the lines of, 'plastic chicken.' "

"You've got no respect for your elders."

Amid hoots of laughter, they made their way up to Anna's first floor office, which had been converted into something they could loosely call an incident room.

Inside, the two walls not already covered in bookshelves had been cleared of any paraphernalia and presented a blank, pale green canvas. Anna's desk remained but was clear of distractions. Ryan hitched a hip onto the edge, grateful that it wasn't a self-assembly job and liable to collapse under his weight.

He picked up a squeezy plastic oddment in the shape of the Leaning Tower of Pisa, which Anna used as stress-relief when she was working to a deadline. He tried it out and then flipped it from hand to hand while he began to order things in his mind.

"Alright, let's just get everything out in the open," he began, skipping the pleasantries. "We all feel bad sneaking around like this—"

"I don't," Phillips threw in, and then shrugged when heads swivelled in his direction.

"With the exception of *Phillips,*" Ryan continued, "the rest of us are probably feeling awkward."

The silence that followed told him he wasn't far off the mark.

"Here's the deal," he said. "This may not be the way we normally do things, but the situation is important enough to justify deviation from our usual methods. If anyone's got a problem with that, there'll be no hard feelings, but it would be better for all concerned if you speak up now."

He waited, but the silence stretched. This time, it was a comfortable one.

"In that case, let's crack on. Consider this a 'safe space.' What we discuss here goes no further. Agreed?"

There was murmured assent.

"We've got three cases running concurrently," he dived straight in. "MacKenzie and Lowerson are still investigating Bowers' death. Meanwhile, Phillips and I are looking into the attack on Gregson and the apparent disappearance of his wife sometime yesterday afternoon. Finally, we're all looking into the Circle. Who they are, *what* they are and to what extent they connect with current and past investigations."

"This is going to rack up some overtime," Phillips joked.

"Yeah, yeah," Ryan waved it away. "It's going to be a gigantic motherfucking bitch of a job, for no extra pay, but somebody's got to do it."

"You're not selling it very well," Anna said.

Ryan flashed her a brief smile, then his face fell into grim lines, eyes dark and compelling as he scanned the faces of his friends and colleagues.

"I don't know what we will uncover, not for certain. That being the case, things could get hard and they could get personal. We should all be prepared for that. The people we're dealing with are likely to be in positions of relative power. How else have they avoided discovery? They'll be desperate to stay hidden and they'll fight dirty. If anybody has a skeleton or two rattling around in their closet, you might as well be prepared for it to jump out and bite you on the arse." He paused, adding, "I'm currently a suspect for murder and I barely dodged being dismissed from my job. On the upside, I've had an unexpected holiday, so life ain't all bad."

They smiled in solidarity but none of them were fooled into thinking that the past six weeks had been anything but a living nightmare for him.

"MacKenzie tells me that the investigation into Bowers' death is heating up. Analyses of blood samples found around the body point to historic crimes chalked up to Patrick Donovan. That man died six weeks ago, which is too damn close a connection for it to be accidental."

"The lab team are working around the clock to get through the rest of the samples," MacKenzie put in. "It will take longer to match them with the right missing person because the database didn't store DNA data before 2010—too expensive. We can always cross-match with the relatives of the women on Donovan's list, see if we get lucky and find a familial match."

Ryan nodded. It was exactly what he would have done.

"Good stuff," was all he said. "What about the telephone records?"

MacKenzie understood that if it could be proven that Ryan did not send any messages to himself, it would go a long way towards clearing him.

"The telephone company confirmed that you made the calls to Bowers' home and place of work at the times you stated. The outgoing calls were made from the mobile phone you turned over to us, which has been verified as your primary phone—"

"I bet that's been a pain in the arse having to turn in your phone," Phillips interjected. "I keep all my games on mine."

MacKenzie threw him a look that could only be described as loving despair.

"When do you ever have time to play video games?"

"On the netty," he replied, with a wink.

"They're still working to triangulate the source of the text message you received purporting to be from Mark Bowers," she continued, turning to address Ryan once again. "Which is trickier since it was sent from a prepaid mobile phone rather than something on a monthly contract. We still haven't found Bowers' mobile, although he did have one, but in any case the message you received didn't come from there. The minute I hear anything further, you'll be the first to know."

"I appreciate that, Mac," Ryan said quietly. He looked away for a second, formulating what he wanted to say next. "I, ah, want you to know I appreciate you—all of you—being here now. I know what it means, and what it could cost you."

Before they had a chance to answer, he was off the desk, rising to pick up a marker pen. Anna opened her mouth to object to the use of permanent marker on her walls, but closed it again as she watched him draw a long black line along the length of one side. She supposed her study was due a fresh lick of paint.

"This represents Bowers' timeline," he explained, adding in Bowers' movements from Friday and Saturday, leading up to his death on the Sunday. "This is what I'm aware of, so we'll leave it at that. MacKenzie, Lowerson, carry on with your own board back at CID, it's important to keep things looking normal."

"You mean in case somebody checks up?" Lowerson asked.

"That's exactly what I mean," Ryan agreed. "Anything you find relating to previous victims, previous cases, bring it here. That might relate to the Circle. Everything else, keep it at the office."

"Understood," MacKenzie said.

"What about ballistics? Have you found a murder weapon?" Anna chimed in, feeling a sense of camaraderie as she was drawn into their work.

MacKenzie reached into her wide leather bag and pulled out a black file, retrieving a couple of printed copies of the ballistics report summary. She handed one to Ryan and referred to the other while she spoke.

"I had a report waiting in my inbox this morning, which tells me that Jepson was working through the night to complete it." She thought of George Jepson, their go-to ballistics expert. What he didn't know about hand-held machine weaponry wasn't worth knowing.

"Upshot is, we still have no weapon but at least we have a better idea of what we're looking for."

"Which is?"

"Jepson assessed the lead ball, the black powder, the size and extent of the injuries," she explained. "There were small powder burns on Bowers' face, which suggests there was a spark of some kind. Putting it all together, Jepson tells me the weapon we're looking for is likely to have a flintlock mechanism. That's what Pinter thought, too."

"A flintlock mechanism?"

MacKenzie held up a finger while she rifled through her notes.

"It was developed in the seventeenth century in France. Basically, it's a type of lock belonging to pistols and rifles during that era. You get a piece of flint which is held in place by these miniature jaws, on the end of a short hammer. You pull the hammer back into a 'cocked' position," she used thumb and index finger on her left hand to illustrate. "When it's released by the trigger being pulled, the spring-loaded hammer moves forward, which causes the flint to strike a bit of steel called the…" she checked her notes, "…the 'frizzen.'

"The motion pushes the frizzen back and opens the cover of the pan containing the gunpowder. As the flint strikes the frizzen, it creates a spark, which falls into the pan and lights up the powder."

"Then everything goes 'boom'?" Phillips finished for her.

"Indeed," MacKenzie's lips twitched. "The flame burns through a tiny hole in the barrel of the gun, ignites the main powder and causes the weapon to fire."

"That would explain the smell of sulphur," Anna commented. "Up at the church. There was a lingering smell of sulphur."

MacKenzie raised an eyebrow but was perfectly capable of putting two and two together and producing the correct number.

"I take it you went on a little expedition?" she asked sweetly.

Anna lifted her chin.

"Mark was my friend."

MacKenzie rolled her eyes heavenward.

"We've thrown out the rule book, remember?" Ryan reminded her.

"Well? You might as well tell us if there's anything we missed."

"It wasn't like that, Denise," Anna replied. "I'm not trying to tread on your toes, I'm trying to make myself useful."

"She saw someone, up there," Ryan added, overriding any smart comment on the tip of MacKenzie's tongue.

Four pairs of flat, cop eyes turned to Anna expectantly.

"I went up there around eight-thirty last night. The sun had set and the place was pretty dark. I couldn't see any other cars parked nearby, so I thought I was alone." She took a sip of coffee to warm her lips. "I made my way up the hill."

She remembered how insignificant she had felt atop that secluded hillside.

"When I reached the entrance, I noticed that a couple of the gas lamps were burning inside. At first, I wondered if there might be a police presence to guard the scene—"

"Faulkner completed his sweep of the immediate area on Tuesday," MacKenzie supplied.

"Ah. Well, I figured if your guys were still around I would have seen a police vehicle parked at the bottom of the hill." She lifted a shoulder and let it fall again. "I decided to go inside."

She heard Ryan's irritable sigh from across the room.

"I know it was dangerous. I guess I wanted to see where he had died, just to be able to visualise the space."

"And?"

"I took some pictures—"

"Which you will hand over," MacKenzie interjected firmly.

Anna smiled serenely and continued to recount her story.

"I became…*aware* of someone else in the church. I didn't see anyone when I first entered."

"Do you think they came in via the vestry?" Ryan prodded her. "Or were they concealed elsewhere?"

"There are very few hiding places in a church that size and there isn't a vestry," Anna said. "I hid in one of the shadowed corners. Even then, I anticipated being discovered sooner or later. I would have to say they came in through the main door, quietly."

"Which is also blocked by a police line," MacKenzie clarified, just for the record.

"What did they look like? Male? Female?"

"I really tried to get a good look but I didn't want to give away my position, just in case," Anna replied, apologetically. "Everything about this person was average: height, gait...although the way they stroked the wall almost made me think of a feminine caress."

Anna laughed at herself.

"It sounds silly."

"Not necessarily," MacKenzie averred. "Can you describe his actions?"

"They seemed to be looking for something on the floor beside the altar. Then, when they stood up, they seemed focussed on this one bit of wall. They stared at it for a couple of minutes and ran a hand across it, tenderly, if you like. It just somehow seemed like a feminine action."

"Mm hmm," MacKenzie's eyes were sharp. "Then what?"

"I must have made some small sound because they whirled around and seemed to see me. I just ran. I didn't stop, I just ran out of the church back to my car."

"Did they give chase?"

"I didn't see anyone when I made it to my car but I didn't stop to check. I just lit out of there like a bat out of hell."

"They saw you," Ryan said flatly.

Anna nodded, just once, while the other members of the room worried for her.

"Yes," she said quietly. "It was impossible for them to miss me, and I wasn't wearing clothing designed to conceal my face."

"Which means that somebody knows that we're checking up, going behind the lines."

"Not necessarily," Phillips interjected, his voice a model of calm reason. "Anybody who knew Bowers would know Anna was like a daughter to him. Only natural that she would want to know what happened to him. There's a chance they'll leave it at that."

"Yes, that's true," Anna was hopeful.

"What did I just say about desperate men resorting to desperate measures? If they think you saw their face…" Ryan's jaw snapped shut and he looked away, giving the Tower of Pisa a vicious squeeze.

MacKenzie turned back to Ryan, who was working very hard not to imagine Anna streaking over blackened fields, filled with fear.

"I'm going to ask Faulkner to go over the area around the altar again," MacKenzie said. "See if our mystery person left any prints."

"Gloves," Anna said with a flash of inspiration. "They were wearing gloves. Dark, black probably but could have been a dark brown. They looked dirty. Dark hat pulled over their head, all-weather coat with the collar up. Some kind of dark riding boots."

"Alright," MacKenzie nodded. "We might be able to work with a police artist, come up with a visual if you're willing?"

Anna nodded.

"I'll ask Faulkner anyway, see what we see."

"What did he want with the wall?" Lowerson looked up from his task of recording the notes of their meeting. He flushed slightly when attention turned to him. "I just mean—why was he so impressed with the wall?"

Ryan pointed a finger at him.

"It's that kind of clear-sighted thinking that makes you a detective, Jack. Damn good question. Why was he…or she, so taken with the wall?"

"You said it was beside the altar but on which side?" MacKenzie asked Anna.

Anna reached across for her phone and brought up the images she had taken last night, scrolling through until she found the right one.

"Here," she handed it over. "It's the eastern wall, to the right of the altar."

MacKenzie studied the image, before handing it around to the others.

"That wall lies directly behind where Bowers was found, nearest to his head."

She didn't need to spell out the fact that it would have been covered in bloodstains.

"Perhaps he was interested in the blood," Anna said, tonelessly, her skin turning pale. Ryan frowned and poised to go to her, but she shook her head, warding him off.

"Or it could be something else," Ryan suggested. "We need to check it out in person. For now, we know that the church has been used as a kill site. We know Bowers is the most recent victim to die there. We know the kind of weapon we are looking for—is Jepson doing a run on weapons recently sold or acquired matching his description?"

"Yep," MacKenzie nodded. "He's reaching out to his sources. He'll keep us in the loop."

"Good enough. Still, it doesn't give us a clue about motive. Why would someone want Bowers dead?"

"The pathologist was clear on the fact that there was no evidence that the wound was self-inflicted, although he's still waiting on some of the analysis coming back from the lab. All the same, he did find a sizeable brain tumour. We're waiting for access to Bowers' medical file, which is a pain in the arse to get hold of."

"Data protection," four voices spoke in unison, with varying degrees of sufferance.

"Mark never told me about a tumour but he didn't seem to be himself. Something was out of the ordinary and that could have been the reason. It still doesn't make sense, though. He was attacked, not the other way around."

"What about the family connection?" Phillips asked.

"His sister hated him," MacKenzie said without inflection. "She's been a selective mute since her accident and she's partially blind, amongst various other ailments. I went to see her at a private nursing home not far from here. She displayed no sorrow whatsoever when I told her that her brother had died."

"I—I can't believe it," Anna stammered. "He told me they were fairly close, that he loved her."

"During my visit, Judith Bowers spoke only three words, when she wasn't cackling hysterically at the news of her brother's death," MacKenzie spoke directly to Anna, thinking that it was important to dispel this particular myth as quickly and painlessly as possible. "And those words were, 'Rot in hell.' "

The sounds of traffic from the other side of the river filtered into the room as its occupants processed the information in silence.

"So, he wasn't Mr Popular, after all," Phillips was the first to speak. "But he still gets the same treatment from us."

Ryan met Phillips' eyes and some unreadable message was exchanged.

"On which note, let's move our discussion on to the next contestant for Mr Popular. Namely, Arthur Gregson, currently occupying a bed in the Intensive Care Unit of the Royal Victoria Infirmary, fighting for his life."

CHAPTER 15

Arthur Gregson lay motionless in a private room attached to the ICU. While the bored young police constable sitting beside him flipped through a measly selection of dog-eared tabloid papers more than six months out of date, Gregson remained sweetly oblivious to his surroundings.

Tubes rose like tentacles from the cannula in his wrist and monitors whirred and bleeped in time to the sound of his beating heart. Urine dripped into an almost full bag hanging from the underside of the bed, connecting to the catheter hidden beneath the neat white covers. His face, which had regained a small measure of colour overnight, was held rigidly in place by a large brace reminiscent of a Medieval torture device, to allow the wound on the back of his head an opportunity to heal.

Arthur was aware of none of it.

In an induced coma, he floated into the sublime recesses of his unconscious mind. He was a young man again, fit and healthy, with a gaggle of women vying for the attention of the newest inspector on the block. He was back in the eighties and at the height of his powers, hair blow-dried and sporting an impressive moustache in the style of Magnum P.I.

Ah, the good old days.

He was on the island again, sharing a cigar with Mark, who was younger by a few years and enamoured with a local girl. What a beauty she had been.

"*Leave it alone,*" he had counselled the young Bowers. "*She's taken.*"

"*I love her,*" Bowers had replied, tucking his hands into slim, bell-bottomed jeans while his pageboy haircut flapped in the breeze.

"*Don't risk it, lad,*" he'd said. "*Andy isn't just a friend, anymore. He's our leader.*"

A few years later, Sara Taylor was found at the bottom of a flight of stairs and he'd intervened once again to stop Bowers, who had been wild with grief.

"*He's a dead man,*" Bowers had vowed, vibrating with anger.

"*As far as we know, it was an accident,*" Gregson had tried to soothe the younger man, thinking that if Bowers knew who had really been responsible there would be no coming back. Things were precarious as it was. "*Look at Andy. He's devastated. He couldn't have killed her.*"

Gregson remembered the look in Bowers' eye as he had turned to face him, the mild-mannered historian suddenly no more, replaced by something fierce, something terrible.

"*He's a dead man,*" he had repeated, with stark finality.

Soon after, they'd found Andy Taylor washed up on the shore and Bowers' prophecy was fulfilled. Gregson never asked Mark what had happened. He could imagine.

Steve Walker had been the next to fill Andy Taylor's shoes as leader of their elite group, but that had been a mistake. How could they have known that the ordinary doctor would become such a liability? Bowers had been ready to step into the vacant position, once the police had taken Walker into custody. Now, Steve Walker spent his days staring at the walls of a high security hospital for the mentally ill.

The persistent *bleep bleep* of the hospital monitor grew faster as Gregson's mind relived the memories, until finally they brought him back to the inescapable present.

Bowers was gone. He had been a formidable man, one who did not brook disappointment or forgive easily. Gregson was certain that, if he had lived, Bowers would have killed him.

Perhaps, he would still manage it.

Gregson's eyes flew open and he gasped for air, his brain battling against the drugs towards the clear, cold reality awaiting him.

* * *

Jane Freeman was adding the finishing touches to a speech she was preparing to give that weekend on the topic of her new textbook, *Sex, Scandal and Northumbrian Legend.* Of course, the title had bugger all to do with the content of the book. If she had been so inclined, she could have included all manner of anecdotes relating to men and women of influence in the region, past and present. Instead, she had threaded her book with scraps liberally laced with gossip and fully intended to pass it off as academic history.

Then she would sit back and wait for the accolades to roll in.

She tugged a pile of freshly printed copies towards her and admired the glitzy cover, traced her fingertip over the embossed text spelling out her name, and flipped the first one open. In a flamboyant script, she added her signature to the title page and moved on to the next.

She thought of the one book she would have liked to have in her grasp but reassured herself that all good things came to those who wait. She should know.

Freeman signed twenty or more books before she heard the rumble of the little black mobile phone she kept hidden in the side pocket of her enormous leather handbag.

"Freeman."

"He's woken up," the voice informed her. No names were exchanged, as per the rules, but Freeman recognised instantly the nasal tones of one of the junior police constables assigned to CID.

"Who knows?"

"Only me," the PC replied. "The nurses haven't come in to check him. What do you want me to do?"

Freeman considered for a moment, thinking that it would be far more satisfying to watch Gregson suffer and squirm. Arthur Gregson would recognise instantly that he was being watched and would also recognise the danger of blurting out any pertinent details about their circle. That made the probability of him blabbing very low. Besides, she remembered that she had made an agreement that he would meet his end in a very particular way and she considered herself a woman of honour—mostly. She would keep her word, so long as it suited her.

"Keep an eye on him, for now. Let me know if anything changes."

She ended the call and checked the time. *Nine-fifteen.* In another hour, she expected to receive some more good news.

* * *

Ryan called a break, during which time MacKenzie telephoned CID to excuse her temporary absence, explaining to the curious detective constable assigned to the Bowers investigation that she and Lowerson were 'following a potential lead.' She issued instructions that he should continue to chase up the telephone records and trace any recent sales of flintlock pistols. Meanwhile, Anna stepped out to satisfy her own lust for baked sugar and came back with a tray of warm pastries from the bakery down the lane, much to the delight of Phillips, who declared loudly that if she ever wanted to cheat on Ryan, he'd throw MacKenzie over and run away with her. Lowerson sniggered at that and, after a brief toilet break, continued to scroll through the messages on his smartphone to keep track of incoming data. Once a reader-receiver, always a reader-receiver. Between mouthfuls of pastry, Phillips checked with the hospital to ascertain Gregson's condition and Ryan liaised with relevant parties to trace Cathy Gregson's last known whereabouts.

As far as Ryan was concerned, that woman was long gone. Every instinct he possessed was on high alert when he thought of the pretty, plump woman with the ready smile and the shaky hands. She liked to drink, he remembered. The telephone company had already informed him that no calls were recorded as incoming or outgoing on her mobile phone, which they had found on the coffee table at 17 Haslemere Gardens, aside from three text messages to her husband explaining that she had locked herself out of the house. Presumably, they had not been sent by Cathy Gregson, though they couldn't determine that for sure until they found her, or at least her body. There had been no activity on either her debit or credit cards in the last twenty-four hours, other than authorising an online grocery shop at 10:04 the previous morning. They found her purse inside her handbag in the master bedroom but no cash. Her car remained parked on the driveway outside her home, alongside her husband's.

Funny, Ryan thought. A person rarely left the house without any method of transport, payment or communication unless they were suffering from a serious mental health episode. He had seen those before; lonely and depressed people who simply wanted to vanish. *That didn't ring true in this case either.*

Ryan requested the CCTV footage from the camera he'd seen perched in one of the bay trees at the entrance to Haslemere Gardens and hoped it would give them some answers. There had been no hospital admissions matching Cathy's description, nor had there been any new additions to the mortuary roster.

One step at a time, he thought, while he drafted the press release in his head.

Once everyone had re-assembled, Ryan drew a second line on the wall and thrust his hands in the back pockets of his jeans.

"Phillips has already brought you up to date with the circumstances of Gregson's attack, so I won't go over it again. Gregson made it through the night, which doesn't surprise me."

Cockroaches can survive almost anything.

"They've got him sedated, but he woke up briefly earlier. Seemed agitated, so they upped his pain medication," Phillips put in. "He slipped back into unconsciousness."

"What are his chances?"

"Much better than they were," Phillips replied. "Doctors say it was a miracle he didn't have a major heart attack, considering the blood loss and shock. They gave him fluids, a transfusion, stabilised him enough to operate last night."

"He's got nine lives, that man," MacKenzie murmured.

"Aye," Phillips agreed, scratching at his ear. "He was in the operating theatre for several hours while they patched him up."

"Shit."

"They're monitoring him every fifteen minutes and they're planning to lower the morphine, to get a better idea of how he's bouncing back."

Idly, Ryan began to roll up the sleeves of his blue linen shirt in deference to the rising temperature inside the small room. Taking it as a cue, Lowerson shrugged gratefully out of his suit jacket.

"Nobody has heard a thing from Cathy Gregson for over twelve hours now. We've gone through the usual channels and come up with nothing. Let's get a press statement out ASAP and draft in a full CSI team to work over the house."

"Faulkner's still overseeing the work at Bowers' home," MacKenzie said, "but he should be free to assist in another day or so."

Ryan gave a quick nod and tapped the wall behind him with the end of his marker pen.

"We've got no information on why Gregson was attacked or by whom. It's a waiting game until we get some clues," he smiled, slowly and deliberately. "In order to apprehend the dastardly criminal who attacked our superintendent, the Chief Constable has sanctioned the use of a warrant to look into Gregson's personal life, including his finances."

"I'll get on to a magistrate," Lowerson offered, half-rising from his chair, but Ryan gestured for him to sit back down.

"No need," Ryan produced a crisp sheet of paper from the file on his desk. "As it happens, I spoke with a magistrate last night. Phillips and I will start to action this warrant today."

He could hardly wait to start peeling back the grimy layers of Gregson's life.

"Now, to the next interesting problem," he moved to the remaining empty wall and drew a large black circle with a question mark in the middle.

CHAPTER 16

Steven Walker, formerly the general practitioner of Holy Island and now resident of Rampton Maximum Security Psychiatric Hospital, made his way back to the single room he had been assigned and prepared to spend the next hour engaged in 'reflective quiet time.' According to the psychiatrist in charge of his care pathway, that meant spending time meditating, being mindful of his thoughts and seeking internal calm. All of this would be possible thanks to the *insightful* sessions they spent talking over his childhood and the reasons why he had been motivated to kill. The psychiatrist called these discussions a move towards 'gaining empathy,' whereas he knew that was a thin excuse for her own ambitions towards writing a biographical expose on the mind of England's latest ritual killer. He could see it now, he thought peevishly, "*My Time with Doctor Death.*"

What a load of horseshit.

How much longer before his brothers would come to save him from this purgatory of involuntary sharing and enforced medication?

At first, he had agreed with the overpriced lawyer he had hired to represent him at the trial. Diminished responsibility on grounds of insanity, ensuring his convictions were reduced to manslaughter rather than outright murder, seemed better than a lifetime spent in a maximum security prison with the scum of society. This way, if he played his cards right and went along with the good doctors, he might be pronounced 'cured' and given an early release date. It might even be easier for his friends to organise his escape long before then.

Over the last eight months, he had come to realise that the reality of his situation was very different to what he had hoped for.

Sure, there was table tennis and television, even a gym and a swimming pool if he followed the rules, but that's where the comforts ended. Security at the hospital matched that of a Category A maximum security prison. Trapped inside the body of a man presumed to be mentally ill, they deemed him an extreme threat to the outside world and at the rate he was going with his so-called therapy, he would never be a free man again.

He hated everything about the place. He hated its chlorine-scented walls. He hated the offensive, condescending shade of turquoise they had been painted, their garish colour seeming to yell, "Hey, you, look at me! I'm a cheerful colour! Try not to kill anybody today!" He hated the names of the different units, designed to sound unthreatening. His own unit—the *Peaks Unit*—was the only remaining specialist care centre for patients suffering with severe personality disorder in the U.K.

Whoop-de-fucking-doo.

In short, it meant that every day of his miserable life was spent surrounded by men who were even crazier than him.

Except he wasn't crazy. It was important to remember that.

Often, he consoled himself with thoughts of how the Master might reward him for his stoic attitude in the face of such demeaning conditions. Like a good servant, he kept his mouth shut and was thankful that the law considered it unethical to administer some kind of 'truth' drug. He knew that none of his brothers or sisters could visit him here; it would present too much of a risk to the Circle should any of them be seen. He understood that and he respected it.

But he hated every last one of them for walking free, continuing to live their lives like kings and queens while he festered here like a forgotten nobody. He was their *leader*, a man appointed by their Master. Had they forgotten that?

Had they forgotten *him?*

He would find a way to free himself. He woke up each morning thinking of escape and he went to sleep still thinking about it. Between times, he was too souped up on medication to know where the hell he was and he resented bitterly the removal of his basic ability to think clearly.

He raised a friendly hand to one of the psychiatric nurses, who gave him a keen, all-over inspection.

"How you doing today, Steve? All good?"

"Oh, top of the bill!" He forced a smile.

Like he didn't know they wished he would just kill himself and rid the world of his so-called evil. He nearly laughed but managed to stifle the sound. He didn't want that self-important nurse to come and ask him whether he was hearing the voices again.

He reached the relative sanctuary of his room and wished that he could slam the door shut, just to get a little peace and quiet, but that wasn't policy for this time of day. Open doors on this corridor, he remembered, just so that a nurse could stop by and check up on you when you least expected it. A man couldn't even take a fucking shit without some wanker or another barging in to watch.

And they called *him* a sadist.

He could feel his breakfast anti-psychotics starting to kick in, softening his mood. He headed over to his squat, safety-approved bed with the vague intention of lying down to plot the many and exciting ways he planned to kill DCI Ryan, when he saw it.

Atop the regulation cerulean blue bedclothes, a collection of little white pills had been arranged in the shape of an inverted pentagram, which was the sign of their Circle. With an ecstatic smile, he snatched them up and began to gobble them down, content in the knowledge that whatever happened to him was all part of the Circle's plan to free him.

* * *

While Steve Walker was choking on his own vomit on the linoleum floor of his bedroom at Rampton Hospital, his name was being written in clear black capital letters on the wall.

"We know for a fact that Walker was one of the Circle's leaders," Ryan was saying. "He refused to talk about it. In fact, every one of his followers has refused to talk about it, which tells us an important thing: they're loyal. Even when faced with prison or a high security mental hospital, these people keep schtum."

"They're either loyal, or they're frightened," Anna pointed out.

Ryan met her eyes and nodded.

"You're right. What ensures loyalty? Expectation of reward or fear of punishment. It's basic behavioural psychology."

"They won't be getting much in the way of a reward, unless they count being able to watch a bit of telly for an hour at the weekend," Phillips said, popping a stick of nicotine gum in his mouth. Eight months since he'd given up the cigs and he was still hankering for a drag.

"Unless their families are being rewarded," Ryan argued. "We don't know how all these people connect or who is the hand that is feeding them. There's no chance of us being able to get a warrant to look into the financials for Walker's wife or his son—"

"Alex Walker isn't involved." Anna was very clear on that. There were some things you had to believe in, your friends being one of them.

"I agree with you," Ryan acknowledged the friendship. "When he was pushed into a corner, he did the right thing and that speaks volumes. But…"

"…You have to tick all the boxes."

"Right."

"If we can't look into their families, how about re-visiting the people we already know about? There were a bunch of them convicted as accessories," MacKenzie thought aloud.

"I think that's a good starting point," Ryan agreed. "We don't want to attract too much attention, that's my concern. Their visitors will be logged and probably leaked."

MacKenzie shrugged.

"I've been in disguise before, I can do the same again. Keep things low profile."

"Alright," Ryan nodded. "Take Lowerson with you and don't mention it to anybody. Let me know before you go in."

"It won't be until the start of next week," MacKenzie said. "Too much happening on the Bowers case."

"Understood. Let's schedule a trip to see Steve Walker at the start of next week. Put it down as personal time off, no questions asked. I'll sign it off."

Once that was agreed, they moved onto philosophy.

"If we work on the theory that Patrick Donovan connects to the Circle in some way, looking into his background and his murders might tell us a bit more about how they operate. Since I've had six weeks to dwell on it, you'll be pleased to hear I've researched the life and times of Doctor Paddy Donovan with a fine toothed comb."

None of them bothered to mention that he should not have had access to confidential files while on suspension from CID, and Phillips trained his gaze on the ceiling to avoid eye contact with MacKenzie, whose accusing eyes burned into the side of his head.

"I won't bore you with his childhood, or his adolescent years, which were predictably dire, full of the usual abusive traumas consistent with the makings of an adult psychopath," Ryan said drily. "But I will pause to mention that he struggled to find reputable positions as a psychiatrist while he still lived in Ireland and his career only seemed to take off when he moved over to Newcastle. Suddenly, he was appointed to a senior clinical position at the hospital and a lucrative private practice followed that."

"Not to mention his attachment to Northumbria Constabulary," MacKenzie said. "That would have earned him a pretty penny over the years."

"And, of course, he was on very good terms with our own DCS Gregson," Ryan finished.

"Gregson is now trying to deny they were all that friendly," Phillips commented. "Since Donovan popped his clogs, he's been spinning a yarn about him being just another nut-job."

Ryan laughed shortly.

"I don't recall playing golf with him at the weekends or taking ski breaks to Austria, do you, Phillips?"

"Can't say we ever ate fondue together, now you mention it," Phillips grinned.

"Whereas Gregson *did*."

"If Donovan links to Gregson, this could be huge," Anna said slowly, as the full implications set in. Fear made her stomach jitter. Desperate men with a legion of armed police at their fingertips? Accidents could happen, and she didn't want Ryan to be one of them.

"Potentially, this is enormous," he agreed, with a spark in his eye. "But Gregson has wound up in intensive care. That could mean he's fallen out of favour."

"We might be able to use that," Phillips popped his gum. "He's vulnerable and he's alone, so he might be willing to do a deal."

"No deals," Ryan said firmly. "He'll get everything that's coming to him, nothing less and nothing more. There's a PC guarding him around the clock, but I don't know him. Lowerson?"

He turned to Jack.

"Who would you trust in the junior ranks? A lot of them are new and a bit green."

Lowerson sat up a bit straighter at the thought of no longer being lumped with the newbies. Here, his opinion mattered.

"Yates is good," he said, choosing to ignore the fact that she had turned down an offer of dinner and the movies. He was still working on it. "She's professional and calm under fire. She's looking to get ahead."

Ryan frowned.

"Ambitious in a good way, or in a 'I'm going to convert to the Circle' kind of way?"

"Oh, the first one," Lowerson said quickly.

"Right." Ryan reached over to the desk phone and made a call, barked out some instructions to PC Yates' superior, softened it with promises of tickets to the match next weekend, then replaced the receiver with a satisfied expression. "Yates'll be standing guard over Gregson as of thirty minutes from now."

"We've got possible connections," MacKenzie picked up the thread of the conversation, "but we don't have any idea what their credo is. Is it like Freemasonry, only murderous?"

"Donovan had a thing for Milton," Ryan answered. "Quotes were threaded through the notes he kept on the women he killed and he kept mementos everywhere."

He thought of the little copy he had found on Bowers' bookshelf and caught Anna's eye. There were shadows from lack of sleep and he felt an outpouring of love for her. He moderated his next comments because, if Bowers was involved—and that was a certainty in his opinion—it would mean more heartache for her. He couldn't put it off forever but he might be able to give her another day or two so that she could regain her strength.

"I've never read any Milton," Lowerson admitted, feeling like a philistine.

"Who has?" MacKenzie laughed, pulling up short when Phillips began to recite a passage.

"*Better to reign in Hell, than to serve in Heaven,*" he pondered, tugging artistically at his lower lip while MacKenzie looked on in fascination.

"Frank? When in the blue blazes have you ever found the time to read Milton? The most I see from you is the *Sunday Telegraph,*" she blurted out.

"There was many a long and lonely year before I met you, my flower."

"There was many a long and lonely pint down at the *Blue Bamboozle,*" Ryan corrected, with a grin. "But he's right. Donovan concentrated his notes on the first part of Milton's poem, which concerns Satan. Obviously, that ties in with what we already know about the Circle's satanic leanings."

Anna nodded, thinking of her own brief and terrifying experience at the hands of men and women in animal masks. Memories drifted in, flashing images of Steve Walker looming above her with a knife in his hand, his face half animal, half human in her drugged vision. The Circle had watched from their knees, chanting in botched Latin.

"Initially, we thought that they were a pagan group," she spoke up. "Some of the practices we saw on Holy Island leaned more in that direction."

Ryan remembered.

"Yes, there were elements, such as burial practice, dousing the body in camphor, the fact that the solstice is an important date in the Neo-Pagan calendar. All of that made us think about some sort of rogue paganism which had moved away from its roots."

" 'Pagan' first started out as a derogatory word," Anna clarified. "Used by other major religions to describe those who did not subscribe to the norm. Nowadays, some modern pagans use the word to describe themselves, but there's no real consensus on a unified religion. There are disparate divisions."

"You think the Circle could be a division?"

"It's possible," she mulled over the idea. "Perhaps it started out that way. Maybe the Circle started out as a group of people who believed in the Old Gods, who believed in praying for a good harvest, and it was never intended to become violent. But the markings we found etched into the bodies weren't pagan. They're commonly associated with satanic practices."

Ryan reached inside his folder and found the images of those who had died on the island.

"The inverted pentagram wasn't always viewed as an evil symbol," Anna explained, getting into her subject. "Once again, it's a case of pagan beliefs being associated with evil ones. Unfortunately for all the harmless followers and sun-worshippers, what we seem to have stumbled across is a group of people who are fusing it all together into something malevolent."

Ryan slapped the folder shut again, suddenly frustrated by it all.

"I'm not getting drawn into it any more than necessary. Whoever or whatever they worship, they're men and women at the end of the day. Flesh and blood, which means they'll fit a pair of handcuffs."

Phillips' laughter rumbled across the room.

"It's useful if we can get inside their heads, because it might help us to track them and stop them," Ryan elaborated. "But even if we don't understand their voodoo shit, we'll still stop them."

"How?" Lowerson asked, innocently.

Ryan smiled wolfishly.

"Because, Jack, killers make mistakes. When they do, we'll be waiting with a big fat net to catch them."

* * *

They agreed to a three-pronged approach. During 'daylight' hours, MacKenzie and Lowerson would continue to work on Bowers' murder, while Ryan and Phillips shed light on Gregson's attack and his wife's disappearance. When she wasn't teaching, Anna would research everything she could about cult practices in Northumberland, under the guise of her next academic project. When they had a spare hour or two, they agreed to meet at Anna's house to discuss developments. At all times, they needed to be careful. Not knowing how far the Circle reached, not knowing which members of CID were affiliated, or whether the barman at the pub, the man who ran the Pie Van or even their next door neighbours were involved created a creeping sense of paranoia.

Ryan suffered from this the least. He was already a man in the habit of looking behind the eyes of a person to study what made them tick and was no longer surprised by the depths that humanity could plumb.

"You scare me, sometimes," Anna confessed, while they were preparing to go about the rest of their day. "There's a coldness, a detachment you have which I don't think I could emulate, even if I tried."

Ryan's hands stilled on the buttons of his coat and his eyes were remote when he turned to face her.

"I wasn't always this way," he said quietly. "I used to be hot-headed, with everything swimming on the surface."

Anna wanted to tell him that his emotions were still swimming there, if one knew where to look.

"Then she died, and everything changed." He spoke of his sister. Beautiful, bright Natalie whose life had been taken for no other reason than to teach him never to interfere in the work of a serial killer on a spree.

"When she died, something inside me died as well. I know that sounds clichéd," he added. "I hear myself say it and I want to laugh but it's true. Something just snapped, Anna, and I don't know how to get it back, the feeling. I'm cold inside."

Anna reached out and folded her willowy body against him.

"You're getting warmer, every day," she murmured, rubbing soothing circles across the taut muscles of his back.

CHAPTER 17

"Gregson's awake."

Ryan glanced briefly across at Phillips, then back at the road ahead as they drove from Durham to Newcastle.

"We'll head there first, see if there's anything he'd like to tell us."

The road dipped into the valley where Newcastle and Gateshead nestled on the banks of the River Tyne. They passed the *Angel of the North,* the enormous rust-coloured industrial monument towering over the city with wide, aeroplane wings. It was no faerie, no classical folly, but an impressive structure that was both jarring and compelling in its engineered beauty.

"You think Gregson's killed her, don't you?" Phillips asked, watching the sun break through the grey clouds to illuminate the proud city of his birth.

Ryan slowed the car while they edged past some road works and drummed his fingers against the top of the steering wheel.

"Yeah, I think so. Maybe not with his own hands."

"He hasn't got the balls for it," Phillips declared.

"Maybe." Ryan leaned his arm against the edge of the window as traffic came to a standstill.

"There had to be a third person," he frowned, imagining what might have happened in his mind's eye. "Somebody to help him clean up the mess."

"Aye, but they wouldn't have cracked his skull in," Phillips was incredulous.

"Wouldn't they?" Ryan murmured. "I wonder."

"Nah," Phillips made a sweeping gesture with his hand. "We're reaching too far with that. Might have been the wife, it could really be that simple. She's still missing and she might have sent those text messages to Gregson, luring him home."

Ryan released the hand brake as traffic started moving again.

"Give me five minutes in a room with him," he growled, "and we'll see if the superintendent feels talkative."

Phillips sniggered and slid back in his seat as the car picked up speed.

* * *

"Gotcha!"

MacKenzie looked over at Lowerson, whose exclamation interrupted their drive back into the city.

"Jepson's come back to us with two possibilities for the pistol we're looking for," Lowerson elaborated. "Two nineteenth century flintlock pistols. One recently sold at auction to a local buyer, another reported stolen from the inventory at Bamburgh Castle."

Feeling excitement lick through her veins, MacKenzie edged the speedometer higher.

"Stolen?"

"Aye, an early nineteenth century officer's pistol, by a manufacturer called 'Durs Egg.' That went missing over a month ago, apparently."

"Could be worth a follow up," MacKenzie said, but Lowerson's face held the excited look of one who knew something that she didn't.

"I think we should look into the other missing pistol first, Mac," he shuffled in his seat, full of beans, and she huffed out a sigh.

"Go on then. Who was the buyer at auction?"

"You're going to love this."

MacKenzie gave him an exasperated look, which told him clearly that she wasn't in the mood for parlour games.

"Alright, alright. It's registered to 'Daniel Mathieson.' "

MacKenzie's fists clamped harder on the steering wheel.

"You're having me on."

Lowerson put his hand on his heart.

"I swear! It's right here, in Jepson's e-mail. One flintlock holster pistol by Davison's of Newcastle, circa 1830, sold at Bonhams Auction House on July 3rd."

"Recent purchase," MacKenzie murmured. "Find out everything you can about the buyer. There's more than one 'Daniel Mathieson,' surely."

"Yeah, but it's another strange coincidence, you can't deny that."

"Oh, it's strange, all right. Not least because the Daniel Mathieson *we* know is tucked up safe and warm at Her Majesty's pleasure and in no position to be buying antique pistols," MacKenzie said sarcastically.

The city came into view as the car descended into the valley. A feeling akin to maternal protectiveness washed over MacKenzie as she thought of the people living their everyday lives, working hard to carve out a future. They had seen enough of this, she vowed. Enough of a small minority playing their local government like sock puppets, killing off their women like flies whenever it suited them and making deals to cover up their crimes.

Maybe there was another person out there who was feeling protective. Enough to shine a light on two killers, potentially more. If they had some kind of guerrilla vigilante on their hands, intent on insurrection or payback, that would be a whole new can of worms to deal with. They had enough to worry about within the ranks of CID, without having to consider the prospect of an unknown reprobate killing off people he deemed to be wrongdoers. In MacKenzie's world, taking an eye for an eye only meant everyone ended up blind.

"Let's get a hustle on," she said aloud.

* * *

Antique weaponry was the last thing on Daniel Mathieson's mind. Unlike Steve Walker, he would gladly exchange his present living conditions for a life spent under the influence of anti-psychotic medication at Rampton Hospital. Eight months spent in confined quarters with the filth of society had not been a bed of roses. Sex offenders, particularly *child* sex offenders, were not popular amongst the other residents of H.M. Prison Frankland on the outskirts of Durham.

From the very first day, he had been extended a warm and personal welcome from his fellow inmates. They had followed the press reports of his trial to the letter, it seemed, and were not shy to make their disapproval known.

Once, between stints on the medical ward, Mathieson had made the foolish mistake of pointing out the inherent hypocrisy of violent criminals pronouncing judgment upon him, given the extremity of their own crimes. At least he had loved his daughter, he'd told them with dignity.

They begged to differ, and that particular episode had cost him four cracked ribs and a broken jaw.

He had tried to harden himself, he really had. It simply was not in his nature. He had never been an alpha male; he could not conceive of spending hours in the gym to beef himself up into a grotesque, tattooed monstrosity in order to turn the tables on his attackers. He was a softly-spoken former schoolteacher and there was little he could do to change that.

The prison officers eventually moved him into solitary confinement for his own protection. There had been no further attacks but there had also been very little contact with another living soul. He exercised alone, he ate alone and he watched television alone. He refused to play video games on principle. He wanted to sign up to a continuing education course so that he might see other people—even if it meant repeating basic mathematics—but it was deemed too risky given his widespread unpopularity.

Slowly, he could feel himself slipping away.

Often, he caught himself muttering, carrying on conversations as if two or three people shared his cell.

But there was only him and the four walls.

Then, there were the memories. They came to him day and night, images of Lucy lying dead, her lifeless blue eyes staring back at him. He would cry out in terror, imagining that he had seen her watching him from the reinforced window on the door to his cell.

Every few weeks, his lawyer contacted him. She told him that the police were still interested in any information he could provide about the Circle. Each time, he knocked her back and rejected the small bribes that were offered.

It was not because he remained loyal to the Circle. He was starting to move past his basic fear of what might happen if he broke his silence. Perhaps the revelatory moment had occurred while he had lain naked, in the foetal position on the shower room floor, as four of the inmates kicked him repeatedly in the crotch. He had screamed like a baby, the pain indescribable, but nobody had broken it up until he had passed out. There, on the wet tiles, he had truly wished for death. He had welcomed it with open arms and, in doing so, forgot to be afraid.

The reason he did not speak was simple: once he had given up his remaining secrets, there would be nobody to call him. Nobody would visit and nobody would seek him out or care about what he had to say. The years would stretch before him with the minimum of human interaction, which was a dreadful prospect.

He could end it all, just switch off the light and solve the problem himself.

Sadly, he was too much the coward even to do that.

* * *

Arthur Gregson did not even know which day of the week it was. His perception of the world extended only to his understanding that it consisted exclusively of pain. Hard, stabbing pain that sang through the complex web of nerves in his spinal cord, up into his brain. It spread through the optic nerves into his eyes so that the act of opening them became an enormous effort. Blurred voices told him that his morphine drip had been reduced to allow the medics an opportunity to assess his recovery but he would have handed over his entire fortune for an extra drop of the good stuff.

He mumbled something unintelligible through chapped lips. His voice scraped over the parched skin of his throat and he wished for water, cool and clean to wash away the sensation of burning.

He tried opening his eyes again and winced against the immediate discomfort. Everything seemed hideously bright.

"Lllifght," he rasped. "Lllifght!"

Mercifully, he was understood and the overhead light was switched off. He screwed up his eyes so that they were nothing more than slits in his face as he tried to bring the hospital room into focus.

Greying ceiling tiles were the first things he saw. The same, cheap kind of suspended ceiling they had back in CID, with brown stains denoting old water leaks.

A young female nurse was the next to grace his line of vision. Like soldiers might have felt during the Crimean War, he looked upon her as Florence Nightingale.

"Pfank yoof," he managed, when she offered him a sip of water from a plastic cup with a colourful straw. He sucked greedily, spluttering a bit as the first taste flushed through his oesophagus after the drip was removed.

The nurse made him as comfortable as possible and then turned to the two men standing out of his line of sight beside the doorway.

"Two minutes only," she said, sternly. "He's still very unwell."

Ryan nodded and stepped out of the shadows. Like a panther, he moved to stand a foot or so from the bed where Gregson lay, his face almost the same colour as the sheets. He looked haggard and frail, Ryan thought, remembering suddenly that the superintendent was nearly sixty. His usual vivacity spoke of a man at the top of his game, not someone who was only a few years off retirement.

"Gregson."

Arthur might have shrunk away from him, but his body was strapped into position to prevent further damage to the wound to his head, so he was trapped.

He closed his eyes, the only form of escape he had left.

"What happened, Gregson?"

Ryan did not raise his voice and nothing in his demeanour could be described as threatening, but nonetheless Gregson felt it.

Ryan waited a beat, then another, before stepping closer to the bed.

"You want us to find out who did this, don't you?"

Gregson's eyelids flickered, remembering the shock of that first blow on the back of his head. Ludo's heavy feet stamping against his skull.

"Where's Cathy?"

Gregson's eyes opened involuntarily and Ryan was waiting for him, ready to catch any small tell-tale sign of guilt. Gregson found himself staring into the unforgiving silvery eyes of his hunter and he began to shake.

"That's enough!" The nurse rushed forward, fussing with the covers, checking Gregson's pupils. "He's not ready to answer any more questions."

"He hasn't answered any, so far," Phillips pointed out, from the back of the room.

Ryan remained where he was, watching the panic pass over Gregson's face, then leaned forward to take one of his hands in a gentle grip. Surprise frittered in Gregson's eyes, followed swiftly by fear.

Ryan smiled slightly and then leaned in further to speak into Gregson's ear.

"Get well soon, superintendent," he said quietly. "You can't hide in here forever."

He stood up again and allowed himself to be ushered out by the nurse.

CHAPTER 18

As Jimmy Moffa had predicted with prescient accuracy, the forensic team at 17 Haslemere Gardens managed to find blood beneath the bleach. As consummate professionals, he and Ludo had succeeded in making it more difficult to distinguish, but ultimately blood didn't lie.

If that wasn't enough, the CSIs also happened to find tiny traces of the masking tape they had used to strap plastic sheeting over the carpet and the floor of the garage. That's what happened when you used cheap tape; it did not peel away easily. It left behind an unmistakeably suspicious set of circumstances, factoring in the reported sightings of a medium-sized, grubby white van seen parked beside the garage doors for half an hour. The neighbour, Mrs Sisodia, claimed to have seen a large, thuggish-looking man getting in and out of the van on the passenger side, but that was it. She presumed Cathy Gregson had called out an engineer, or a plumber, to take care of some small household matter.

While Ryan awaited confirmation that the blood type they had found matched Cathy Gregson's, alongside DNA samples taken from her clothing and bed sheets, he put a statement out to the press which would be plastered over the local lunchtime news:

Northumbria Police are appealing for information to help trace a missing woman who has not been seen since the morning of Tuesday 4th August. Mrs Cathy Gregson (56) went missing from her home in Haslemere Gardens, Newcastle. Following a brutal attack on her husband, prominent Detective Chief Superintendent Arthur Gregson of Northumbria CID, police remain concerned for Cathy's welfare and urge people to come forward with any information regarding her disappearance.

Technically speaking, it was ahead of schedule to order police divers to search the river, but Ryan made the call regardless. If Cathy Gregson was hiding somewhere in the city of Newcastle alive and well, he would sprout wings and fly.

* * *

Phillips spent an hour grappling with the compliance officer at the bank where Cathy and Arthur Gregson hoarded their money, during which time he called upon his many and varied skills in the art of persuasion. Eventually he slammed the desk phone back into its holder with unnecessary force, after issuing a final parting shot along the lines of the smarmy pen-pusher being hauled into jail for obstructing the course of justice if he didn't pull his finger out of his arse and comply with the bloody warrant.

In the name of Holy Newcastle United F.C., was it too much to ask for a bit of civility these days?

Phillips took a couple of deep breaths and moved onto his next task, which was to chase up the CCTV footage overlooking Haslemere Gardens. Luckily for him, the residents tended to be overly concerned with matters of personal security, given the costliness of their possessions. Woe betide anybody who threatened their top-of-the-range barbeque or even *considered* nicking off with their telly or designer frocks.

Phillips sighed, thinking of his own humble beginnings. He had grown up in a poor part of the city, where many of his schoolmates still remained, on the dole or working long hours at minimum wage. His own father had been a labourer, his mother a housewife and proud of it. Hardworking and tough, they had brought their only son up to be the same. Frank Sr. had a bit of a rep around the estate but he wasn't known to be mean; he never hit his wife or his son but he didn't shirk at planting a fist in somebody's face for stealing what was his, or for peddling drugs to the kids on the corner.

He had a code.

Phillips thought about the time his father had frog-marched him to the front doors of the police station and instructed him to hand over the packet of cigarettes he had taken from the corner shop. His father asked the bobby to give him a few hours' informal community service and Frank remembered spending those hours cleaning up cigarette butts from the street outside the same shop where he had shoplifted. That was justice in action, and he had never done it again because his father's disappointment had been too heavy a burden to bear.

"We earn our way in this life, son, and don't you forget it. There's them that have more, and them that have less," he'd declared. *"But you're only a poor man if you choose to be. You just remember that, lad."*

Phillips felt a stab of yearning as he remembered his father, the kindness wrapped up in a toughened shell, the workman's hands and gravelly voice just like his own.

Long gone, now.

He looked back at the paperwork in front of him and couldn't blame the street kids for trying to get a taste of middle-class living, if only to shake up the people who deliberately drew a mark in the sand.

* * *

Daniel Mathieson ate his solitary lunch from a metal table in a room that was empty but for the vacant guard who waited for him to finish. He deliberately took his time, drawing out each spoonful, cutting up each bite into tiny squares that he chewed until the sloppy food was almost pulp.

"Hurry up," the prison officer grumbled.

Mathieson ignored him and continued to chew his food methodically.

The room had a view of the exercise yard outside and he watched the other inmates mingling in groups. He caught the eye of one of his former attackers who raised a hand and waved theatrically before providing a coarse re-enactment of lovemaking for his benefit.

Shuddering, he looked away and down at his tray.

After a painfully slow lunch, the prison officer escorted him back to his cell and Mathieson heard the door shut behind him with palpable relief. Alone again, Mathieson stood for a moment and thought of how he might end it all.

He thought of his ex-wife and the divorce papers that had come through, neatly folded in a brown paper envelope. He thought of the island and closed his eyes to block out the reality of his cell so that he could imagine the wind and sea. Like an endless reel, the memories flooded in. Lucy born, Lucy toddling across to him after taking her first steps, Lucy shivering and crying as he'd paid his first visit to her bedroom. The wallpaper had been *My Little Pony,* he recalled, while tears spilled down his face. All the lies he had told his wife, all the threats he had whispered into Lucy's perfect shell-like ears, until she had turned around one day and stood up to him. She had fought back, for the first time in years, and taken him by surprise. She didn't want any part of his perverted circle, she had screamed, she didn't want any part of *him*.

His fingers trembled as he relived the sensory memory of her pulse fluttering wildly before it had died in his hands.

Behind him, the locks unbolted on his cell door and he turned, rubbing the tears from his face.

An hour later, the prison officer found Daniel Mathieson on the floor of his cell, curled up as if asleep.

Only he wasn't asleep.

He was dead.

* * *

Jane Freeman felt marvellous. All of her ducks were lining up in a neat little row, with the exception of one or two larger ones who stubbornly refused to cooperate.

They would learn. They all would.

She walked the short distance from her car to her regular appointment at an exclusive beauty salon located on one of the premier streets in Newcastle. Long gone were the days of mousy hair and imperfect teeth. Over the years, she'd implemented a few subtle and some not-so-subtle changes and, even if she said it herself, she was very pleased with the results.

Whoever said you had to accept what your gene pool dictated?

She certainly didn't ascribe to that philosophy. Out-dated thinking would have consigned her to a life of mediocrity, stuck inside a body she hated, begging for recognition from her peers.

Now, they deferred to her. She was the last word on all things historical in the region and she was never short of a charming escort if she wanted to go to the theatre or to the opera. She preferred them rich, with good manners and taste in clothes. It didn't hurt if they were younger, with plenty of stamina.

Jane had grown up as Plain Jane Freeman and the concept of 'late blooming' didn't begin to cover her adolescent experience. Her middle-class parents had given their daughter everything they could. An expensive education, trips abroad, big flashy parties for her birthday. Only a handful of people used to turn up but she didn't care. They were all inferior anyway.

Now, when she held a gathering, people clamoured for an invitation. Experience had taught her the art of patience, the value of hiding the burning ambition that consumed her and motivated every action she took. People didn't understand that kind of need, she reasoned. They feared it, *feared her,* she thought smugly, and her success.

People had always been jealous of her.

That stupid psychiatrist had once called her a sociopath, right to her face. Didn't he know that she couldn't accept that kind of insult? Did he imagine that she would forget? The years had passed but his words were as fresh as if they had been spoken that morning.

Patience and planning, that was the key, and she congratulated herself on a job well done. Hadn't she encouraged the Circle to make sure he came to a tragic end in his cell? What if he talked? *He was off the rails,* she had whispered, like a rabid dog which needed to be put down for its own sake as well as those around him.

That had been too easy, she reflected, but Donovan only had himself to blame. If he wanted to take it upon himself to kill young brunettes, that was none of her business, but he ought to have had the good sense to remain undetected. By taking those girls around the same date each year, he had endangered the secrecy of their organisation and he even kept notes.

Fool.

She had obtained copies of his notes—of course she had. It was fortunate that he at least had enough good sense not to name names, but there was plenty of navel-gazing nonsense in there to arouse suspicion if your name was DCI Ryan.

Which was why, she thought with a small measure of regret, he must be stopped. She paused to fluff her hair in the hallway mirror as she entered the salon and then greeted the smiling receptionist who invited her to take a seat in one of the plush chairs in the waiting area. Ryan wasn't hard on the eyes, she thought, as she selected a magazine from the glass coffee table. Had circumstances been different, she might have made a play for him. It was a crying shame to destroy anything so downright beautiful, but she had to think of Number One.

Against that, he was no competition at all.

CHAPTER 19

Brad Pitt's younger brother was sitting at his desk.

That was all Ryan could think as he strode into the open-plan office at CID Headquarters. There, looking comfortable and confident, was a bronzed, blonde-haired fusion of a Hollywood star and a character from *Baywatch* swinging back and forth on *his* desk chair. He was wearing the appropriate gear, too: a tightly fitting summer t-shirt displaying a slogan which warned one not to 'Hassle the Hoff' and faded jeans moulded to his muscular legs. A pair of wraparound sunglasses were propped in his voluminous quiff, which swayed as he spoke animatedly to a gaggle of female police support staff who had miraculously relocated from their usual workspace to congregate around the new attraction.

Ryan slung his file bag onto the desk with a thud and watched the golden-haired man turn with a broad, toothy smile.

"Ryan!"

He stood up and enveloped him in a hard hug, which took Ryan by surprise. Public displays of affection often did.

"Alex," he said easily. "Good to see you."

Alex Walker stepped back and surveyed the Chief Inspector with a pair of arresting green eyes which held just a hint of sadness. As the coastguard on Holy Island, he had met Ryan under extreme circumstances. He had been a suspect for murder and he had lost the man he had loved to a brutal killer who turned out to be his own father.

It didn't get much worse than that.

Ryan's voice remained light but his gut was beginning to roll. That very morning, they had made plans to visit Steven Walker at Rampton Hospital and by lunchtime, Walker's son was paying an unsolicited visit to CID. He smelled a rat.

He turned to the group of people hovering beside his desk, ogling the coastguard.

"Did crime take a day off? I must have missed that memo," his voice dripped with sarcasm and he watched them scatter back to their own desks with mumbled apologies. He turned back to Alex with an indulgent smile.

"Looks like you've still got it," he said.

Walker grinned widely and affected a modest expression, which he didn't quite manage to pull off.

"What brings you to the mainland?" Ryan cut to the chase. They could socialise later.

Alex looked away for a second, gathering himself together and when he met Ryan's level gaze, his laughing green eyes were serious once again.

"I had a phone call about an hour ago," he said in a blank tone. "It was from the forensic psychiatrist at Rampton. She was calling to tell me that my father took a fatal overdose just after breakfast. They found him dead on the floor of his room."

Ryan's face did not betray any emotion whatsoever but he processed the words and searched the other man's face.

"I'm sorry," he offered.

Alex barked out an angry laugh.

"I'm not," he said vehemently, but in truth he was in turmoil. He had spent the last eight months hating his father, coming to terms with the life-changing knowledge that everything he thought he had known about Steven Walker had been a lie. He had killed, repeatedly and without mercy. Alex had seen his mother's devastation at the unbelievable news about a man she had loved deeply, had shared a bed with and borne a child to. There were no words, only a gradual shift towards accepting the truth of what Steven Walker had done.

Now, he was dead. Hundreds of miles away inside a maximum security psychiatric hospital in Nottinghamshire, his father had chosen to end his life. Part of him felt relieved that the world was now rid of him, but the other part, the small boy who stubbornly refused to forget a childhood spent playing football on the beach, mourned.

Inexplicably, he mourned.

Alex scrubbed his hands over his face and felt tired, all of a sudden. He sat back into the chair and Ryan settled himself on the edge of the shiny beech desk to listen.

"I hated him for what he did," Alex said clearly. "He was a monster. But he was still my father. I don't know how to feel about this. About any of it."

Ryan put a hand on the man's shoulder, all he could think of to show support.

"You didn't ask to be a part of it," he said. "And you need to remember that you're different, Alex. I don't believe in all this 'sins of the father' crap."

Walker smiled, but it didn't reach his eyes.

"You don't get to choose," he said softly.

* * *

They kept rolling with the punches throughout the afternoon, beginning with an update from Faulkner.

"We've had another breakthrough," he told MacKenzie, his voice wobbling down the line. What had begun as a single suspicious death was beginning to snowball and with each new discovery demanding forensic attention, Faulkner's pool of resources grew smaller.

MacKenzie felt a knot rise in her own chest as she waited for him to elaborate.

"We've finished the preliminary sweep of Bowers' house on the island," he said. "And…God, Mac, we've found more blood stains. At least two different types, in large quantities on the floor of his basement. We swept the house for any other signs of blood and there was a trace on the big sword hanging over his mantelpiece, although it looked clean to the naked eye. If I were a betting man, I would say it was used to kill at least one person."

MacKenzie switched the phone to her other ear and scribbled down a note which she held up to Lowerson, instructing him to "FIND RYAN." He hustled out of the incident room and down the corridor without needing to be asked twice.

"What about prints on the sword?" she asked.

"Only one set of prints, which we've already confirmed as belonging to Bowers."

She looked up as Ryan walked into the room, a concerned expression marring his handsome face. She asked a couple more questions of Faulkner, then ended the call and pressed her fingers over her eyelids to give herself a moment's respite.

"What's happened?"

She opened her eyes again.

"They've found blood at Bowers' house. Lots of blood," she added. "Two types, neither of which belong to him. They've matched the samples to traces found on the ornamental sword above his fireplace."

Ryan's eyes darkened.

"He used the sword to kill?"

MacKenzie swiped a hand over her neck, to ease the psychosomatic ache which had begun to throb at its base.

"We don't know for sure..." she stopped and licked her lips. "Yeah, it looks a lot like that."

"Have you got a match?"

MacKenzie shook her head and looked over at Lowerson, who was standing looking as if his eyes would fall out of his head.

"Jack, I'm going to ask you to handle that search. Faulkner has enough on his plate. In fact, we're all starting to drown under the weight of this."

Ryan shuffled through his mental files and felt a soft *click* as something fell quietly into place.

"Lowerson, save yourself time and start by looking out the details of Mike and Jennifer Ingles," he ordered. "They're the only two people known to be missing from the island, the only two unaccounted for recently."

He recalled the vicar of Holy Island and his wife, who had been responsible for supplying hallucinogenic seeds to the Circle. They had both vanished, never to be seen again. Although an all-ports warning had been in place for months, there had been no sightings, no trace of them at all.

"We assumed they went abroad—" MacKenzie interjected, but Ryan shook his head.

"I think I'm starting to understand what's happening here," he said. "Somebody is taking us on a magical mystery tour, helping us to tie up loose ends because apparently we're too ignorant to handle it ourselves."

His jaw ticked and he thrust his hands into the back pockets of his jeans.

"I don't like being drip-fed," MacKenzie's fingers tapped against the desk, betraying her annoyance.

"Somebody is ticking persons of interest off the list. People who have been involved, somehow, in the Circle. For instance, guess who's sitting at my desk, right now?"

MacKenzie frowned and shook her head.

"Alex Walker," Ryan said shortly. "His father died this morning. Apparent overdose."

"Christ Almighty!"

"What about Daniel Mathieson?" Lowerson threw in, worriedly, turning to Ryan. "The pistol—ballistics came back to us this morning with two possibilities. One of them was bought at auction and the sale was registered in the name of Daniel Mathieson. Could be another arrow, pointing us towards him?"

Ryan's head whipped around and MacKenzie drew out her mobile phone, scanning the numbers quickly for her contact at H.M.P. Frankland in Durham.

"Get over there, right now!"

Lowerson left the room at a run.

* * *

They were too late.

The ambulance was parked outside the service entrance when Lowerson and MacKenzie pulled up in front of the prison at speed. If he hadn't been concentrating on the road, Lowerson might have enjoyed the novelty of the flashing blue light shouting out its cacophonous message that other road users should get out of his way.

They watched in silent dismay as a black body bag was hefted from a stretcher and into the waiting ambulance, its occupant having been pronounced dead at the scene. MacKenzie met the flustered prison warden at the door.

"What happened here?"

"You got here quick," he said, dazedly. "We only rang it in a few minutes ago."

"Never mind that," MacKenzie snapped. "What happened?"

"That was one of our inmates, Daniel Mathieson. Seems he was attacked."

"What? He was in solitary—"

The warden scratched the side of his chin.

"Look, love," he began in the kind of patronising tone which made MacKenzie's fingers itch. "He was in and out of the medical centre. We do our best, but if some of the blokes in here want to rip a piece off him, they're going to find an opportunity to do it. Mathieson was lucky he came away with the injuries he had, rather than a fatal stab wound before now."

"How did they gain access? I want to know who was in charge of his section."

"Now, don't get your knickers in a twist," the warden said, and had the nerve to pat MacKenzie's arm. "We'll look into all of that, no need for you to worry—"

MacKenzie regarded him with narrowed eyes.

"A man died under your care," she breathed. "He was attacked despite being sectioned away from the other prisoners, and to make matters worse, you moved the body."

She nodded towards the ambulance.

"I'm not a bloody doctor," the warden said, defensively. "How should I know whether to move him? They might have been able to save him."

Lowerson stepped in when it was on the tip of MacKenzie's tongue to turn the air blue.

"This is under our remit, now. I want you to set aside an interview space and we will be speaking to each of the prison officers on duty. I'm sure I don't need to tell you to keep them apart until we've spoken to each of them in turn."

The warden rubbed the heel of his hand over his own chest, which was starting to contract in sympathy for the dead man.

"Alright."

"I presume you already know who is responsible for the attack?" MacKenzie asked, considerably calmer than a moment ago.

The warden shrugged.

"Got a few names on the list but they're all accounted for," he said, vaguely.

MacKenzie looked at him for a long moment and watched him shuffle his feet under the scrutiny.

Then, she leaned forward, so that only he could hear her.

"They can't protect you," she whispered and caught the recognition flash in his eyes.

The warden rubbed a hand over his face and wondered if he should tell them. One look into the hard eyes of DI MacKenzie told him that she was a terrier. It might be best to get it off his chest now and have done with it.

"I—I don't know what you're talking about."

"Perhaps," MacKenzie said portentously. "On the other hand, perhaps not. Get the interview room ready, I'll be starting with you."

The warden nodded and thought wearily that it was going to be a long day.

* * *

Ryan had known it would not be possible to hold off the media bloodhounds for long. MacKenzie had kept Bowers' name out of the papers, although it was enough that the local news speculated on the man found dead in suspicious circumstances at a rural church on the same night as the annual pilgrimage. The attack on Gregson and his wife's disappearance was intriguing to say the least, and Cathy Gregson's picture was splashed over local television news and the early evening editions of the *Evening Chronicle* and *Northern Echo*. The moment that word reached the regional news desks that both of the Holy Island killers had died within hours of each other, things went nuclear.

Sharp-eyed journalists hungry for a scoop swarmed the car park of CID Headquarters, scurrying over the tarmac like ants. Chief Constable Morrison watched them gravely from the window of her office on the second floor.

"What progress has been made?"

Behind her right shoulder, Ryan stood with his feet hip-width apart, as if poised for action.

"Forensic evidence from the crime scene at Heavenfield has elicited several unexpected lines of enquiry, ma'am," he answered. "The circumstances leading to Bowers' death remain unclear but MacKenzie is pursuing all the evidence available to her."

Morrison watched the reporters set up their cameras, jostling amongst themselves for the best view of the entrance to the building where she was due to address them in twenty minutes' time.

"Unexpected lines of enquiry?"

Ryan rubbed his lips together, considering how much to say. Morrison seemed solid but he had thought the same of Arthur Gregson. Until he knew for certain, it was a case of trusting nobody but himself and his team.

"There were blood stains on the altar at the church which match the DNA of several missing women. They have been identified as possible victims of Patrick Donovan but we won't be able to say for certain until their bodies are found."

If they are found, he added silently.

"You feel there's a connection between Bowers' murder and the deaths of these women?" Morrison was a quick study.

"Possibly, ma'am. Until DI MacKenzie's team get to the bottom of Bowers' death, it's anybody's guess."

Morrison turned away from the window and surveyed her chief inspector, who swiftly donned an impressive poker face that was entirely devoid of expression.

"And Gregson?"

Ryan shifted his weight but not his appearance. It was important that he maintained a neutral outlook.

"DCS Gregson's condition has stabilised. The forensic team are in the process of sweeping his home, as we speak. We have not been able to locate Mrs Gregson and have executed the usual procedure for high risk missing persons."

"Your opinion on her disappearance?"

Morrison regarded him with a shrewd, birdlike expression and Ryan was reminded briefly of his mother, though the two women were unalike in every other respect. He found himself feeling just a little guilty for deliberately omitting to tell her the extent of his suspicions concerning Arthur Gregson, but reminded himself that his reasons for doing so were good.

"Neighbours report having seen a white van outside the property during the afternoon and there appeared to be some jewellery and other items missing from Gregson's home. Current thinking suggests a botched burglary of some kind."

Morrison was not persuaded.

"You're telling me that there is no connection between Gregson and any of these other crimes?"

Ryan's eyelashes swept low, shielding his eyes so that his face took on a guarded expression.

"I wouldn't care to speculate, ma'am."

Morrison laughed shortly.

"The man had you on trumped up charges of misconduct and is gunning for you to be charged with Bowers' murder, yet you won't say a word against him?"

Ryan remained silent and, after a moment, Morrison moved to take a seat behind her desk. She spread her hands over the material of her slacks, while she pondered how best to draw out the enigmatic man in front of her.

Finally, she surveyed him again.

"Ryan, I admire your circumspection," she would not say *loyalty*.

"Thank you, ma'am."

"You'll keep me informed of any facts which may come to light and relieve you of the present obstruction in your throat?"

Ryan's eyes flashed appreciatively.

"*Yes, ma'am.*"

While Morrison dished out sound bites for the press, Ryan spent the better part of an hour chain-calling his list of prison contacts. If there was somebody intent upon administering their own kind of rough justice to known or former members of the Circle, it was imperative that those convicted as accessories and currently serving their time in prisons around the country should be protected. He needed them alive, for the information they may yet be able to give him.

The large plastic clock on the wall showed four o'clock as he made the last call.

CHAPTER 20

Blissfully unaware of the gaggle of reporters charging the gates of CID Headquarters, Anna drove north along the coastal road from Newcastle. To the east, the North Sea spread out a brilliant steel-blue. Far off in the distance, ships chugged slowly over the water and dark clouds began to form in the sky above, signalling the onset of summer rain.

Anna zoomed along winding roads, expecting that at any moment her Mini would be forced into the hedgerows by an SUV hurtling towards her from the opposite direction or a trundling tractor with a death wish. Then, unexpectedly, it appeared before her. Like a mirage, Bamburgh Castle materialised on the horizon, its pink-hued stone glowing in the hazy afternoon sun. It was the stuff of legend, of kings and folklore, she thought mistily. As a child, she had looked out across the water from Holy Island and dreamed of living there one day. Those childish dreams had faded with the passing years but Anna's love of Northumbrian history had not. It called to her, she realised, this thirst for knowledge.

The village of Bamburgh was quiet, with only a few elderly residents out walking their dogs, heading towards the dunes which beckoned to the expanse of golden sand beyond. Children living out the last few weeks of their summer holidays charged across the castle green and sprawled over the benches bearing engraved memorials. Anna pulled into the car park resting at the foot of the towering whinstone crag upon which the castle had been built. Thousands of years earlier, volcanic activity had thrust the dolerite upwards to form the rocky plateau and, centuries later, men had seen its defensive possibilities. Improved and upgraded over the years, now a magnificent stone castle rested atop the volcanic rock, seamlessly blending with earth and sky. One hundred and fifty feet below, the sea crashed against the impermeable cliff-face, an unstoppable force meeting an immoveable object.

With a longing look towards the wide, sandy beach, Anna began to make her way along Vale Typping, the ancient road winding up the craggy incline towards the castle gates. Families chattered past her, saturated by historical tours and ready for the cups of tea and jam-loaded scones which awaited them in the village below. Anna smiled and continued upwards, passing through a series of fortified gates until she entered the main castle compound. She went in search of a guide who could direct her to the offices of Professor Jane Freeman, Chief Archaeologist for National Heritage in the North-East.

The woman in question watched Anna from her vantage point in the library, which formed part of the clock tower, one of the smaller towers overlooking the excavation works in the southernmost part of the castle compound. Its central position afforded her an excellent view of anybody entering or leaving the castle and, given that some of the castle workers were also minor members of the Circle, it also gave Freeman the illusion of being mistress of all she surveyed.

Now, she watched Anna walk in the direction of the clock tower with long-legged strides. She reflected that it must have been fate that led her to look out of the mullioned library windows at that moment—*no,* she corrected, not fate. The Master. It was He who had given the signal that she should rise from her desk and look out to see who had entered her domain.

Anna Taylor had come to find her.

Though the world of local academic history was a small one, their respective specialisms were too polarised for their paths to cross very often. For her part, Freeman remembered teaching Anna from her days as a doctoral student at Durham. She might have forgotten her, were it not for the fulsome praise Bowers had heaped on the girl. Freeman considered it a personal insult, considering that she and Bowers had been burning up the bed sheets at that time. It was hardly an aphrodisiac to hear a man waxing lyrical about another woman—especially a younger one.

"*If you're so enamoured with the girl, get out of my bedroom and go and crawl into hers!*" she had screamed, during one particularly heated argument. Bowers had risen from her bed and dressed in complete silence. Even now, Freeman remembered his control, the incredible self discipline he had possessed which had been such a turn on.

Now, the girl who had driven a wedge between them had grown into a woman and she had come to ask questions; questions that Freeman did not want to answer. Various possibilities occurred to her and temptation reared its ugly head. It would be so simple,

Freeman thought, to arrange an accident. The winds were strong on the battlements and Anna Taylor would not be the first poor soul to lose her life to the sea.

* * *

The rain started. It fell in fat droplets over the people of Newcastle, casting a shadow over the sky. It drummed against the thin window panes at CID Headquarters and washed away the media throng who retreated to their vans and to their deadlines. It pattered melodically against the single window in the incident room and gave comfort to the people within.

"Telephone company has come back to us."

MacKenzie looked up at Lowerson.

"About bloody time," she muttered.

"They've managed to triangulate the source of that text message sent to Ryan, the one he says was from Bowers."

"And?"

Lowerson grinned and swung his chair from side-to-side.

"It couldn't have been him! Ryan received the message while he was at Anna's place in Durham on Sunday afternoon but the company say that the text message was sent from a throwaway phone within a range of five hundred metres from a location in Newcastle. Here, let me show you."

He skipped over to the map on the wall of the incident room and stuck three red pins onto it, indicating the three closest telephone masts.

"These are the closest masts to pick up the text signal, which aren't far apart since we're in a built-up area."

MacKenzie picked up her mug of tea, now stone cold, and made her way across the room. Immediately, she noticed another pin which fell squarely within the area Lowerson had demarcated.

"Interesting coincidence again, Jack. The text directing Ryan to make his way out to Heavenfield on Sunday was sent from a mobile phone within five hundred metres of these telephone masts. Look what else lies within that zone," she tapped a finger against the map. "17 Haslemere Gardens."

"You think Gregson might have sent it, to set Ryan up? That he arranged for Bowers to be killed, then set it up so that Ryan would be the first on the scene?" he asked, fiercely.

MacKenzie took her time sipping her tea.

"At this point, nothing would surprise me. One thing I am prepared to do is cross Ryan off the list, once and for all."

Lowerson did the happy dance.

"If he turns out to be a murdering maniac, I will stand corrected," MacKenzie tagged on.

* * *

The body count was piling up. They had no killer, no weapon and no real explanation or motive as to why men were dying or being attacked left, right and centre. Ghosts from previous cases visited him with unnerving frequency and his team was stretched to the limit of its capacity.

Ah, God, how he'd missed this.

Phillips glanced across at Ryan, who looked stupidly pleased with himself.

"Don't know what you've got to smile about," he grumbled. "I've had those press hounds up my arse for hours, I've got nothing but bad news to tell them and all you can do is sit there grinning like a monkey!"

Ryan's smile grew wider, until it was almost blinding.

Phillips shook his head and adopted a sympathetic expression.

"It's the strain, isn't it? Now, there's no shame in admitting when things start to get on top of you—"

"Phillips, d'you know something? It feels good to be alive."

Frank leaned back in his olive green desk chair and linked his fingers across his paunch, settling down for the chat.

"Well, now, that's just dandy. I'm glad you're having some sort of spiritual epiphany but we do have quite a few things to do today. Nothing urgent, just investigating three suspicious deaths, grievous bodily harm and a missing person."

Phillips made a dismissive gesture.

"You know, the usual."

Ryan linked his hands behind his head and looked at the little framed photograph of Anna which he kept on his desk to remind him of the good things in life.

"D'you know what else?" he said, dreamily, ignoring Phillips' tirade.

Frank huffed out a breath.

"I have a funny feeling you're going to tell me."

"After this is all over, when these people are behind bars, I'm going to marry that girl."

Phillips' eyebrows shot into his receding hairline. It wasn't quite fair to say that Ryan was afraid of commitment, not after he had existed for the last eight months in a co-habiting relationship with a grown woman, but in all the years Phillips had known him, Ryan had never been a man to talk of marriage, or relationships generally for that matter.

"What's brought this on?"

"I think it's what they call being 'happy,' Frank. I'm unfamiliar with the feeling, in general, but recently I've been experiencing this odd sort of contentment. The kind that makes me want to get up in the morning. If I can feel this good when all the world is crumbling around me and I nearly lost my job, I must have Anna to thank for that."

Phillips' chest puffed out in pride. His boy was growing up.

"That's good, lad. That's really good."

* * *

Keith Thorbridge watched the news on his ancient television set. He listened intently to the grainy sound of the newscaster who reported that the two Holy Island killers had been found dead in their cells on the same day.

Suicide, it looked like. Suicide and a violent prison attack.

Thorbridge grunted and took a swig of ale.

Neither of those two would ever have ended themselves. Not without a bit of help, at least. It took a real man to top himself, not that soft-palmed doctor from the island. As for the other one, he didn't have much sympathy for nonces.

He stubbed a finger on the remote control to turn the screen off, hefted himself out of his armchair and then tramped up the stairs, which creaked underfoot. He turned left along the tiny landing and pushed open the second bedroom in his two up, two down cottage. He flicked on the weak light with its cheap paper shade and eco-friendly bulb, which shone a gloomy white light over the room. Outside, the sun found a gap in the grey clouds and shone beams of light over the hills but Thorbridge didn't notice.

He took out his special box, a tattered cardboard affair he had found outside the supermarket. First, he selected four sheets of dog-eared white paper, covered in scribbled biro. He laid them out on the mouldy carpet to form a complete diagram, showing a wide black circle with names listed along its circumference. He rummaged in the box and found a biro, then carefully struck a line through two names.

Steven Walker and Daniel Mathieson.

* * *

Anna made her way up the stairwell of the clock tower at Bamburgh Castle to the upper floor, which housed a splendid library and served as an honorary office space for Jane Freeman's exploits. She tapped on a door bearing a brass plate with the woman's name and, soon after, it swung open.

"Professor Freeman? I don't know if you'll remember me. My name is Anna Taylor."

"Doctor Taylor?" Freeman nodded kindly. "Do come in. Of course I remember you. You were in one of my classes at Durham, isn't that right? And, of course, I've read your work since. Very impressive."

Anna was surprised by the warmth of her welcome. Perhaps she had misjudged the woman.

"Thank you," she murmured. "I, ah, this might not be the best time—"

"Not at all. Why don't we get comfortable?" Freeman suggested, leading the way across to a seating area, which was grandly furnished. "This part of the castle isn't open to the public. The owners have graciously allowed me to use these rooms as a suite of offices."

Freeman tried not to let the words choke her. Perhaps in a few years, with a strong army of loyal followers, she would be able to make the owners of this stone fortress an offer they couldn't refuse. Then, everything would be hers.

Anna accepted a seat beside the fire, which had been lit to offset the draughts which managed to permeate the walls despite the fact they were metres thick.

"It doesn't feel much like summer anymore, does it?"

Freeman looked out of one of the windows across the choppy sea. She could hear the waves crashing against the rocks below as the winds rolled in from the east.

"It's powerful," Freeman said, regally.

She turned back to Anna and crossed one leg over the other, holding court.

"It's a pleasure to meet you again," she continued. "As you know, I deal mostly in Roman archaeology which means our paths haven't crossed too often in the years since we were both at Durham."

"Yes, I took a different route," Anna agreed. "But, actually, that's partly why I came to see you."

"Oh?"

"Yes, I wanted to ask you a couple of questions about your doctoral paper, if I may. I'm hoping to explore some similar themes in my next project."

Freeman adopted a guileless expression.

"By all means, if it interests you, but I haven't looked at that old paper in many years."

"Of course, I understand," Anna assured her. "It's simply that I believe there may be some crossover between our respective areas of interest. In researching the early religions operating in Northumbria during the first few centuries A.D., I have found myself drawn to more recent examples of similar practices."

"I've always found pagan history very interesting," Freeman smiled.

"Well, in your doctoral paper, you discussed certain high-profile Roman figures who occupied the region during the construction of Hadrian's Wall," Anna said. "You suggested that several commanding officers in the Roman garrison were recorded to have died in what we might call suspicious circumstances, implying some kind of pagan ritual."

"I'm afraid I can't recall, off-hand."

"I have the names here," Anna tugged her notebook out of her bag and recited them.

"My, you are prepared," Freeman said. "But the fact is, if you read my more recent publications you will see that I have largely discredited my own findings in that first doctoral paper. It was somewhat speculative of me to imagine that the deaths of those garrison officers amounted to anything other than a local discontented population or a simple dispute."

"I see," Anna said slowly, gnawing her inside lip.

Freeman surveyed the young woman sitting across from her, the firelight gleaming on her dark hair. Hatred rose from deep within her belly and she touched a hand to her stomach, to settle it.

"When I was a younger woman, Anna, I was less cautious in my style of writing. Perhaps I was too assertive," she forced an apologetic smile. "But I made a case for the evidence I thought I had in my possession. As I say, further excavations and research in the years since have convinced me otherwise."

Anna nodded and decided to try another direction.

"I was very sorry to hear about Mark," she said softly.

Freeman arranged her face into sad lines.

"It's a terrible, terrible thing," she agreed. "Mark was a friend of mine and I know that you two were very…*close* over the years."

Anna watched an undefined emotion pass over Freeman's face.

"Yes, he was like a father to me."

Freeman held off a snort of disbelief. Had this woman really no idea of how Bowers had felt? *No,* she thought, it was all part of Anna's simpering, little girl lost act. She would have to be an imbecile not to have realised the man was in love with her.

Then again, Jane reminded herself, not everyone was as insightful as she.

"It's a tragic loss," she said benevolently.

"I wanted to ask whether you'd seen him, recently?"

Freeman's eyes narrowed.

"No, not for some time, dear," she replied. "Why do you ask?"

"Oh, no reason," Anna said quickly. "I'm trying to understand his last movements, whether there was anything troubling him, anybody who had a grudge—"

Freeman almost laughed. She could name numerous people who held a grudge against the late Mark Bowers, starting with herself.

"Surely, that would be best left to the police?"

Anna watched Freeman closely and thought she heard a threat somewhere in her last statement. But when she searched the woman's face, all she saw was a glossy, youthful-looking woman with big, blue eyes. Outside, the wind howled and whistled through the gaps in the stonework and Anna shivered, as if somebody had walked over her grave.

* * *

DC Lowerson stood at the foot of Gregson's hospital bed, watching the man's chest rise and fall. Not so long ago, a vicious crack to the head had consigned Lowerson himself to a hospital bed for six months. As far as anybody knew, he still suffered from amnesia and was unable to remember who had delivered that devastating blow. They probably assumed it had been Steven Walker or Daniel Mathieson.

But Lowerson remembered. Over and over, he replayed the sound of Gregson's voice conferring with Bowers, the pitiless way he had left him lying on the cold ground, assuming that he would die where he had fallen.

Now, it was Gregson lying in a hospital bed, strapped into place to prevent any movement which might jostle the wound at the back of his head. He was sleeping and the monitors bleeped regularly in time with his heart beat.

It was comforting to know that karma really did exist.

Lowerson continued to watch Gregson, trailing his eyes over the collection of expensive machinery surrounding his body, helping him to recover.

He hoped that the superintendent *did* recover, because he was not done with him yet. Not by a long shot.

Lowerson turned and left the room with a nod of thanks to PC Yates, who waited until he had rounded the corner before entering the visit into her log book.

CHAPTER 21

The smell of oven-baked pizza pervaded Anna's cottage, where the team congregated after hours to discuss the events of the day. The rain had eased its fall and pattered against the glass with a tuneful *rat-a-tat-tat.* Night had fallen over the city of Durham and the five members of Ryan's team shook out their damp hair and stuffed carbohydrates into their mouths with grateful abandon.

Ryan uncorked a bottle of rioja and told himself it was medicinal as he poured a few generous glasses for the small group.

"Alright, where are we with Bowers? Aside from the news that I didn't kill him," he said, irreverently.

MacKenzie leaned forward.

"The telephone company could tell us the location where the text message was sent to within five hundred metres, but they can't tell us *who* sent it. The message came from an unregistered, as we know."

"Gregson's house is within that five hundred metre radius," Lowerson couldn't help blurting out.

Ryan nodded, patiently.

"I can tell you that no mobile phones other than Gregson's work phone and his wife's mobile were found at 17 Haslemere Gardens. Cathy Gregson sent three text messages to her husband around lunchtime, asking him to stop by the house to unlock the front door as she'd managed to lock herself out. There's a reply from Gregson to say that he would be on his way; that was sent around twelve-thirty. Both phones are on a monthly registered contract so they don't fit the bill for the phone that was used to text you on Sunday."

"Still, it tells us that Cathy or an unknown third party deliberately lured Gregson home. He didn't stumble into the house of his own volition," Ryan observed.

"He could have," Phillips argued. "Those messages show us why he headed home, but they don't show us what happened when he got there."

Ryan nodded.

"Agreed."

"Even if it wasn't Gregson or his wife, it's reasonable to assume that whoever sent you that message on Sunday got rid of the phone fairly quickly afterwards," MacKenzie said. "Regardless of whether it's at the bottom of the river now, for our purposes it corroborates your story. It's good enough to know that you couldn't have been in two places at the same time."

"It's interesting, don't you think, that whoever sent me the message chose to send it from the vicinity of Gregson's home?" Ryan crossed his arms and leaned back against Anna's desk while he mulled it over.

"Somebody pointing an arrow in Gregson's direction, you mean?"

"Exactly."

"I could have sent the message to Ryan, if we were in it together," Anna broke the brief silence, and four heads turned in her direction. She held her hands up. "I was only thinking aloud!"

"Strewth, woman, are you trying to have me arrested again?" Ryan joked.

"Chance would be a fine thing," she muttered darkly.

"Presuming you didn't conspire to kill," MacKenzie teased, "I'll turn to our next update. I heard from Pinter again today. He's finished the post-mortem on Bowers and the toxicology report has come back nil of unusual chemical substances. That tells us he wasn't under the influence. It also tells us he wasn't taking any prescribed treatment for the tumour."

Which, Ryan thought, *still didn't answer the question of whether Bowers was aware of his tumour, because even if he were, he might have refused medication.*

"He was sober as a judge when he drove up there and remained that way," Phillips meditated on the new information. "We can't find Bowers' mobile phone, which means we can't check to see if this unknown somebody sent him a text message telling him to drive out to Heavenfield, but it has to have been something like that."

"If somebody sent Ryan a message claiming to be Bowers, it is certainly possible that Bowers was sent a message by somebody claiming to be Ryan," MacKenzie said.

"Or claiming to be Anna," Phillips pointed out, turning to where she was perched on a window seat. "Bowers trusted you the most, didn't he?"

Anna nodded sadly.

"However it happened, Bowers must have headed over to Heavenfield because somebody asked him to."

"There were no defensive marks, no signs of a struggle, which suggests to me that he was caught off guard," MacKenzie said.

They ruminated on it, for a moment.

"It's an awful coincidence for the text message to originate practically on Gregson's doorstep," Ryan continued. "We might not have the physical evidence, but we can draw a lot of conclusions from that. The man has spent the last six weeks trying to push me out. Maybe he wanted to make damn sure of it, and this is the best way he could find."

"How do you explain his attack, then?" Anna probed. "His wife's disappearance?"

Ryan lifted a shoulder in frustration.

"Gregson had help from someone, maybe from his friends in the Circle, but they turned against him."

"Any word on his wife?"

Ryan shook his head.

"You must have seen the news. Her face has been all over the television and every local paper since lunchtime. We've had the usual number of quack calls from people claiming aliens abducted her, but no legitimate sightings yet."

"I've looked into vans matching the description the neighbour gave us," Phillips put in. "White Transit, old model. The registration that the neighbour took down is fake, so we're probably dealing with a professional."

"That's interesting," Ryan's interest piqued. "Your average burglar, even the career ones, don't usually cross over into the kind of violence we're looking at. They're all about a quick 'in and out' smash and grab."

"Aye, it's true. There's only a few I know who would know to clean up after themselves like this," Phillips agreed. "And I've already checked out the names on my little list. They're all accounted for."

"That's hardly surprising," Ryan had to point out. "The type of criminal we're looking for would have a ready list of people willing to provide an alibi."

"Be that as it may," Phillips persevered, "there are a limited number with the kind of network and resources to pull this kind of job off without leaving evidence all over the place."

"The people we're looking into, the ones who form part of the Circle, might have endless resources," Anna contradicted him, softly. "We have to think beyond 'ordinary' criminals, now."

Ryan looked across and his silver eyes locked onto hers. He wanted to gather her up against him, to tell her it would all be alright, but he couldn't. Not yet. She didn't even know the worst of it, not until he had shown her Bowers' name listed inside the copy of *Paradise Lost* he kept tucked inside his jacket pocket.

"Anna is right. We can look into the usual suspects, but we're working on a whole new level, with a new cast of characters that we don't even know about."

"Somebody knows them," MacKenzie said. "He knows who they are and he's doing our work for us. First, Steven Walker, then Daniel Mathieson."

"The Chief Constable tells me Walker was suicide and Mathieson was another case of prison violence," Ryan said, idly.

"Bollocks," MacKenzie declared. "How did Walker manage to stash away a bunch of pills? Violent prisoners finding their way past several prison officers into the solitary unit, then back out again?"

She shook her head, disbelievingly.

"We'll have to wait to hear from the pathologist down in Nottingham before we'll know what killed Walker and how. I've had a chat with the SIO down there and he's willing to share information given the previous history. Jeff Pinter is going to look over Mathieson's body as a priority today and see if we can narrow down a pool of suspects. The warden knows who it was, though," she said, and her lips flattened. "He's not being forthcoming, but give me time to work on him. Lowerson has been looking into that pistol which was bought and registered in Mathieson's name."

"The sale was made over the telephone," Lowerson picked up the conversation. "They're tracing the call now but that will take time. The buyer claimed to be Daniel Mathieson and came into the auction house to make payment in cash later that day."

"CCTV—" Ryan began.

"Already requested it, sir," Lowerson was happy to say. "The auction house is retrieving it, as we speak."

"What about paperwork?"

"It was an antique collectible," Lowerson provided. "That makes it exempt from the usual firearms regs, and in any case the guy we're looking for had fake I.D."

"That's good, fast work," Ryan approved. "What about forensics?"

"Faulkner came back with the analytics on the lolly stick and the crisp packet we found at the church. No useable samples whatsoever, they're a dead end."

Ryan stood up to stretch out the knots in his back while he thought.

"Now that I'm off the list of suspects, do you have any objection to me taking a look around the church?"

MacKenzie shook her head.

"Not at all."

Ryan nodded, resolving to do that first thing the next morning.

"What progress has been made to identify the blood samples found at Bowers' house and on the altar?"

"We had positive DNA matches on the altar, belonging to women listed as missing and potential victims of Patrick Donovan. Next of kin have been informed. We'll have to wait and hope that their bodies will be found but all we can do is continue to excavate the site where Donovan was active," MacKenzie answered, glumly.

"As for the blood samples at Bowers' house, the blood types match what we have on record for Mike and Jennifer Ingles, as you suspected. Faulkner's team is retrieving the DNA samples taken from their house on the island and he'll update me if and when he can make a conclusive match."

"Looks pretty cut and dry, if you ask me," Phillips said, then raised an eyebrow in Ryan's direction, which was interpreted correctly. It was time to speak openly about Mark Bowers, which meant it was time to lay his cards on the table.

Ryan looked across at Anna and called a break.

* * *

"No. I don't believe you."

Anna snapped the words out while her eyes sparked angrily.

"Look, I'm not here to smear the man's memory. It's my job to uncover the truth," Ryan said quietly. He had expected this reaction, so was prepared for what would come.

"Seems to be one and the same thing."

He took Anna's shoulders in a gentle grip and steered her across to the sofa, then stepped out of the room. When he returned, he held a pair of nitrile gloves and a small book in his hands.

"Look at this," he offered, deciding to let the words speak for themselves.

Anna pulled on the gloves mechanically and looked at the book, then up into his fathomless eyes. Her fingers shook but she turned the first page.

It was there, a list of recognisable names. Amongst them, she read her father's, Steven Walker's, Mark Bowers'. Her eyes blurred and she fumbled with the next page, her eyes tracking over the passages of Milton's poem. The rain had stopped, she thought inconsequentially. The rain had stopped, along with her childish dreams. Mark Bowers had been no more a saviour than her father. No more a good man than Steven Walker had been, and he had nearly killed her.

Like a veil lifting, she saw it clearly now.

"He gave me the first glass," she whispered.

"What's that?"

"On the island," Anna explained. "Mark gave me my first drink, the night of the wake, the night I was taken by the Circle. It was drugged, and he was the one who gave it to me."

Ryan said nothing, he was too angry, but he took her hand in a firm grip to remind her that ordeal was over. She shed no tears. Her profile was hard as she stared out of the window at her own reflection in the glass and her voice was brittle when she spoke.

"He made me believe that he cared for me like a daughter, but he was complicit. He knew what they would do and he let them take me. He helped them."

Ryan's jaw worked.

"Yes."

Anna closed her eyes briefly and there was a sheen of tears when they re-opened, but she did not let them fall. She would cry no more tears for Mark Bowers.

"If he was killed, it was because of his association with the Circle. Judging from this," her hand hovered over the book lying open on her lap, "I presume Mark was a higher-ranking member of the *organisation,* if we can call it that."

She took a deep breath.

"As was my father," she said, stupefied. She would not have imagined that Andy Taylor possessed the gravitas to command others or to indoctrinate them into a cult, but her vision was clouded through the eyes of a child who had seen him only as a weak alcoholic prone to bouts of violence.

"Yes," Ryan said again. It was all he could manage.

Anna closed the book, re-wrapped it carefully in plastic and handed it back to him. She leaned across to bestow a kiss, then stood up.

"We need to find out whose name should be written beneath Mark Bowers. They're in command now, and are probably responsible for all the violence that has happened this week."

Ryan watched her stride out of the room and up the stairs to re-join his team. Pride and love swelled in his chest, unlike anything he had experienced before. For Anna to suffer such loss, to experience such betrayal, but still to dust herself off and carry on regardless was precisely why he was determined to spend the rest of his life making sure that she would never have to do it again.

* * *

Arthur Gregson was fully lucid as he watched the late evening news. The newscaster delivered his report in solemn tones which barely managed to conceal his excitement at the prospect of weeks of good ratings as he drew out the story of murder and missing women until the people of Northumbria could stand it no more.

For now, they clamoured for as much information as possible.

The people wanted more news on the man found dead up at Heavenfield Church with his brains blown out. More news on the upstanding detective chief superintendent who was brutally attacked and whose wife was missing, presumed dead. They organised community search parties and they appealed for her safe return. They wanted more news on the two killers found dead in their cells. The people whispered about a cult circle and local mafia, about business deals gone bad and prison retribution. They contemplated domestic violence and acts of revenge and came to their own conclusions.

Gregson watched the journalists holding their mics out to passers-by, who tutted and swore that they would hurry to the safety of home and hearth until the police put a stop to all the 'goings on.' The area never used to be so violent, they said, not in the old days, but Gregson knew differently. He could have told them that violent crime statistics were the lowest for decades, in fact the lowest for more than a hundred years.

But they were right about one thing: there *was* a circle. There was a group of people who would never, ever stop, not so long as self-interest and greed remained a deadly sin. There were people who chose to embrace their hedonistic nature rather than try to change it; who passed off their misdeeds as the means to an end, the necessary consequence of working towards a higher cause.

Yes, Gregson thought, the people of Newcastle should hurry home before night fell over the city, if they thought it would save them.

He looked across at the shadowed outline of the police constable manning the door to his private room. He hadn't seen her before but that could be a good or a bad thing. He presumed that Freeman would be keeping tabs on his movements, that she had been informed the moment he woke up. He thought of Walker and Mathieson and of how steel bars were unable to prevent the Circle reaching out to extinguish their miserable lives.

His chest heaved with weak laughter. It would be the easiest thing in the world to administer an overdose as he lay inert and unable to defend himself. Any one of the nurses, or that police constable, could do it. He didn't know who Freeman might have recruited for that very purpose.

He closed his eyes but could not sleep.

CHAPTER 22

Thursday, 6th August

Ryan opened his eyes and realised that he had enjoyed an unbroken night's sleep for the first time in nearly two years, free of nightmares, free from the spectre of anti-anxiety medication. His eyes adjusted to the early morning light shining through the gaps in the curtains and he felt Anna stir beside him. He looked across to where she still slept, her brow furrowed slightly as she dreamt. He wished that he could ease the ache in her heart, that he could lie to her and allow her to keep her fond memories of the past.

But it was not in his nature.

He leaned over to press his lips to her brow and then slipped out of bed to tug on his running gear. With a final look over his shoulder, he padded out of the room and set off for another jog around the city. It was a good habit, and he felt better than he had in a long while.

He followed his usual circuit, raising a friendly hand to the rounds of regulars who wheezed past him, working off the excesses of yesterday. The sky was an unbroken blue this morning and he looked up at it with childish delight, thinking that perhaps it heralded a turning point in their investigation. He didn't believe in a higher power, but it couldn't hurt to imagine that there might be some altruistic, omnipotent being watching out for the lowly human race. It sure beat the alternative, which was knowing that all the vice, violence and death plaguing the world happened for no greater reason than just 'because.'

His feet pounded the pavement and he sped up as he approached the underside of the bridge, working off the adrenaline kicking around in his system. Ahead, another jogger had the same idea, racing towards him from the opposite direction and he raised a hand in sociable greeting.

Ryan didn't see it coming.

He felt no prickle on his neck, no inkling of impending doom. Only at the very last moment did he recognise the face of one of the new police constables assigned to CID.

By then, it was too late.

He felt the sharp burn in his side, the pain of flesh ripping open as the knife tore through his thin t-shirt to find the skin beneath. He twisted away and stumbled backwards, clutching the side of his belly, trying to stem the flow of blood as shock reverberated through his body. He looked up and into the eyes of the young man who stared at him, fascinated by his own handiwork.

"No!" Ryan lashed out one-handed to fend off further blows but he read it in the man's eyes. The decision had already been made.

His legs wanted to buckle but there was no time. In one savage move, the man smashed his fist into the side of Ryan's head and he felt himself falling backwards into darkness. His heart seemed to stop in his chest, suspended in time before the cold water engulfed him.

On the bridge above, a woman pushed a pram and hoped that the motion would rock her new baby into slumber. In one hand, she sipped at a takeaway coffee while she forced one tired foot in front of the other. Another ten minutes, she thought, that should do it.

She heard the hard *clapping* sound of Ryan's body hitting the river water and turned sharply to look over the side of the bridge. She saw him immediately, a tall man in jogging pants and a faded white t-shirt stained with blood, sinking into the murky water.

"Oh my God!"

She looked down at her baby, whose lips quivered at the harsh sound of her voice. She couldn't leave him unattended. Panicked, she looked around for somebody to help, then she spotted a man standing by the water's edge.

"Help!" she screamed, waving her hands frantically to attract his attention. "There's a man in the water! You need to help him!"

Startled, he looked up at her and then backed away from the water before turning to sprint away.

Aghast, the woman watched his retreat and then looked back into the river, where the man had almost disappeared from sight, his body fully immersed in the stagnant water.

* * *

Anna checked the time again and grimaced. She had to deliver a lecture to some summer students at the university at nine-thirty and she was going to be horribly late.

Where was Ryan?

It was well after nine and there was still no sign of him. She presumed he had gone out for a run, because his gym clothes were missing alongside his trainers. His mobile phone, wallet and warrant card still rested on the bedside table upstairs and she knew that he would not leave for work without them.

Automatically, she checked her watch again, but less than a minute had passed.

She had taken her time getting ready, tidying the house and the kitchen, hoping to be able to share breakfast with him before their day began. A creeping, sickly feeling began to spread in her stomach. Something had happened to him, she knew it. She could *feel* it.

She walked to the window overlooking the river and watched the ordinary hustle and bustle of pedestrians making their way to work or catching an early morning view of the city before the crowds swelled through its cobbled streets.

"Come on, Ryan," she muttered aloud, while her insides churned with worry.

She heard the sound of a car engine arriving along the lane at the back of the house and her heart began to hammer so loudly she thought it might break through her chest. She hurried to the front door and opened it before Phillips had completed the short walk from his car to her front door.

One look at his face told her something was very, very wrong.

She reached out and blindly grasped the doorframe to hold herself upright.

Phillips watched the blood drain from her face and leaned over quickly to take her arm.

"Come on, love," he led her back into the house.

Inside, the living room faced west and away from the sun, so the room was dimly lit by a couple of lamps on small Moroccan side tables. Phillips helped her into a chair and sat across from her, taking one of her hands between his rough palms.

"Is he alive?" The words were barely audible but he caught them.

"Aye, he's still alive."

Anna closed her eyes and a single tear spilled out. Air rushed back into her chest and the blood began to pump again, coursing through her veins like wildfire.

"What happened?"

"He was shanked—knifed in his side while he was out jogging. Whoever it was pushed him in the river, about half a mile down the road."

"Did they catch him?"

"No, but we've got a good description from an eyewitness. A woman," he elaborated. "She heard the splash from the top of the bridge, shouted for help and luckily there was a student wandering past. He dived in."

"Thank God," Anna said, shakily. "What if nobody had been there? What if nobody had seen—"

"Ah, now," Phillips tugged her across for a bear hug. "Doesn't do any good to think about all the 'what ifs.' What matters is that they got him out in time."

Phillips didn't bother to tell her that Ryan hadn't been breathing when the student had struggled to drag him out of the water, or that several agonising moments had passed before he finally coughed up a gutful of river water and slipped back into unconsciousness.

"Where have they taken him?" She sat up again, ready to pounce off the sofa. "I need to be with him."

"He's at the University Hospital," Phillips answered.

"Let's go." Anna stood up.

Phillips stayed her arm.

"They've taken him straight into surgery," he told her. "He'll be in there a while."

Anna nodded and grabbed up her things. Once they were inside the car, she turned to him again.

"Frank, I don't care what you have to do, but find whoever did this. Just find them."

"Aye, lass, you can count on it."

* * *

The waiting went on forever. Hours spent in the depressing environment of the family waiting room with its empty water dispenser and strategically-placed leaflets on bereavement, drinking endless cups of coffee until their stomachs revolted and their hands jittered. MacKenzie and Lowerson came and went, and their false cheer for Anna's benefit did a better job of conveying their deep concern than tears ever could.

Anna made the difficult call to Ryan's parents and spoke with his mother, who had already lost one child and whose heart couldn't stand to lose another. They would be making their way north on the earliest flight from Devon to Newcastle.

Three hours trickled by in a haze of whispered trepidation until the surgeon eventually stepped inside the room, still in his scrubs.

"Mrs Ryan?"

Anna stood up on shaky legs and swallowed the weak tears in her throat.

"No, I—um, I'm Ryan's girlfriend. His mother and father will be here as soon as they can."

The surgeon nodded, then looked across at Phillips, whom he had already spoken to in an official capacity.

"Please, take a seat," he urged them both. "Maxwell has come through the surgery well. There was a laceration to his right side but by some stroke of very good luck the knife managed to miss his major organs. It's small comfort to you but from a medical perspective it was fortunate that he was recovered from the water with the blade still entrenched in his abdomen. That has allowed us to remove it safely, to stem the blood loss and seal the wound. He was suffering from advanced shock when he first came to us and his heart rate was very erratic, but it's stabilised since then and I'm optimistic."

Anna let the happy tears flow and Phillips barely held them off himself.

"When can we see him?"

"He's in recovery, under sedation. It'll be another couple of hours before he'll be ready to see anyone."

Anna stood up and reached for the surgeon's hand. As a naturally reserved man, he flushed at the gesture.

"Thank you," she managed.

* * *

Ryan heard her voice first, the gentle sound of it rubbing over his senses like a balm.

"Ryan? Love, it's me."

She watched his eyelashes sweep upwards and she found herself looking into a pair of silver-grey pools, foggy with pain.

"Anna."

His fingers groped for hers and she clasped them firmly. He was so pale. His skin held a greyish tinge and his lips lacked their usual healthy pink bloom. It was an affront to see this man in a hospital; his strong face with its hard planes and angles was so drastically out of place here, amongst people who were weak and dying.

"You'll be out of here in no time," she said briskly, giving his fingers another quick squeeze. "Your mum and dad are coming up to see you. They'll be here any minute, now."

Ryan watched her putting on a strong front and smiled faintly. She leaned over and fussed with the blanket, careful to avoid his bandages.

"Anna?"

"Mm hmm?"

"Would you do something for me?"

"Anything," she said.

"Marry me."

Her hands froze on either side of his chest.

"What?"

Ryan smiled, the fine lines crinkling at the corners of his eyes. His head felt fuzzy and his body was numb but he was thinking clearly. Near death experiences tended to clear out the mental junk, leaving only what mattered most.

"I know it isn't the most romantic of settings."

Anna looked at him for a full minute. He was serious, she realised, as warmth began to spread through her body.

She eased onto the edge of the bed and took his hand again.

"Is this the morphine talking?"

"I think they injected me with a love potion," he said. "Bloody medics."

Anna's smile spread.

"Seems wrong to take advantage when you're weak and vulnerable."

He tilted his head to one side and gave her the 'look.'

"Oh God," she moaned. "Don't look at me like that, you know I can't stand it."

"Like what?" he said innocently. "Here am I, an injured man. My only request is that you agree to spend the rest of your life with me, and you're stalling."

Anna pursed her lips.

"There'd be a big dress," she said, eventually.

"I'd expect no less."

"And a fancy party, with lots of people we barely know getting drunk at our expense."

"It's only right and proper."

She leaned across to press the gentlest of kisses to his pale lips.

"It's a deal."

Phillips rapped on the door to the recovery room and a moment later his face appeared.

"Any room for a little one?"

He didn't wait for an answer but stomped inside, coming to a hasty standstill when his antenna picked up the unusual atmosphere.

"What's going on here?"

"Anna's just agreed to make an honest man of me," Ryan said.

It took a few seconds but, after the initial surprise, the worry lines cleared from Phillips' brow and a gigantic grin broke across his face.

"Well, pet, I hope you know what you're letting yourself in for," he said, walking across to plant an affectionate kiss on her upturned forehead. He reached across and took one of Ryan's limp hands in his broad palm and pumped it briefly.

"I'm happy for you, mate. You've got one in a million sitting here. 'Course, the only reason she's marrying you is because I was already taken."

"Naturally," Ryan agreed.

* * *

Ryan's parents arrived and there were tears of distress at the sight of him wounded, followed expeditiously by tears of sheer maternal joy at the thought of a wedding in the near future. Eve Finlay-Ryan reserved a very special place in her heart for Anna. She, who had lost a daughter, opened her arms to the girl who had lost all the family she had ever known. From that first telephone call, Eve had warmed to the softly spoken woman with enough backbone to stand up to her son who, she admitted, could be remote and stubborn at the best of times.

After some none-too-gentle cajoling from the nurse, they were ushered outside. Loath as he was to admit it, Ryan was tired. His body was broken and needed time to heal. Nothing would be gained from pushing himself too hard too quickly, except a stunted recovery.

Phillips lingered at the end, the frivolity draining from his watchful brown eyes now that the others had left.

"Anything I can get for you, lad?"

Ryan felt his eyelids drooping and forced them open again.

"It was one of ours," he whispered. "One of the new PCs. I don't remember his name."

Phillips listened to Ryan as he recounted his ordeal, heard the catch in his breath as he described the sensation of falling backwards into the cold water of the river and it did not take much to imagine the horror. It was there in the man's eyes, where the shock of it all replayed like a film reel. Ryan's tone never faltered as he gave his statement with the kind of cold precision he was famous for. If there was fear, it was banked down beneath the surface. To acknowledge it would be to acknowledge how close the Circle had come to succeeding.

"They're escalating, Frank," Ryan was saying. Gratefully, he accepted a sip of water from the cup Phillips held to his lips. Collapsing back against the pillows, he turned grave eyes to his sergeant.

"Whoever is in charge now doesn't take any prisoners. They're not afraid of making a try for me," he wheezed out an incensed breath of laughter. "They're obliterating any potential threats and they don't seem to care about showing their hand."

Phillips cleared his throat and felt emotion overwhelm him.

"You're a pain in my arse most days," he looked away, then back again. "But God knows you scared me today, boy."

A small muscle in Ryan's jaw ticked as he held his own emotions in check.

"It'll take more than a piddling little flick blade to see me off, Frank."

"Aye, and what if they pull something bigger, next time? They want you gone."

"Well, we can't always have what we want, can we?"

Phillips bellowed out a laugh and waved away the nurse who tapped her watch and pointed at the door.

"Get some rest," he said, then gave in to the temptation to ruffle Ryan's black hair. It was probably the only opportunity he would get. "We're watching out for you, son."

"Thanks, Frank."

CHAPTER 23

Arthur Gregson had been terrified before but now he was almost paralysed by fear.

Ryan's attack dominated the late morning news as the latest in a long line of strange and violent incidents to happen within a matter of days. Freeman had reached too far, Gregson thought, in her quest to stamp out any threat to her authority. Too many deaths, too many high profile attacks to be overlooked. The Circle was coming out of the shadows and into the light.

Gregson did not know why they allowed him to live. Day by day, his body regained its strength. All that he knew about Freeman told him that she did not tolerate outsiders to their cause, and she considered him an outsider now. Years of loyal service meant nothing in the face of her indomitable leadership.

Gregson's lip quivered, self-pityingly.

It could only be a matter of time before they came for him. The silent stab of a syringe while he slept his drug-induced sleep. The painless overdose of intravenous sedative to ensure that he never woke to tell the sorry tale of a life spent worshipping the Master.

It sounded unbelievable, like a fantasy story. But he had seen the power of the Circle first hand. He had lived while others had paid the ultimate price for betrayal. Complacently, he had looked on and said nothing, done nothing to prevent it. Stupidly, he had believed he had risen too high for them to touch him. He believed he was untouchable.

Gregson's head throbbed against the bandage and he knew that a hospital attendant would be arriving shortly to wheel him along the corridor for another MRI scan. Nobody was invincible, he thought, not he, not even the mighty DCI Ryan.

Gregson wondered if Ryan was lying in his bed feeling the same brand of terror. Did he worry that the Circle would find him again and finish the job?

If he wasn't, then he should.

* * *

Jane Freeman blamed herself. Like a field marshal, she took responsibility for the failure of one of her infantrymen. She should not have entrusted such an important task to a young police constable who had not yet been initiated but had seemed so eager to prove himself and be accepted into their circle.

Uncharacteristic sentimentality led to poor decision-making, she concluded.

But what to do about it?

Her sources told her that Ryan was now fortified behind a barrier of police staff, hand-picked by his sergeant and under constant supervision by the snivelling Detective Constable Lowerson. There was another one on her list, she thought venomously, but he would be for another day. The problem of how to infiltrate remained.

They would be searching for the young constable who had turned on his own chief inspector, but she didn't worry too much about that. She might have been sentimental but she wasn't stupid. That young man had already been dealt with, punished swiftly for his failure.

She would not tolerate damp squibs.

Freeman allowed herself to imagine briefly what life might be like with a man like Ryan by her side, a worthy partner to walk beside her…well, perhaps a pace behind. With his strength and her charisma, they would be unstoppable.

Desire fluttered at the prospect. She thought of how it would feel to bring him to heel and convert him to their way of life. He would be a good lover, too. Better than the usual fare, she was sure of that. Perhaps she had been short-sighted in giving the order. She had not fully considered the possibility that he might convert and in doing so, she had not given adequate weight to her own extensive skills in the art of manipulation.

But then, modesty had always been her failing.

* * *

Phillips strode along the corridors of CID Headquarters like an angry bull, fit to tear into the first unsuspecting detective constable who so much as looked at him cockeyed. This wasn't his city anymore, he thought bitterly. This was not his heartland, the land of industry, of ship-building craftsmen to the east and land-lovers to the west. The people of that landscape were, for the most part, an honest and open tribe. They did not sneak around the hills and groves dressed in black capes, flapping around like a poor man's Batman. They did not worship the devil, chanting nonsense in front of bonfires. And if they killed, or injured, or stole, or lied, they had the decency to be upfront about it afterwards. It was a sorry state of affairs, Phillips thought, when the character of his own people came under threat from a band of fanatics who fancied themselves above everybody else. Well, he would be happy to bring their feet back down to solid ground with a vengeance.

The truth was that he was frightened. Easy enough to face your foe when they came at you head on but how could he fight against the Circle if he didn't know a thing about their origins or their number?

With these gloomy thoughts circulating, he turned towards the main bank of desks in CID and bumped straight into MacKenzie.

"Frank! I was just looking for you," she said. "How's Ryan?"

Phillips' agitation slowly melted away. It was impossible to keep hold of a good bout of anger when faced with the dulcet tones of Denise MacKenzie.

"He'll do," he said shortly.

MacKenzie gave him a lopsided smile of understanding.

"I'm worried sick," he tugged at his ear, self-consciously. "I know he's got his family there, and Anna—"

"But you still worry," MacKenzie finished for him.

"Aye, I do. He said himself they're turning up the heat. Never in a month of Sundays did I think they'd take a shot at him, but here we are."

MacKenzie's lips firmed.

"Pinter rang me while you were at the hospital. The remaining analysis has come back on Bowers and it turns out there was glue residue on his right hand."

"Glue?" As she had hoped, news of progress in her investigation distracted him from thoughts of Ryan.

"Yes, that's the composition. I've no idea what the significance is, yet, but it's another piece of the jigsaw, isn't it?"

Phillips nodded.

"I also heard from Bowers' GP, who finally sent through the medical records. Turns out Bowers had only known about his tumour for around a month but the prognosis was terminal from the outset. Chances of radiotherapy or chemotherapy reducing the size of the tumour were very low and Bowers was offered information on respite care instead."

"Bumps up the probability of suicide," Phillips commented, but MacKenzie shook her head.

"I thought about that, but all the other evidence points to a third party and we're still missing a weapon."

Phillips tugged at his lower lip as he thought.

"What about the pistol registered in Mathieson's name?"

"Lowerson checked that out and the CCTV footage is useless—it was pointing in the wrong direction. All the auction house can tell us is that the pistol was paid for in cash by a man claiming to be Daniel Mathieson. The make and model are both so old that they're exempt from the usual legislation requiring a certificate and he didn't buy any ammunition, so they had no need to ask for paperwork of any kind. He showed them I.D. and the sale was registered in Mathieson's name."

Phillips frowned into the distance, imagining the different pieces of the jigsaw.

"But we know it wasn't Mathieson, because he was in prison and now he's in a body bag. Either someone sorted out fake I.D. in Mathieson's name in advance or he had access to Mathieson's belongings. Still, it'd have to be someone who resembled him, at least a bit," Phillips said. "Dark, greying hair, in his fifties. Put on a pair of glasses, wear the right clothes…it's possible."

"We know quite a few men who match that description."

Phillips scrubbed a hand over his eyes.

"You said there was another possible weapon matching the type used to kill Bowers—a pistol missing from Bamburgh Castle?"

"Yes, that's right. Lowerson spoke to the curator up at the castle, who says it went missing a few weeks ago. They went through the usual channels and reported the theft, got a crime reference number. Upshot is they think it was swiped by a tourist when the castle was busy. The kind of duelling pistol we're looking for was displayed on the wall in the armoury there."

"So far, every new link has been deliberate, to point us towards another person of interest. I'm wondering whether there's something or somebody up at Bamburgh we should be watching out for?"

MacKenzie racked her brain for an answer.

"There's a National Heritage office up there," she began.

"There's the link," Phillips unrolled a new line of nicotine gum. He was going to need it. "Bowers worked for National Heritage, and there's bound to be somebody in the office who links to him. I seem to think Jane Freeman is based up there."

"Bowers worked on an excavation at Bamburgh," MacKenzie added. "It was the last one before he died."

"Let's get cracking."

* * *

Jane Freeman drew the next batch of books across the desk towards her, pen poised to scribble her name inside. She spent a few minutes happily engrossed by how pretty her own name looked on the front cover, when her eye fell on a small brown parcel resting to one side.

She picked up a silver letter opener and slit open the thick paper. A copy of her new book, alongside a notecard and a folded pre-paid envelope fell onto the desk in front of her. She read the notecard first:

Dear Professor Freeman,

I have been a great admirer of your work for many years and am very much looking forward to reading, 'Sex, Scandal and Northumbrian Legend.' Unfortunately, I am unable to attend your forthcoming appearance and book signing, much to my regret. However, I would consider it a great honour if you would kindly autograph the enclosed copy and return it via the pre-paid envelope provided.

Yours faithfully,

Professor Gregory Chambers

Freeman's lips curved and her hand lifted unconsciously to smooth her hair. She had heard of Professor Chambers, though she had never met him in person—yet. He was a popular figure in the public eye following several successful history documentaries he had fronted for the BBC and her avaricious mind spun with the thought of the doors that such an admirer could open for her.

She tapped her fountain pen against her lips as she imagined herself leading a series of glamorous historical documentaries based around Northumberland. Just as quickly, anger and pique followed at the realisation that she had not been asked already.

The nerve of it.

Who did those television producers think they were? Didn't they know who she *was?* She closed her eyes and told herself to remain calm. Rome was not built in a day and neither was a Northumbrian empire.

She thought for a moment, then wrote a short note inside the book:

For Professor Chambers,

From one historical expert to another, with warmest regards.

J.L. Freeman

She decided that she would give it a couple of days, then follow up with a personal call to his offices in Cambridge. The more she thought about it, the more she realised how limiting it would be to confine her talents to the North-East.

With a feeling of deep satisfaction, she ran her tongue along the flap of the pre-paid envelope and set it aside to be posted along with the other mail.

CHAPTER 24

Gregson lolled between sleep and wakefulness as the hospital attendant wheeled him back from his MRI scan, accompanied by the ever-present PC Yates, whose footsteps squeaked against the hospital flooring in time with the metal clang of the gurney's wheels. Soon after, a doctor stepped in to inform him that he was making an excellent recovery and could expect to fully regain his speech and fine motor skills over the next couple of weeks. Two nurses assisted in removing his brace and changed the bandages at the back of his head, which felt impossibly heavy now that his neck was once again required to support its weight.

After they left, Gregson strained to hear PC Yates' muted telephone conversation in the corridor outside. He couldn't make out whether she was updating a member of the Circle or one of the team handling his case in CID. Not knowing for certain on which side of the battle lines she rested was slowly driving him insane. He watched her mouth moving and tried to make out what was being said through the gap in the blinds but eventually he snatched his gaze away, frustrated by his inability to lip-read.

The clock on the wall read three-fifteen. At four, another constable would be along to relieve Yates from her present shift. That was their pattern, he had noticed. Usually, one of Ryan's own trusted team replaced Yates to guard his door but he suspected that would not be possible today. The man himself was recovering in another hospital a few miles yonder and, though Gregson was still the man's professional superior, he was under no illusions that he outranked Ryan in the pecking order, especially when it came to safeguarding his life against a mob of Satan worshippers.

That was another illusion, he thought. Ryan claimed the guard on his door was for his own protection but Gregson knew it was little more than house arrest.

He let out a laugh which bordered on hysteria, then glanced at the clock again.

At four o'clock, the constables changed their guard. Then, around four-thirty, the medics would do their usual rounds. There might be a small window; just a few minutes, that's all he would need.

Gregson's fingers clutched and unclutched the bed sheets as he thought of all the possible outcomes and concluded that the longer he stayed here like a sitting duck, the more chance there was that somebody would come along to shoot him in the pond.

Gingerly, he raised his head from the pillow and battled the searing pain. He retched but managed to half pull himself upright, leaning heavily on one arm which shook under the weight of his torso. Determination propelled him upwards and he swung his legs heavily over the side of the bed, where they hung like dead weights for a moment while the pins and needles tingled in his feet. He didn't need any doctor to tell him that he wasn't fully recovered, he could feel that for himself. But he needed to know if his legs would support him and if escape was even worth contemplating.

He slid off the bed slowly like a newborn fowl, the greying hair on his legs quivering as his body worked against the pain. He swayed for a moment and thought he might faint but his body seemed to right itself and his vision cleared again. He shuffled a couple of steps forward and checked the blinds to see that Yates was looking in the other direction.

She was.

Gregson tugged on an imaginary rope in the air, counting out each step between gritted teeth until he reached the bathroom. Only a few steps from his bed but he felt like he had just crossed Antarctica.

He leaned against the doorframe for a moment and clutched at the wide plastic handles that were conveniently placed to help ailing men like himself to make it to the toilet, but he wasn't concerned about his bladder. The doctors had removed his catheter the previous day and he had already endured that first humiliating pee into a cardboard bowl, to make sure his system still worked. He had never felt more *base,* lying there with his withered old dick in his hand, peeing in front of a young nurse who looked at him as if he were a specimen, not a flesh and blood man.

He exhaled a weak sob, then gripped the doorframe harder before he pushed away again, making for the bag which held his meagre belongings. They had taken his mobile phone, car keys and wallet for 'safekeeping,' and his clothes had gone to the lab for analysis in connection with his attack. But he had some small change, a free toothbrush from the hospital and some basic clothing the police had brought from his home in the event that he would need something other than the pyjamas he now wore.

It took fifteen minutes to remove his pyjama bottoms, don jogging pants, then replace the pyjama bottoms on top of them so as not to arouse suspicion. If a nurse happened to look underneath the bedclothes, they would notice the difference immediately, but he hoped it wouldn't come to that.

He dragged his feet back to the bed, clutching socks and some cash in his hands and when Yates glanced back through the crack in the window blinds, she saw Gregson lying under the bedclothes, apparently asleep.

She turned back, to await the change of guard.

* * *

As the clock struck four, Anna returned to the University Hospital with a small bag of essentials for Ryan. She was relieved to find that DC Lowerson was seated outside the door to Ryan's room, eyes trained on the corridor to assess any new visitors that approached. He had already turned away a number of resourceful journalists over the course of the day but now he relaxed at the sight of a familiar figure.

"Hi Anna," he stood up to greet her, uncaring for once that his new suit was badly wrinkled or that he would have liked to freshen up his aftershave.

"Hello, Jack. How's the patient?"

"Doctors came round about half an hour ago," Lowerson said. "They've reduced the painkillers and checked his stitches. Everything's looking good, so far."

Pent-up breath whooshed out of her body.

"Let's take a look at him, then," she smiled.

Inside, Ryan was starting to feel the effects of reduced pain medication. The wound on the right-hand side of his abdomen was tender and he could feel the stitches beginning to burn. The constant stream of news on the television screen fixed to the wall flickered with muted sound and he watched the broadcasters delivering their reports at the foot of Heavenfield Church. Their message was always the same: the police knew nothing, the police had solved nothing, it was all connected to the cult circle and now the people's champion—Ryan himself—had fallen. They likened his attack to that fateful arrow which had brought down Achilles. They prophesied the downfall of the people of Northumbria, while Ryan watched from his hospital bed with a growing sense of annoyance at the unnecessary drama of it all.

So, he had been knifed and thrown into a river.

So, three, possibly four people had died in as many days and another had been attacked and was drinking through a straw at another hospital a few miles away.

Alright, Ryan acknowledged, it didn't sound good. But he would be out of these clinical walls in no time, back in the thick of it. All he had to do was be patient—ha ha—and let the dust settle, then he would have a nice, friendly chat with one of the doctors and convince them that he was only taking up bed space. He was determined to sleep in his own bed again as soon as possible, serious injury or not.

The impotence of being forced to remain inactive subsided when Anna walked into the room, armed with spare clothes and a carrier bag full of non-hospital-regulation goodies which he spotted immediately.

"How's the invalid?" She leaned down to press her lips to his.

"Grumpy and irritable," he replied.

"No change, then."

"Humph," he muttered. "Have you come to torment me?"

Anna smiled and snuck him a chocolate bar, which he snatched out of her hand like a toddler.

"Knowing you as well as I do," she continued, "I'm fully aware that even though it's only been few hours since you nearly *died,* you're probably wondering how soon you can get out of here."

Ryan chewed the chocolate in silence.

"You're probably *also* wondering if you might be able to use your charms to convince one of the unsuspecting junior doctors to discharge you in time for dinner. Am I right?"

A smile tugged at the corner of Ryan's mouth.

"Know-it-all."

"There's no way you're getting discharged before you're good and ready," she said flatly. "*And* it would be over my dead body, so you might as well stop thinking about how you can rush back to work."

Ryan glowered at her.

"However, since you can't go to work, I thought I might bring a bit of work to you, as long as you're not too tired."

"I knew there was a good reason I was marrying you," he said, smugly.

"I don't see a ring on my finger, yet."

"All good things…" he grinned, eyeing the bag she had brought for the familiar outline of a police file.

Following his eyes, she shook her head.

"Everything we need for the work I have in mind is in *here,*" she tapped the side of her head.

* * *

Richard 'Rick' Upton was a junior doctor at the Royal Victoria Infirmary. He had a good, friendly rapport with colleagues and patients alike, in part thanks to the innocent, open-looking face he had been born with. His big brown eyes and average features instilled trust and he was possessed of a well spoken voice that conformed nicely with what most people expected of a middle-class doctor.

In his present role attached to intensive care and acute medicine, he was never known to grumble over the long shifts or lack of resource, over rude patients or incompetent judgment calls from his fellow staff. He went about his business in a tireless fashion, greeting each new patient with professional cheer.

But beneath the harmless façade, there festered a burning desire for recognition. He didn't want to spend the rest of his days at the beck and call of stinking drunks who had fallen over their own feet, or drug addicts with their gaunt, staring faces. He wanted to rise above the rabble, to take his true place in society. He had earned it. He hadn't slaved away for all these years to save *these* people.

He wanted to be the man the celebrities called upon. He wanted to be the consultant in the three-piece suit standing outside the private hospital where a royal baby had just been born, giving a self-deprecating statement to hoards of press.

Over the first few years spent on the wards, he had realised a very important thing. It was down to him whether these people lived or died. He made the order to operate in time, or he didn't. He could lean on a tube, block an airway, 'miss' something vitally important and people wouldn't lose sleep over the loss of an old tramp who, to him, was just taking up oxygen.

Then, one night last Christmas, he had seen the news. Three ritual murders on Holy Island and the discovery of a cult circle. The police claimed it was all over, that the circle had been disbanded, but Rick had been inspired. He knew then, there was another way. A better way.

He'd searched for them but come up with nothing. He'd gone to the island and stayed there during his summer vacation, gone out walking late into the night, hoping to stumble across a ceremony.

Nothing.

Then, to his amazement, they found him, and the rest was history.

"*The Master seeks you out,*" they'd told him. "*Because he senses your devotion.*"

Now, Rick made his way up the hospital's service stairs, conscious of the small window of opportunity the Circle had given him. There would be a change of police guard, a mere five minutes when Gregson would be unattended. It was his only chance, that had been made very clear from the outset. At four-fifteen exactly, the police constable would take himself off for five minutes and would return at four-twenty. By four-thirty, Rick was due back on his rounds and would be one of the first to 'find' Gregson's body. He panted slightly as he ran up the final flight of steps and stepped onto the ward, with a nervous glance in either direction.

Four-sixteen.

He moved quickly along the corridor, eyes focussed on the door which stood unguarded, as promised.

In his right hand, he held a syringe, already prepared with a lethal dose of morphine.

Four-seventeen.

He heard footsteps in the distance and froze, but the sound melted away and he continued onward. His face was set into hard lines and his eyes were clear. There was no question of him altering his course now.

Rick reached the doorway and he didn't pause but opened it quickly, his movements smooth and practised. His eyes locked on to the huddled figure in the bed in the centre of the room. Rick slid his thumb to the top of the syringe and closed the distance, needle poised to finish the job.

Then his arm fell away again, the syringe clattering to the floor so that he had to stumble around and pick it up.

The bed was empty.

Confused, disappointed, Rick stared at the bed. He spun around to check that Gregson was not hiding in the bathroom but the little en-suite was empty too. Sweating now, Rick threw the covers back over the bunched-up pillows and slipped out of the room to make his way back to the service stairs.

In the empty stairwell, he looked down at his hands, which were trembling. *Adrenaline,* he thought automatically. He wondered how he would ever face them, and how long it would be before the Circle found out that Gregson had escaped. It wasn't his fault, he thought, he couldn't be blamed for that. He had been there, right on time, ready to kill the man.

It wasn't his fault.

But his palms sweated and his bowels loosened as he recalled the warnings he had been given of the consequences of failure, no matter how unavoidable. There would be no sympathetic nod of understanding because, in his new unforgiving circle of friends, there was always somebody else waiting to step into his shoes.

Doctor Rick Upton slid down to the floor and dropped his head into his hands.

CHAPTER 25

"In *Paradise Lost*, Satan is a very seductive character."

Sixteen miles further south of where Rick Upton sobbed in an empty stairwell, Ryan leaned back against the plump pillows of his hospital bed and considered Anna's statement.

"He's portrayed as a great orator," he agreed. "By the end of the poem, you almost feel sorry for him."

Anna nodded.

"That's just it. He has a kind of infectious rhetoric, a way of making his followers believe that God is really some kind of despot, whose power is arbitrary."

"A lot like Steve Walker," Ryan remarked. He didn't bother to point out the similar traits in Anna's father, or in Mark Bowers. Some things didn't need spelling out.

"Yes, a criminal profiler might say that the men who have led the Circle had naturally similar traits to Satan, in Milton's poem." She laughed shortly, then added, "I'm sure he had no idea that his poem would spark such a following."

"Wouldn't be the first piece of prose to be used for unscrupulous ends," Ryan pointed out. "Nietzsche is probably fairly pissed off, for example, as he turns in his grave."

"Interesting that the leader is always a man. Why does Satan have to be male?"

"Well, nobody ever said that misogyny was confined to normal society. It happens amongst the crackpot elements, too."

Anna covered her face with her hand but couldn't hold back the laugh. *Crackpot?* Her beloved had such an elegant turn of phrase.

"Do you think the new leader is a man, too?"

"I thought for a while that it was Gregson," Ryan answered seriously. "He has—or *had*," he smiled unkindly as he made the distinction, "unparalleled access to case files, personal data on almost anybody. He's well connected and had a force of police staff at his fingertips. It made sense that he would be a contender.

"I still think he's involved, but I can't see the Circle attacking their leader and not finishing the job. Their outlook is very black and white; they either offer unstinting support, or they kill without mercy. There aren't shades in between, which is why Gregson being allowed to live and recover in hospital makes no sense to me."

"Somebody else, then?"

Ryan huffed out a breath but despite the nagging pain and the mountain they still had to climb before they found the answers, he was enjoying himself. Brain work was better than being forced to watch daytime television any day of the week.

"Let's work on the basis that the Circle's new leader is male, for now. They're a traditional group and they like their old sources, like Milton. Getting back to that," he shuffled to make himself more comfortable. "And assuming I suspend my disbelief to imagine the existence of God, or any of these characters, let me see if I've got this right: according to *Paradise Lost*, Satan started out as one of the most important angels in Heaven. Turns out, Satan had beef with God. That beef was jealousy at the fact God is the boss of the universe. He started bitching about God and rounding up a bunch of other angels who felt the same way. Satan started a war in Heaven, angels against angels, which he ultimately lost. As punishment for being such an almighty pain in the arse, God consigned him to Hell, hence Satan's famous 'fuck you' quote, *'better to reign in Hell, than to serve in Heaven.'*"

Anna laughed appreciatively.

"I would have loved to see you in your student days," she muttered, and Ryan wriggled his eyebrows suggestively.

"That can be arranged."

She threw him a mocking look, then turned firmly back to the point.

"In simple terms, yes, that's the basis of the poem. We know that the Circle used it, otherwise they wouldn't have listed their leaders on the inside of that early edition you took from Mark's house."

"Agreed."

"Well, what you may not know is that there's a related legend around Holy Island. Locals believed that when God knocked Satan's battle axe out of his hand during the battle in Heaven, the axe fell to the Earth where it hit the North Sea and became the island of Lindisfarne—Holy Island. If you look at the shape of the island, it looks a bit like an axe."

Interested, Ryan leaned forward and then winced as pain flashed from the wound at his side.

"Don't get too excited," Anna chided him, pushing him gently back against the pillows.

"It all feeds into their warped thinking," he said. "It helps them to believe that they're special or that there's a higher cause. What else?"

"Well, there are so many different historical sources which could be read in different ways. If you're looking to find support for your own crazy mission, a lot of the old texts could be misread. Take the War Scroll, from the Dead Sea Scrolls," she shrugged a shoulder.

Ryan waited for more but apparently she had made the mistake of assuming he knew the first thing about...well, anything historical.

"Ah, you're going to have to spell that out for me."

"Oh, sorry. Um, well the War Scroll was one of the texts found amongst the Dead Sea Scrolls, in the caves on the West Bank. It describes a war between the 'Sons of Light' and the 'Sons of Darkness,' who are part of the army of 'Belial.' That's an old Hebrew word for the Devil."

"Another bit of text describing a war between good and evil?"

"Exactly. The Sons of Light and the Sons of Darkness are representatives of either side of the battle on Earth," she said slowly. "They're a human army. It strikes me that, if I supported Satan, if I genuinely convinced myself that there was a higher purpose for why I liked killing innocent people, I might imagine that I were a Son of Darkness fighting on Earth."

Ryan sighed and looked up at the plain white ceiling of his hospital bedroom.

"I found references to old pagan gods, which have since been appropriated by Christianity, or Judaism," Anna added. "Wherever you look in pagan history, you'll find a harmless old ceremonial ground now has a church built over it, or it's been otherwise claimed by an 'orthodox' religion."

"I think I'm following you," Ryan's eyes flickered. "Paganism might have formed the basis for the cult, in the early days. In more recent times, they've veered into more dangerous territory after deciding that their allegiance should be to a more powerful master?"

Anna said nothing, only listened with darkened eyes.

"Maybe they're angry that their old pagan sites have been taken over and they want to take them back," Ryan concluded.

"Which would explain why bad things keep happening on sites of religious significance," Anna agreed. "Holy Island, Heavenfield..."

"There must be hundreds of sites like that."

"Yes," Anna said, imagining what could be uncovered over the following months, or years. "But I've been asking myself—why Heavenfield? Why not another church, or somewhere bigger or flashier, like Durham Cathedral?"

Ryan waited for the answer.

"These sites are all part of 'St. Oswald's Way,' " she provided. "The pilgrimage starts at Holy Island and takes people along the coast past Bamburgh Castle, over the fields via Rothbury. Eventually you end up at Heavenfield. It's where Oswald defeated the 'pagan' Mercian army, which is why it's particularly significant."

"To put it another way," Ryan said dryly, "if you want to give orthodox religion the finger by killing in the name of Satan, the best place to do it would be at a site of a famous Christian victory? Even better if you manage to kill someone on the one day of the year dedicated to St. Oswald." Bowers had died on St. Oswald's Tide, after all.

"Yup."

There was a momentary pause while they took a synchronised sip from cans of sugary soft drinks, most definitely not sanctioned by the hospital.

"So, do I need to get myself some kind of magic battle axe?" he said eventually.

Anna grinned.

"Get yourself well again," she said quietly. "That's enough for now."

* * *

While Anna left Ryan to rest and made her way back to Durham to look after his parents, whom she had convinced to stay at her cottage rather than smothering their irritable son with well-meaning affection, Arthur Gregson stepped onto a northbound bus. The rickety pale green double-decker was occupied almost exclusively by dour-faced pensioners returning home after a day out in the Big City and equally dour-faced young teenagers who returned to their village homes in time for curfew. The appealing lights of the cinemas and fast food restaurants in the city centre were a distant blur and, as a light rain began to fall, the only sound was the trundle of the wheels against the tarmac and the swish of oversized windscreen wipers. Now and again, a crackling advert came to life on the LED screen touting the benefits of herbal remedies during the onset of menopause.

Gregson rested his head against the grimy window, eyes open but red-rimmed after days without proper sleep. He had salvaged a filthy woollen hat bearing the logo of a local football team, which mostly hid the bandage at the back of his head. He still wore his pyjama shirt, tucked into grey jogging bottoms. Now and then, the bus swerved wildly around the zigzagging road towards Bamburgh and his head cracked against the glass. Passively, he ignored it and continued to watch the drizzle from haunted eyes in an ashen face.

"Next stop, Shilbottle!"

The bus driver bleated out the name of the next village and Gregson looked up briefly, then hunkered down again in his seat. Still a way to go yet, until he reached his destination.

Soon, he thought, *soon he would reach the promised land.* There would be plenty of supplies and money; lots and lots of cash money. Enough to get him out of the country, enough to buy a false passport and passage across the sea, if necessary. Freeman could consider it severance pay if she liked but he was damn well taking it. She could rouse up Hell's Fury, for all he cared, he wasn't leaving that sodding castle without a bagful of fifties and an apology for all the pain and hardship he had been through.

He enjoyed his newfound bravery but the better part of him knew that he had absolutely no intention of facing down Jane Freeman. He was as weak as a kitten and she wouldn't need to call upon any of her minions to chuck him over the battlements at Bamburgh, she could probably manage it herself.

No, it would be much safer to just slip in and out as quickly and quietly as possible. The bandage on his head needed changing, he needed fresh clothes, food and water, not to mention a good night's sleep. But he didn't yet have the means. Perhaps he would splash out on a cheap hotel before making his escape across the water, he relented, thinking of blissful white sheets and a warm meal.

His eyelids closed and his head continued to drum against the window pane. The ancient green bus continued its painstaking journey through the countryside and the sky began to dim from an overcast grey to a deepening charcoal as the sun began its slow descent.

* * *

Further ahead on the same road, DI MacKenzie and DS Phillips headed towards Bamburgh with considerably more speed than the regional bus service. A brief telephone conversation assured Phillips that Ryan was still resting, safe and sound at the University Hospital in Durham and recovering better than ninety-nine per cent of similar victims of knife crime. Phillips put that down entirely to Ryan's refusal to show any kind of weakness, even following a near-death experience.

Stubborn as a mule, he thought proudly.

Another telephone call to the Royal Victoria Infirmary in Newcastle told him that their other charge, DCS Arthur Gregson, was sleeping peacefully and should be well enough to answer questions at their earliest convenience. It was a sad thing not to harbour any real sympathy for a man he had known for decades, had served under and admired, but that was life, he supposed. People weren't always who you believed them to be.

He glanced across at MacKenzie, who was driving with the kind of ability which came from certification in advanced police driving skills. For his part, he liked getting from A to B with his remaining hair still intact and he didn't feel the need to drive at anything other than his own pace. As the music shifted to the next acoustic version of something moody from the late nineties, Phillips was reminded that perhaps the biggest downside to riding shotgun was not having first dibs on the radio.

"Doctor says that Gregson'll be ready to talk whenever we are," he said.

"About time," MacKenzie replied. "He's been hiding behind that head injury for days but I'll be damned if he doesn't know what happened to his wife."

"Aye, there's still no sign of her," Phillips was sad to say. Cathy Gregson might have made a questionable choice of husband but she had always been a decent woman. "The local news stations are still running the statement we gave them yesterday but they've been badgering me all day for something new."

MacKenzie's lips firmed.

"They'll have to wait."

"Aye, no sense in pontificating about bugger all," he said, wisely.

"I heard from Faulkner earlier today and he tells me they've confirmed the blood found at Gregson's house is a conclusive match to Cathy Gregson's DNA type. It looks very bad," she turned down the radio, much to Phillips' relief.

"He's bound to say there was a burglar, or something," he reasoned. "No way he could have bashed the back of his own head, for one thing."

"Fair point," MacKenzie acknowledged. "But I'll be interested to see what his financial statements will reveal."

"I've been chasing up the bank," Phillips unwrapped a boiled mint sweet and offered her one. "The data is slowly trickling through, but unless he's a complete dingbat, Gregson won't have anything dodgy going through his current account. It'll all be laundered through something or other," he said, dreading the prospect of trying to unravel an elaborate financial carousel. They could get some support from the financial crimes unit for that, couldn't they?

He hoped so.

"I had a good chat with Anna, while we were waiting for Ryan to come out of surgery. She agrees with us about the geographical points being significant to the Circle. There's all kinds of history behind it but we're singing from the same hymn sheet," MacKenzie told him.

"She's a good lass," Phillips mumbled, negotiating speech around the boiled sweet he was sucking. "If she says there's a plausible reason behind these incident sites, we're likely on the right track."

MacKenzie nodded.

"Right enough." She pressed a bit more heavily on the accelerator, then added, "It's the funniest thing, Frank, but I've got a queer feeling that we're going to find something bad waiting for us, up at Bamburgh."

"It's not funny at all, because I've got the same feeling myself."

They looked on as the castle emerged from the murky landscape, a blurred outline behind the rain that pummelled their windscreen.

CHAPTER 26

"Denise, it's starting to feel a bit like Cabot Cove around here."

"I know what you mean," MacKenzie murmured, as they looked upon the rigid body of Jane Freeman with dispassionate eyes.

She lay where she had fallen, slumped across her shiny desk, surrounded by copies of her latest book. There was an uncomfortable odour in the room which told them she had lain undetected for at least a couple of hours while the stench of blood-stained vomit fermented in the air surrounding her lifeless body.

"No signs of attack," MacKenzie commented, in a small, detached voice. "Better call it in, Frank."

While Phillips moved away to put a call through to the Control Room, MacKenzie sought out the young castle guide who had directed them here. She turned out to be a twenty-two-year-old work experience student named Charlotte and MacKenzie found her perched at the foot of the stairwell which led up to Freeman's offices, biting her fingernails.

"Charlotte?"

The girl raised glassy, shocked eyes in the direction of MacKenzie's voice.

"I-I didn't hear anything," she stuttered. "I didn't see anything, either."

MacKenzie retrieved a tissue from the depths of her tan leather bag and handed it to the girl, who blew her nose loudly.

"Let's just take this one step at a time," MacKenzie said, her eyes watchful. "You've been working with Professor Freeman?"

Charlotte swallowed.

"Yes. Yes, I've been doing a summer placement with National Heritage. Professor Freeman invited me to work as one of her personal aides."

"That was kind."

The girl swiped at her nose again.

"How long have you been helping her?" MacKenzie asked.

"Oh, since the beginning of July, when classes stopped on my Masters course. I've got a thesis to write but I thought I'd get some practical experience over the summer."

"I see. How did you find it, working for Professor Freeman?"

The girl bit her lip and started to shred the tissue. MacKenzie noted the action.

"She was very knowledgeable."

"And on a personal level, how would you describe her?"

"Very professional."

MacKenzie almost laughed but instead she sighed deeply and came to sit next to the girl on the bottom step while she waited for Phillips to return.

"You know, Charlotte, there isn't much to be gained from being polite, not at a time like this. You're not going to get an 'F' for telling me she could sometimes be a bit of an uppity madam," she said, casually, then felt it necessary to add, "I'm not here to judge the woman but I do need to find out why she might have died."

Charlotte shredded the remaining tissue and then clutched at the pieces. Thoughts of retribution swarmed her young mind, of what the Circle might do to her. They might think she had killed their leader and *then* what would they do?

She began to blubber and, silently, MacKenzie offered a second tissue.

"Honestly, I don't know how this has happened!" The girl sniffled. "She was fit as a fiddle the last time I saw her!"

"Which was when?"

"Um," Charlotte hiccupped and thought back. "It was around two…yes, two o'clock. I delivered some books for her to sign ahead of her event this weekend, at the Literary Society in town. She seemed happy enough, so I left her to it."

"What did you do then?"

Charlotte gulped and began to shred the next tissue. Should she admit that she had snuck off to the dunes for a clandestine meeting with one of the young archaeology students currently excavating the eastern side of the castle grounds?

"I went for a walk on the beach," she said instead.

MacKenzie watched guilt play over the girl's face and shook her head, wondering if they would ever learn.

"I take it that somebody can vouch for you during this, ah, beach walk?"

"Yes, he...yes."

"I'll get his name later," MacKenzie said, wryly. "But, for now, tell me this: was Professor Freeman expecting anybody, later in the afternoon? Had anything, or anybody, upset her?"

Charlotte thought hard about what she was at liberty to say.

"No, she seemed fine," she said, truthfully. "The last time I saw her really blow a gasket was after she had a visitor yesterday."

"Oh? Do you remember the visitor's name?"

"Doctor Anna Taylor."

* * *

Night was setting in by the time Gregson finally reached the village of Bamburgh. He dragged his aching body upwards and shuffled off the bus. The driver waited patiently until he had eased himself onto the pavement on the village high street and bade him a friendly farewell before moving off again to motor the return route back into the city.

Alone, Gregson cast a wary glance in either direction along the street and tugged the woollen hat further over his head. There would be people here who would recognise him, he knew that. In fact, there would be people throughout the county who knew his face, publically and privately.

Across the road, the castle was a dark outline against the sky, which was a magnificent royal blue blending into deep midnight navy. The rain had stopped and the skies were clear once again, a cloudless blanket where stars would soon begin to twinkle. His stomach was rumbling and his head was light but Gregson began the slow walk towards the castle's southern entrance, known as 'St. Oswald's Gate.' It was the oldest entrance to the castle and gave access to a natural harbour on the seaward side, as well as the castle itself. It was not accessible via an ordinary pathway—tourists used the main entrance to the north of the castle along Vale Typping instead. Only archaeological staff, castle workers and members of the Circle sometimes hiked up the steep grassy incline to use the old gateway.

Bamburgh had been used by the Circle for generations. A castle which had once been home to the first kings of England and had replaced ancient burial grounds with commemorative monuments to Oswald and his Christianity was now infiltrated by the enemy. It was one of the perks of being the High Priest—or Priestess—to occupy the castle, in one form or another. Mark Bowers had spent his year in office under the legitimate guise of excavating Bamburgh's southern walls. Freeman had taken over that responsibility and had gone one stage further to secure a suite of permanent offices for herself inside the clock tower.

Gregson lumbered along the underside of the western walls of the castle, then stopped and looked up and over the grassy incline ahead of him until he found the small stone archway demarcating St. Oswald's Gate. It appeared nothing more than a black hole, small and insignificant against the taller castle walls built around it. Shamefully, his legs began to weaken. The grassy verge might as well have been a mountain to climb and for a moment he considered swallowing his pride and fear by prostrating himself at Freeman's feet, begging her forgiveness, appealing to her softer side.

Then he remembered that she didn't have a softer side.

There was nobody around and the village was quiet, particularly at this end which led away from the pubs and the holiday cottages. The air was still and there was barely a breath of wind from the sea as Gregson stood shaded by the castle's outer walls. Looking upward, he felt like an interloper, David to the castle's Goliath.

He dug one tennis shoe into the grass and leaned forward to grasp two handfuls of the long straw to find purchase. He fell forward and his knees hit the hard ground but he was hardly a foot away from the pavement, with over a hundred feet yet to cover.

Gregson fisted his hands and began to climb. First thing he was going to do was to get his hands on a mobile phone, so that he could contact Ryan and strike a bargain.

* * *

It had taken a short, hard exchange of words with the consultant, but Ryan lay atop his hospital bed with his faculties returned to him, free of the drugging effect of strong painkillers. It wasn't the first time he had suffered a knife injury. He knew the score and he could handle the pain.

And, God, it was painful.

It wasn't all about pride, he admitted. He hated feeling out of control, not being in charge of his own senses. Between the facile drone of prime time television and the painkillers, he hadn't been able to think clearly.

Now, the television was firmly off. They meant well, he was sure, but he didn't need the banal background noise of a reality TV show to keep him company. The characters inside his head were enough for any man and, failing that, there was always Lowerson to talk to.

"Jack!"

Lowerson turned at his voice and was inside the room in a heartbeat, casting suspicious glances around its walls for signs of intrusion.

"Calm down," Ryan said, conversationally. "Pull up a pew."

Lowerson shut the door behind him and dragged the visitor's chair over to Ryan's bed.

"How're you feeling, Chief?"

"Like I just got stabbed and thrown in a river, but I'll live," came the predictable reply. "Give me an update, detective."

Lowerson shifted in his seat.

"Ah, now, Phillips said you weren't to be bothered with anything—"

Ryan fixed him with a cool, ice-grey stare.

"Who is of higher rank, Jack?"

Lowerson pursed his lips. In terms of authority and respect, there wasn't much to choose between Ryan and Phillips except a couple of letters at the front of their names.

Ryan caught the look and had to smile.

"Alright, that's an unfair question," he relented. "But let's say for argument's sake that I'm a higher ranking chief inspector whereas Phillips is only my sergeant. In those circumstances, you'd be obliged to override his orders, wouldn't you?"

Lowerson met him stare for stare.

"Well, that wouldn't account for the fist which might end up planted in my face if anything happened to you on account of me ignoring the order of a mere sergeant."

Ryan tried to look stern but failed miserably.

"Damn it, man, you're all in this together."

Lowerson reached across to dip into the bag of goodies Anna had brought earlier and began to unwrap a chocolate bar.

"Oh, and now you're robbing me of my private stash of life-enhancing chocolate," Ryan said peevishly, before dipping back into the bag himself.

"Seriously, though," he gestured with a *Twix* a moment later. "I'm going mad in here."

Lowerson was a sucker for emotional blackmail, Ryan thought. Sure enough, the younger man folded like a Hallmark birthday card.

"Well, alright," Lowerson said. "Phillips and MacKenzie are up at Bamburgh Castle now. They wanted to poke around a bit, have a word with Professor Freeman—"

"Good thinking," Ryan interjected. "She has to be connected, somehow. Senior position…"

"Well, ah, she's dead."

Ryan chewed the last of his chocolate very slowly.

"Christ Jesus," he murmured. "Who knows?"

"Only Pinter and Faulkner."

"And if anyone in their teams is affiliated with the Circle, that means a bunch of dangerous psychopaths might also know that they've lost another one of their number."

"Freeman might not have been with the Circle," Lowerson objected.

"And the Pope might not be Catholic," Ryan said darkly. "She had to be. It has to be the reason she's dead. How'd she die?"

"Phillips says it looks like some kind of poisoning. Crime scene doesn't show any signs of an aggressor."

"That's interesting," Ryan ran his tongue over dry lips. "Anna's theory is right, by the way: whoever is leading this onslaught is picking sites of historical significance. We wondered what Bamburgh would hold and we're too late, again."

Ryan drummed his fingers against his thigh, obviously frustrated.

"Gregson is still under twenty-four hour surveillance at the RVI?"

"Yes, sir. The last I heard was that he's awake and lucid. We can ask questions whenever we're ready."

Ryan thought of the resources and of how many hours Lowerson had been sitting outside in the corridor, guarding him like a lap dog. It was time he returned to ordinary duty.

"Jack, I want you to head over there and start asking him some pertinent questions. I want to know who cracked his skull and I want to know who killed his wife. It's her blood all over their kitchen and I want some answers. If the Circle are involved, they could be coming back at any moment to finish the job and we can't guard him forever. He needs to start talking."

Lowerson was torn between competing desires.

"I can't leave you here, unattended."

"For pity's sake, Jack, I'm in the middle of a crowded hospital. This is important," he crooned. "I couldn't trust this to just anybody."

Lowerson flushed with pride, even though he wasn't fool enough to miss the obvious flattery.

"I won't be more than an hour. I'm going to call in a replacement to stand in for me, while I'm gone."

"Forget that," Ryan snapped. "Get going. The sooner you leave the sooner you can return."

Lowerson had been gone less than ten minutes when Ryan received the message.

I'm at Bamburgh. Meet me at St. Oswald's Gate if you want the answers. Come alone. G

There was a saying somewhere about being wary of Greeks bearing gifts and this was not the first time a text message had led Ryan along a sinister path. But it told him one crucial fact that could not be ignored: whether or not Gregson had sent the message himself, he was no longer under police guard at the Royal Victoria Infirmary. He may not even be alive.

Ryan spent a quiet moment considering the best course of action, then bowed to the inevitable. He raised his phone to his ear, intending to call Lowerson back from his journey across town, but the man himself burst back into the room.

"I got into my car," he explained urgently, slightly out of breath. "And I got a call from PC Yates. She went off shift at four o'clock, to get some rest, then returned at eight-thirty when the shift changed again. She opened the door and—"

"Gregson had vanished?"

Lowerson looked deflated.

"How do you always *know* these things?" he asked, dumbfounded.

"I'm psychic," Ryan replied, then eased his legs out of the hospital bed. Lowerson surged forward, as if to catch him.

"Sir? What are you doing?"

"I've been summoned, Jack, and you're helping me bust out of here."

"I can't—"

"Lowerson, shut up and get over here. Lend me your shoulder, there's a good lad."

* * *

You wait half an hour for a bus and then three arrive at once.

For days, Ryan's small task force had been waiting for key information and then, with typically bad timing, the results of various tests and diagnostics all filtered through when nobody was manning the incident room to deal with them. First, MacKenzie took a call from the pathologist to confirm that Daniel Mathieson had died from acute respiratory failure following two collapsed lungs and a cardiac arrest. Swabs had been taken from Mathieson's body and the pathologist was hopeful that there would be DNA evidence identifying the inmates who had been responsible. For now, that was all he could tell them.

While Pinter's bookish voice imparted the news, MacKenzie's eyes strayed to a brown package on Jane Freeman's desk, close to where her body had recently lain. Though Faulkner and his CSI staff were appropriately attired, she shouted out a warning that they should approach it with extreme care. Freeman appeared to have been poisoned and, until they found the source, she didn't want to see anybody else falling foul of it.

Phillips took a similar call from his sources at the hospitals—both of them. One to say that DCS Gregson had vanished from his bed during a change of police guard and another to tell him that DCI Ryan had discharged himself against the better judgment of the medical staff and with the assistance of a young man bearing a striking resemblance to their very own DC Lowerson.

He would wring the lad's scrawny neck, Phillips swore it.

Phillips hesitated but ultimately decided to call Anna on the off-chance that Ryan had returned to the bosom of his home and family, only to be told in worried tones that she knew nothing about him leaving hospital. If he was any judge, Anna would be hounding the life out of their illustrious chief inspector if he didn't turn himself into her tender care. It was a small comfort to know that.

Damn stupid thing to do, Phillips thought angrily. What had possessed him to leave the hospital, in his condition? What had possessed either of them, for that matter?

The world was going mad.

His phone rang again and he snatched it up, ready to snarl obscenities in the event that Ryan was on the other end of the line. Instead, it was a member of the tech team back at CID. They were in the process of going through Arthur Gregson's financial statements received from his bank and they had found some unusual activity. Several large deposits recently made into his current account, of all places.

Phillips shook his head. The world had definitely gone mad if a detective chief superintendent couldn't take a better stab at covering up the proceeds of his crimes. At least try to make it difficult for them, Phillips thought.

"Who made the deposits?" he asked.

This was a slightly trickier question, since the numbered account used to transfer the funds into Gregson's account was based overseas. They would need some time to trace the account holder who made the payments but, on the face of it, the funds didn't appear to have any legitimate source and that was a further black mark against Gregson.

Phillips ended the call and frowned. What use would the money be to Gregson if he couldn't access it? His house had already been sealed off and a patrol car had checked for signs that he had returned there but 17 Haslemere Gardens was in darkness, not a hair out of place. All important documents pertaining to Gregson and his wife, including their passports, had been confiscated in accordance with the search and discovery warrant. Therefore, if Gregson had left the hospital, he would have very little to sustain him in the outside world.

MacKenzie came out of Freeman's office and stripped the plastic shoe coverings from her feet, dropped them into a plastic evidence bin, then walked down the stone stairwell to join Phillips. The lamps had been lit around the mezzanine floor beneath and spread a warm yellow glow around the room, which offset the howling wind rocking the windows on the eastern side as it rolled in from the sea, contrasting sharply with the relative calm a short while earlier.

Phillips let out a sigh.

"Gregson's given Yates the slip, while she was on her break. Some idiot constable left his post to nip along to the gents and Gregson disappeared."

"How long has he been gone?"

"We reckon at least three hours."

"And this other constable—who?—didn't notice before Yates returned? Bring him in for questioning."

"Already done," Phillips answered. He'd thought the same thing himself. "The hospital is going through their CCTV cameras now, to see which direction Gregson headed and if he had help. One of the doctors who was supposed to be doing the rounds on Gregson's ward is also missing, apparently—that's why the hospital didn't notice that Gregson was gone."

"He must have had help. There's no way he could manage on a few quid and the clothes on his back."

Phillips rolled his aching shoulders.

"Desperate men," was all he said. "They've already checked his house and there's been no sign of him. Without some clue about where he's headed, your guess is as good as mine."

"We'll have to tell Ryan."

"Fat chance of that, since he's discharged himself from hospital and isn't answering his phone," Phillips growled.

MacKenzie didn't bother to ask any more questions. It was clear from the look on Phillips' face that he was already none too pleased about it.

"Freeman's death is looking like poison," she commented, "and there was a package on her desk. They'll run tests, but I've just spoken to the courier. The sender on their records is listed as Arthur Gregson, though the letter inside apparently came from some history boffin down south. He doesn't know anything about it," she added, thinking of the short telephone call she'd had with Professor Chambers. "He's never heard of Freeman and definitely didn't send her a package. If Gregson is responsible for this, we've got hard evidence against him now."

"He's a bloody nutcase," Phillips reeled. "I've told the boys back at CID to put out an all-ports warning. They'll arrest him on sight."

He turned to look at MacKenzie, who was starting to show signs of strain. He took her elegant hand in his broad, knobbly fingers and smiled at the difference between them.

"Ryan and Anna are tying the knot," he said quietly, looking intently at her.

"Ah, that's grand," she said, her face clearing into a smile. "There's nothing like young love to cheer up an otherwise crappy day."

Phillips gave her fingers a squeeze and looked down at their joined hands. It was enough, for now.

"Come on, let's go and find some killers."

"You're such a romantic, Frank."

CHAPTER 27

Gregson watched the flashing blue lights heading back towards Newcastle and shivered. His body was exhausted, his energy supply depleted after a difficult climb which had almost finished him off. Several times, he had fallen forward, his face buried in the damp grass, somewhere between consciousness and unconsciousness. He thought that was the end, there on the grassy hill leading up to St. Oswald's Gate. It had felt oddly appropriate that he should meet his Master at a place which had played such an important part in his life.

But the Master was good. Gregson had risen up again and found the strength to carry on, scratching and tearing at the grass as he clawed his way to the top. He supposed that was appropriate, too, considering that was what he had done for most of his life. Always clawing his way up the ladder, reaching for more success, more money, more women. He wondered what the blokes at the tennis club would think of him now, a shrivelled fugitive.

At first, he presumed that the blue lights had come for him, that they had found him already. He sobbed at the thought of all that wasted, painful effort coming to nothing and had let himself into one of the disused passageways at the base of the castle walls, staggering through the tunnels to hide from the sirens. After a while, he heard the faint sound of their retreat and he had surfaced again, letting himself into the clock tower to look out of one of its diamond-shaped windows. There was an ambulance and two police cars remaining, and he thought he recognised the familiar lines of Faulkner's CSI van.

Who had died?

He heard shuffling on the floor above and voices in the stairwell. He shrank back against the stone wall, holding his breath.

Phillips and MacKenzie, he realised. He listened for a moment, enough to know that they were looking for him now and that Freeman was dead. He frowned and shook his head to clear it. He thought they had said something about him sending a poisoned package.

Freeman was dead? He couldn't believe it. Who would kill her? His head was spinning. Who else might be lurking in the tunnels? He must move quickly, take what he needed and leave. He would make for the vault, help himself to whatever he could find and get out of the castle *now.*

All bets were off.

The voices became louder and he retreated back to the tunnels, melting into the castle's walls like an apparition.

* * *

The vault was empty.

The hollowed stone with its heavy iron door had served as a purpose-built secure space for Circle business since the late eighties. Gregson had been here a hundred times before, deep in the cellars beneath the castle, to make a deposit and more often to make a withdrawal. But now, gone were the boxes of cash, the trays of false identification documents, the armoury and special manuscripts recording the Circle's evolution.

It was all gone.

Desolation swept over him and tears swam in his eyes. Dreams of escape, of starting a new life and rebuilding his small empire evaporated. He was just an ageing man standing cold and alone, deep under the ground. The thought of just finding a quiet spot and curling up there, of handing himself over to whichever Power would have him, appealed to him unlike ever before.

Bitterness rose in his throat like acid, hard and strong so that it nearly overwhelmed him. He hadn't come this far, he hadn't lied, cheated, stolen and swindled, sanctioned murder and covered up his own wife's murder, to die in an underground tunnel. Gregson was damned if that was how he would go out, while men like Ryan lived on to bask in the sunlight, swanning around the countryside lapping up the adulation while he rotted underneath the earth.

He tugged the iron door shut again and thought that it was time to do a little more borrowing from the people who roamed inside the castle.

* * *

Ryan was pale as a ghost after the drive north, albeit Lowerson had driven like his maiden aunt, taking each turn at what felt like five miles per hour. The act of sitting upright placed pressure on the new stitches at his side and he held the seatbelt away from his torso to avoid the painful crush against his flesh. When the car finally came to a standstill, his forehead was clammy and his jaw was rigid with control. He let himself out of Lowerson's black Fiat and waved him away while he threw up his earlier chocolate bar into a nearby hedge, his stomach muscles contracting to cause even more pain in his abdominal stitches.

Lowerson watched him with a look of extreme worry on his boyish face.

"Sir? What can I do for you?" *He should never have listened to him,* he fretted.

Ryan took some deep, nourishing breaths before turning around again.

"You can stop mothering me, for a start," he snapped, but the statement lacked its usual assertiveness and did little to allay Lowerson's fears.

"At least let me call Phillips," Lowerson begged.

"I was told to come alone."

"Let me drive you up to the castle gates," Lowerson turned, as if to usher him back inside the car. "You can't manage that hill, not in your condition."

The thought was tempting but Ryan considered the risks which may lie ahead. Already, he carried the guilt of having put Jack Lowerson in the path of danger too many times before. He wouldn't—couldn't—do it again.

"Stay here," he said firmly. "Trust me to do my job, I know my limits."

He almost flinched at another twinge from the wound at his side, but managed to control the muscles of his face, enough to convince Lowerson to step away while he limped towards the castle mount.

* * *

Like a slumbering giant, the castle waited for Ryan to ascend Vale Typping through the great arched gates to the inner courtyard. Lights from the clock tower shone a welcoming glow and cars were still parked outside, which told him that MacKenzie and Phillips were still on the premises. There was a small prick of guilt as he turned deliberately away to skirt around the perimeter, away from where people congregated, away from the safety of numbers.

He made for the southern side of the castle grounds, towards the site where archaeologists were excavating. The prospecting sites were abandoned now, and moonlight cast a thin light over the trenches. Even to his practical mind, they transformed into shallow graves and his stomach shuddered as he wove between them, expecting to see men in steel armour rising up with pale faces from the past. Light and shadow played over the castle walls and there was only the crash of the sea and the sound of Ryan's own thundering heart for company as he walked over the ancient ground.

St. Oswald's Gate lay further ahead, a gaping archway in the western perimeter wall of the castle which opened out onto a chasm of air and sky, with a hundred and fifty feet of steep ground between where he stood and the road far beneath. Standing just inside its arch, Ryan narrowed his eyes against the darkness and tried to make out the visitors' car park where Lowerson waited, but could only see a dark abyss which held certain death if he should fall into its vacuum. Still, he drew strength from knowing that the young constable was safely inside a locked car, somewhere in that darkness.

The wind whistled through the cracks in the stone and knocked against him, taking him by surprise. Ryan threw out a hand to steady himself and pulled away from the archway to lean back against the inner wall, flinching as his coat snagged against the aching wound underneath. He sucked a breath between his teeth and prepared to wait.

* * *

Lowerson slammed the car door shut behind him and set off at a run. Halfway up the hilly road leading to the castle's main entrance, he paused to shake off his suit jacket, which he discarded in a heap by the road and sprinted the rest of the way to the top unhindered.

He ducked under the archway gates and entered the main courtyard, stopping to scan the area for signs of Ryan, but he was nowhere in sight. Lowerson stood there panting, partly from the exertion and partly from panic. He *knew* he should have gone with him. He should never have listened to Ryan in the first place; the man was ill and should never have been taken from the hospital.

Only a prize moron would have taken him out, Lowerson thought with self-loathing.

He ran a fraught hand through his hair and wondered which way to turn. The castle compound was enormous—one of the largest in the country—and there were several different entrances. His eye was drawn to one of the smaller towers where lights blazed in the windows and, with a sob of heartfelt relief, he recognised MacKenzie's red fiesta parked beside two other police vehicles.

* * *

Ryan listened intently to the wind. It carried the scent of the sea and was loud enough to obliterate most other sounds but, if he really concentrated, he could make out the whisper of birds nesting in the cliffs beneath the seaward wall. He closed his eyes and let it brush against his face while he concentrated on emptying his mind and blocking out the pain radiating from the wound at his side.

Then, he heard another sound and his eyes snapped open again.

Stone scraped against stone and there was a rustle somewhere up ahead, from the dug-out trenches dotted between the crumbled stone walls. Ryan focussed on the direction of the sound and then, as he had feared, a man seemed to rise from the earth. The figure unfolded its body to stand a few feet away, nothing more than an inky shadow without a face.

The world seemed to pause as they did; each recognising the presence of another, instinct guiding their senses while their eyesight hurried to catch up. Ryan stared into the gloom and watched the figure walk towards him, slowly negotiating the potholes and the uncovered soil. He pushed away from the wall to stand with his feet slightly apart, arms by his sides, ready to defend or attack if necessary.

Gregson could feel his body wilting, ready to give up on him, but his mind refused to allow it. This would not be his end; he would go on to live again, even better than before. The Master would make sure of it, he had to believe that. Hysteria had taken a firm root as all remaining logic flew out of his muddled mind. When Ryan gave him a searching look, he saw a man who had aged ten years in a few days, with cuts and bruises on his face, wearing dirty, mud-sodden clothes. Mania glinted behind his eyes.

"I see you got my message."

There was a tense silence.

"It was you," Ryan ground out. "I wanted to believe I was wrong, but I *knew* that it was you."

To his shame, Gregson felt a frisson of fear at the harsh tone. He wanted to turn away from the look in Ryan's eyes; contempt, mingled with disgust.

"You will show respect to a commanding officer!" he burst out.

Ryan noted that one of Gregson's hands remained in the pocket of his filthy jogging bottoms and braced himself while the wind continued to roll around them and through the gap between them.

"Where's your wife?" He had to shout it, to be heard.

Gregson swiped away the spittle at his mouth with the back of his hand.

"Gone. Cathy's gone," he sliced his hand through the air, as if to draw a line under it, but Ryan ignored the flimsy gesture.

"You killed her. How did you do it, Arthur? Who helped you cover it up?"

"I haven't killed *anyone!* I never did!" Gregson shouted over the wind and Ryan frowned slightly.

"You're full of shit," he returned, taking a step forward.

Gregson wanted to step back, but he held himself firm, reminding himself that he needed Ryan to organise his ticket out of here.

"Why did you kill her?"

"I never touched her!" Gregson shouted again, but he remembered the casual slaps over the years and the change in Cathy's eyes as her love had curdled to hate. He had caused that.

He pushed the thought away.

"I'm taking you back in," Ryan was saying. "Your wounds will be treated, that's the law. But then, you're going to talk. I want names, I want dates, I want to know it all. It's over, Gregson."

Gregson shuffled away and Ryan followed him, impatient and hurting.

"Are you listening to me? I didn't kill anyone!"

He thought of the others who had died, of the men who hadn't been particularly unwilling to sink a dagger into another person and told himself he wasn't responsible. He had known, but he wasn't responsible.

"You're going to help me out of the country," he carried on. "Why do you think I brought you here? I need your help, damn it! I need money and a passport—"

"Are you mad?" Ryan laughed mirthlessly. "Why in the name of God would I help you? You're an arrogant bastard. What gave you any idea that you'd be allowed to walk off into the sunset?"

Ryan moved closer still, baring his teeth, anger in full flow.

"Men and women have *died.* Some of them barely more than girls, because of you. Because of what you have allowed to happen—"

"They'll kill me!" Gregson grasped Ryan's shirt front as they came face to face, so close that Ryan could count the lines on the other man's face. In reflex, he took a fistful of Gregson's cotton pyjama top to even things out.

"Who? Tell me *who,* damn it!"

"I don't know! I don't fucking *know* anymore!" Gregson struggled free of Ryan's grasp and he let his hand fall away from the man's collar. "You don't have the first idea about what you're dealing with. Freeman's dead. Just like Bowers, except I thought she killed Bowers," Gregson said wretchedly. "If it wasn't her, then I've got as much of an idea as you have."

* * *

Lowerson found Phillips and MacKenzie on the first floor of the clock tower, conferring with Faulkner. All three of them turned at Lowerson's shout for help as he ran up the stairs towards them.

Phillips' brows lowered and he was across the room in two strides to grasp Lowerson by the scruff of the neck.

"You're supposed to be with Ryan," he growled, shoving his weather-beaten face into Lowerson's personal space.

Jack nodded and—to all of their surprise—shoved Phillips away with a strength none of them knew that he had.

"I can't find him," he said urgently. "He got a message at the hospital, apparently from Gregson offering him answers if he met him at St. Oswald's Gate on his own."

"And you *let* him?" Phillips shouted.

"He's my commanding officer!" Lowerson shouted back but he was barely holding off tears. The knowledge that he could humiliate himself at any moment made things even worse. "I made a mistake," he said miserably.

MacKenzie put a warning hand on Phillips' shoulder and stepped forward to speak to Lowerson in clear, calm tones.

"He was meeting Gregson at St. Oswald's Gate?"

"Y-yes," Lowerson nodded. "I would have gone there straight away, but I—I don't know where it is," he confessed.

"Follow me," she shouldered him out of the way and ran down the stone stairs.

* * *

Gregson cast a nervous glance around, sniffing the air.

"You said you'd give me the answers," Ryan said flatly. "Has that changed?"

"I want to deal—"

"And I want a unicorn for my birthday," Ryan snarled. "Never going to happen."

Gregson stared at him, trying to judge if there was room for manoeuvre, if there was any way Ryan could be convinced to let him go.

Then he let out a short laugh.

"Bowers was right about one thing," Gregson mused, while he considered his next move. "You could never have been one of us."

Ryan nearly hit him. His fists bunched and it was an effort to loosen them again.

"Yeah, he was right about that. I wouldn't meet the entry criteria," he bit out. Not having a severe personality disorder or a thirst to kill innocent people tended to rule him out.

"You could have risen high," Gregson continued, in the same sleepy voice. "The Circle would have chosen you."

"Aww, now I'm really upset," came the sarcastic response. "Save the bullshit, this has gone on long enough and I'm tired of hearing your whining voice. We both know where we stand. I've got enough evidence to take you in."

Ryan stepped forward and grasped Gregson's upper arm in a firm grip.

"Arthur Gregson, I am arresting you on suspicion of murder—"

With sudden strength, Gregson pulled his arm free and stumbled backwards, fumbling inside his trouser pocket until he found the little dagger, one of the few things he had been able to salvage from the underground tunnels.

Ryan caught sight of the knife and thought of that very morning, which seemed so long ago. He felt sweat trickle between his shoulder blades and the muscles of his abdomen contracted, reliving the pain. For a moment, he was submerged again, water suffocating him as he tried to fight his way back to the surface. He fisted his hands, this time to fight off the anxiety and the panic attack which threatened to overtake him. In his peripheral vision, he saw the blurred lights of the clock tower to the north and knew that anybody who happened to look out of one of the little diamond windows would see nothing but darkness.

Gregson wielded the knife with one hand and swayed, the effects of exhaustion and severe head trauma taking their own toll. They faced one another, two broken men, each holding their own ground.

"What are you going to do with that?" Ryan jerked his chin towards the blade and his voice was steady. "You tell me you've never taken a life. Are you planning to start now? If you take that step, there's no going back," he added quietly.

Gregson jabbed the knife in the air between them, as Ryan made to step towards him again.

"Get back!"

Ryan tried to maintain eye contact, techniques skipping through his mind. *Eye contact, use the suspect's first name, build rapport,* he chanted silently. He just never imagined he would have to employ such methods on his own superintendent.

He watched the man edge backwards, darting swift glances towards the main exit. Ryan smiled and shook his head.

"You'll never make it past the clock tower, Arthur," he said.

"Shut up! Just shut up! I'm trying to think."

"Think fast, because sooner or later they'll figure out where we are," Ryan continued, thinking of Lowerson, of Phillips and MacKenzie so tantalisingly close. "Why did you do it, Arthur? You had a good life."

Gregson turned and the confused glaze in his eyes lifted, replaced with pure venom.

"What would *you* know about it? Tell me what the hell you would know about the kind of life I had before the Circle found me!" he demanded, gesturing wildly with the knife he still held. "Little Lord *fucking* Fauntleroy is what you are! Cushy parents, smug background, pretty boy face," he sneered. "You haven't got a clue how the other half live, surviving day-to-day, week-to-week, living off the dole. You wouldn't know how it feels to be the scummy one at school, who nobody wants to know."

Gregson pointed the knife at Ryan, while he let loose the anger of a lifetime, one he rarely voiced.

"Must be hard for you, always playing the bloody hero! Somebody's in trouble, call out DCI Ryan, he'll take care of business. You've never known what it feels like to be an average bloke, have you, *Maxwell?*"

Ryan said nothing but continued to watch the knife with the silver eyes of a predator preparing to strike.

"Let me tell you, it feels shit! Scrounging for money, trying to get ahead when every door slams in your face—you know why?—because you're not 'one of them.' People can see it on you, it's like they can smell it. Oh, that's Arthur Gregson, his da is serving time and his ma puts it about for money," Gregson spat, then his voice changed into something reverent.

"Then, one day, you're offered a once-in-a-lifetime chance, an opportunity to shine. Important people want to know you. Doors start opening for you and women start giving you a second glance. Well, I *took* the chance," he butted his chest with the heel of the knife to emphasize the point. "And, I'd do the same again. You can sit there in your ivory tower and judge me from here to kingdom come, because I'd do the same again."

Gregson seemed to run out of steam and in that moment Ryan lunged forward. In one swift upward motion, he knocked the knife to the ground. The action stretched his body and cost him a couple of stitches, which burned as they opened, but he set his teeth against the stabbing pain. His objective was to bring Gregson to the floor and he put his back into it, struggling to pin the man's arms.

It took a couple of seconds for him to react but, when he did, Gregson fought like a tiger, spitting and snarling as he reared up against the unexpected ambush. Whatever vestiges of DCS Arthur Gregson that may have remained were gone now. Here was no gentleman fighter, Ryan realised, but a street kid who had grown into a man. Underneath the grey hair, Gregson was the same snivelling boy who resented his lot in life and no amount of power, wealth or women had changed that.

At his heart, Ryan was not a violent man. But he would not back away from a fight if the situation demanded it, and it was demanding it now. He drew back his arm, intending to shove a fist in Gregson's face, but doubled over as he took a vicious elbow to the side. He could feel his wound bleeding through the bandages beneath his shirt and he raised an arm to block a further blow. When Gregson turned to scan the ground for his knife, Ryan forced himself upward, reeling with nausea.

"Where do you think you're going to run to?" he shouted across to Gregson, hoping that the sound would be heard from the clock tower, though the waves made it difficult for him to hear the man standing a few feet away from him let alone if he were on the other side of the castle grounds.

Gregson stood there for a moment and then tried to skirt past Ryan, making for St. Oswald's Gate and freedom beyond. It would be a dangerous night time descent over the steep ground he had climbed earlier, but it was worth the risk.

Ryan intercepted him, grasping his shoulders to thrust him away from the archway.

"Let me pass!"

Ryan stood in front of the archway to block it, trying not to stagger against the wind.

"I'm taking you in," he repeated.

Gregson charged at him with a shout of frustration, his eyes feral and dangerous now that reason had left him.

Ryan anticipated the charge but his body was sluggish to react. He dug his heels into the grass and wrapped his arms around Gregson's middle to prevent his escape.

Gregson punched him squarely in his wound, where the skin was tender and bleeding.

Ryan blacked out for a second, his mind protecting him from the unspeakable pain and he collapsed to his knees, then to the floor. Gregson panted above him, fingers still bunched and ready to administer another sharp jab if Ryan moved. He was about to give him a good kick, just for his own pleasure, when he heard the sound of running footsteps approaching.

CHAPTER 28

Ryan came around almost immediately and knew that his body was starting to go into shock. He was shivering and he could feel himself floating, as if the world were a surreal, distant place. He shook himself and dragged himself upwards, crying out as his skin wept. He pressed a hand to his side and could feel the damp material of his shirt, indicating that he was bleeding badly. He could hear footsteps approaching from the north and knew that his team were not far behind. Across the rough ground, he heard another sound, something akin to a hunted animal tripping over the uneven tufts of earth as it scrambled to get away.

Gregson.

He didn't stop to wait for the others. Ryan staggered forward to stall the man's escape, though he hardly knew how Gregson hoped to manage it. The only thing awaiting him on the other side of the eastern perimeter wall was a sheer drop towards the unforgiving North Sea.

Perhaps that was his goal, he thought fiercely, *but not on his watch.*

Ryan reached across to tear at the seam of his shirtsleeve and tugged at it until he heard it rip apart. He folded the material and held it against his side to stem the blood flow as he loped across the ground in the direction Gregson had turned.

* * *

A cursory glance around the area surrounding St. Oswald's Gate told the three other members of Ryan's team that the man himself was not there. MacKenzie stuck her head through the archway and pulled back again quickly, breathing deeply against the sudden vertigo. Phillips and Lowerson fanned the ground, straining to hear any sound which might give them an indication of Ryan's whereabouts.

"Check the area along the western wall," Phillips began, but Lowerson raised a hand to point in the opposite direction.

They all turned and, there, silhouetted against the moonlit sky, were two figures. They seemed to dance like puppets along the high stone wall which separated them from the safety of solid ground and hundreds of metres of oblivion.

"Christ almighty," Phillips breathed, his heart skipping in panic.

Lowerson moved as if to sprint in their direction but MacKenzie said sharply,

"Don't startle them! They're walking a tightrope as it is."

Phillips' brain reverted back to full power and he pulled out his mobile phone.

"Jack, approach from the southern end, at a safe distance. Try to remain undetected, we don't want Gregson doing anything stupid. Denise, do the same from the north. I won't be far behind."

Both nodded and jogged away, leaving a wide arc so that the two men who skirted the upper wall would be less likely to notice their arrival. Phillips punched in a number and waited while it rang.

"H.M. Coastguard Lindisfarne, receiving. What is your emergency?"

"Walker? This is DS Phillips. We've got a situation on the outer seaward wall of Bamburgh Castle and we could be looking at some kind of fatality. We need assistance from the sea, just in case."

In the Coastguard Station on Holy Island, Alex Walker spat out his chewing gum and kicked his legs off the table top to listen more intently.

"What situation?"

"Ryan and Gregson. Either or both of them could fall."

"That crazy bastard," Walker breathed, then swung into action. "I'll get a boat across, although the water's choppy and we won't be able to get up close because of the rocks."

"Just get over here," Phillips said, then ended the call before heading across to face the two men who edged along the outer wall.

* * *

"You've always been a coward," Ryan said, scathingly.

Gregson looked back over his shoulder to where Ryan stalked him along the stone wall. The wind was strong without anything to shelter him from the gusts, which pounded his weakened body as relentlessly as the sea pounded against the rocks beneath. He wanted to drop to his knees and crawl until he reached the narrow stairwell he was looking for, but he wouldn't give Ryan the satisfaction.

"Are you hoping to climb down and hail a passing boat to China?" Ryan baited him as he tried to close the distance, bending his knees slightly to regain his balance when the wind threatened to carry him away.

"I'm leaving!" Gregson's frantic cry carried on the wind as he ploughed onward, hunting for the stone steps which led down into a natural harbour that hadn't been used for years. "God help me, Ryan, if you come any closer I'll hurl you over the side of this wall."

"Come on, big man," Ryan jeered, thinking of all the innocent victims Gregson had wilfully ignored, of all the victims they had yet to find. "Come and show me what you're made of."

Gregson's teeth ground together and his eyes were wild when he turned back. Ryan was within a few feet of him now and he concentrated on that, and not on the sickening drop to his left. In other circumstances, the view out across the sea would have been awe-inspiring.

Gregson huffed out a satisfied breath as he found the hidden stairwell, moulded into the outer rock and worn almost smooth by thousands of footsteps made centuries ago and the fall of rain in the years since. He dropped to his knees and swung his legs around, feeling for the first toe-hold.

He found it and began to descend the slippery steps, keeping his back to the wall he had just left, the prospect of escape outweighing the bowel-loosening fear of falling.

Then, a strong hand tugged at his collar and yanked him backwards.

* * *

Lowerson was the first to climb atop the seaward wall from the southern end and, fifty metres further along, he spotted Ryan. His blood curdled as he saw the man's precarious position, leaning forward over the wall at a forty-five degree angle with one arm bent downward as he clutched Gregson's neck.

Lowerson pushed forward and focused on gripping the thick stone wall as he rushed to help his friend.

"Ryan!"

The man didn't turn but he heard the sound carry on the air and thanked whichever god was listening.

At the other end of the wall, MacKenzie struggled to move. Vertigo blurred her vision and she froze like a statue, trying to regain control. Her fingers shook against the stone and her stomach heaved. She hadn't known it before, she thought weakly. She hadn't known that this would be a problem.

The fear worked its way through her body and she flattened herself against the top of the stone wall, unable to move either forward or backward.

Phillips found her there and climbed quickly to place reassuring hands over her shoulders.

"Frank," she moaned.

"Alright, pet, don't panic. Frank's here," he said cheerfully, with a taut glance at the drop on the other side. "What we're going to do is moonwalk off this wall."

MacKenzie sobbed out a laugh.

"I'll sing along, if you like," he continued, making sure he had a firm hold of her. "Now, you need to loosen your grip on the wall—"

"I can't," she whispered.

He edged a bit closer until he was almost on top of her, then put his hands over hers.

"I'm not going to let you fall, love. Trust me."

MacKenzie loosened her knuckle-white grip, little-by-little.

"I'm sorry, Frank. I'm so sorry," she murmured, thinking of how she had failed their team.

"Don't worry about anything except listening to my voice," he crooned, then started to hum an old Michael Jackson song as they edged closer to the inside. "Now, I want you to swing your right leg down over the wall until you can get a toe in one of the cracks. OK?"

MacKenzie's teeth were chattering so hard she had to snap them together, but slowly, she followed his advice.

"That's the girl. Now, swing your other foot around, that's right."

MacKenzie gripped the top while her feet found purchase in the crevices of the inside wall and with a grateful smile of thanks, she began to climb down again towards safety.

Phillips waited until her feet thudded back against terra firma, then looked ahead to where Ryan's body stretched at a death-defying angle as he maintained a stranglehold on Gregson's collar.

***

Gregson struggled to release himself from Ryan's grasp without losing his balance against the slippery rock face. He scratched at the man's hand and wrist until he drew blood but Ryan had a grip like iron.

"I'll jump!" Gregson threatened and realised that he meant it. *Why not?* He thought. Where was he running to? He had no friends to help him anymore. No family to shelter him. Only the rest of his life in prison or an eternity with his Master.

"You're not getting off that easy, you pathetic bastard," Ryan managed, as sweat poured down his face and the tendons in his arm screamed for him to let go.

The decision was taken from him.

In one decisive movement, Gregson simply went limp against his hand, stopped struggling and without another word fell forward. Without Ryan's grasp on his collar, he would have plunged face-first into the sea.

"Gregson!"

Ryan nearly careered over the edge of the wall and, from his position a few feet away, Lowerson's heart crashed against his chest, driving him onward like a madman to save his friend.

Ryan threw out his other arm to grip the inner edge of the wall to prevent himself falling over the edge, while his other arm still grappled with Gregson's collar. The man's leaden body dangled loosely in his grasp, strangling him at the neck. Spread-eagled against the top of the wall, Ryan felt himself slipping, felt his grip slacken while his body was torn apart; the remaining stitches in his abdomen ripped open and the pain was incredible. His mind was somewhere else, somewhere pain could not touch. In that moment, his only objective was to ensure Gregson lived. The pain could wait.

It felt like an agonising minute, but in a few seconds Lowerson had bridged the gap. He took his own fear in his hands and lowered himself over the seaward wall, gripping the stone with one hand while he threw his other hand out to grab at Gregson's shirt. No words were spoken; time was precious and in a few more seconds Ryan would have to let go or lose his own life.

Lowerson tried once, twice, a third time.

He grabbed a fistful of Gregson's shirt on the fourth try, and pulled him back towards the wall.

The man was losing consciousness but Lowerson pinned him to the wall with his free hand, lining his feet up against the stone steps so that Ryan could ease his grip.

"Is he secure?" Ryan ground out.

"As much as possible," Lowerson answered, taking in the full danger of his position now that the immediate urgency had passed. Across the water, he saw the bright lights of the Coastguard's lifeboat motoring over the waves, circling to avoid the jagged rocks which lay hidden beneath. A white spotlight shone from the front of the boat, illuminating the water in front of it. Much good it would do them, if they plummeted into the sea.

"Phillips is nearly here," Ryan whispered, almost ready to pass out. "I can hear him. He's nearly here, Jack."

The world went dark.

Lowerson heard Ryan go silent and a moment later felt Gregson stir against his restraining hand. He adjusted his grip and held him upright against the wall with one wiry arm while he waited for Gregson's eyes to open again.

"Open your eyes, you murdering bastard," he muttered.

Gregson coughed and choked, then desperately shoved against the wall in a futile effort to escape from Lowerson's grip and throw himself over the edge. In the seconds before he lost consciousness again, all Gregson saw was Jack Lowerson's clenched fist, right before it connected with his face.

* * *

Anna found herself in the waiting room at the RVI living out what felt like *Groundhog Day* as Ryan's stitches were re-sewn and his body was treated for shock. His parents were in the recovery room with him now but she hesitated before joining them. She had thought that she understood Ryan's life and the kind of danger he would face, dealing with unscrupulous men and women who wouldn't blink at deploying extreme violence to achieve their goals. She had experienced a taste of that kind of psychopathy before and was grateful that she had walked away alive.

But Ryan walked *towards* these people. He actively sought to uncover them, placing himself in danger *voluntarily*. She didn't know if she could ever understand that impetus and she worried for their future together.

Phillips stepped into the room and moved to take a seat beside her. Silently, he offered her a cup of coffee, which she accepted with murmured thanks but didn't drink.

"It's who he is," Phillips didn't bother with the small talk. Not when something important was at stake. "You knew that when you met him."

"He didn't even call me, to warn me. He never told me he was putting himself in so much danger, discharging himself from the hospital…"

"He probably didn't want to worry you."

"I would rather worry about something real, something concrete, than spend hours imagining the hundreds of awful ways he might have died."

Phillips looked down at the cup in his hands and could understand her pain.

"If MacKenzie wasn't one of us, she'd probably feel the same," he said quietly. "Hell, if the tables were turned and I was the civilian, I would worry myself sick."

Phillips smiled across at her.

"It's a double-edged sword. The risk-taking, the focus, it's what makes him brilliant. It's also what makes him a gigantic arsehole, most days."

Anna was silent for a couple of beats, then she visibly relaxed.

"You're not wrong."

"I rarely am," Phillips agreed, with a wink, then slurped the rest of his coffee and stood up to offer her a hand. "Come on, lass. He needs us."

Anna held out her hand.

CHAPTER 29

Two weeks later

There was an expectant hush along the corridors of Northumbria CID, the kind of sensation one would expect from a crowd awaiting the arrival of a matinee idol from the 1920's. Outside, the weather was glorious, a blistering August day which the people of Northumberland enjoyed to its fullest before Autumn set in and they donned thicker coats and wellington boots to kick at the falling leaves.

Ryan and Phillips' footsteps echoed along the tiled corridor which led to the interview suite. A small crowd was gathered outside Interview Room A and in the viewing area, Chief Constable Sandra Morrison, Detective Inspector Denise MacKenzie, Detective Constable Lowerson and inspectors from neighbouring districts gathered to watch. There would be nobody to say that things had not been conducted appropriately; Ryan had been clear on that. He wanted the procedure airtight, with no room for their fish to wriggle off the hook.

With Phillips directly behind him, Ryan stepped into the interview room and started the tape recorder before facing Arthur Gregson for the first time in two weeks. He had recovered, Ryan noted, enough to don a smart suit and instruct a fancy lawyer.

Not that it would help him.

"DCI Ryan and DS Phillips, entering Interview Room A. Also present are Arthur Gregson and his counsel, Amelia Duggan, of Price and Company, alongside constables Yates and Wickham."

He went on to state the standard caution, was assured that it was understood and took a seat opposite Gregson, who didn't so much as flinch.

Ballsy bastard, Ryan thought.

"Well," he said in friendly tones. "You're looking a lot better than the last time I saw you, Arthur, it has to be said."

Ryan wouldn't refer to him by his professional title. He deserved no such distinction.

Gregson did not respond, as his counsel had instructed.

"We've been looking forward to catching up with you," Ryan continued, leaning back in his seat and crossing his arms. "Haven't we, Phillips?"

"Oh, indubitably," Phillips replied, with a broad smile.

"Now, just so we understand one another, you're sitting here because you've been arrested on suspicion of the murder of Professor Jane Freeman, and on suspicion of aiding and abetting the murder of Doctor Mark Bowers and of your wife, Catherine Gregson. You are also suspected of aiding and abetting the murders of eleven women murdered by the late Patrick Donovan, of Lucy Mathieson who was killed by her father the late Daniel Mathieson, and of Robert Fowler and Megan Taylor who were killed by the late Steven Walker." Ryan sucked in a deep breath. "That's just for starters. As you can see, there's quite a list."

Ryan glanced down at it and shook his head theatrically.

"Tut *tut,* Arthur," he scolded. "I see there's also a charge of fraud and conspiracy to defraud, and of perverting the course of justice."

"If you are not planning to ask my client any questions—" the lawyer interjected, in snooty tones, "we'll be making a complaint about police intimidation."

Phillips waved that away with one broad hand.

"You'd know a thing or two about intimidating people, wouldn't you, Arthur?" Ryan's eyes turned flat as he fixed them on the older man's face. "Let's start with that text you sent me on Sunday 4th August."

Gregson's lips firmed, but he maintained his silence while Ryan read out the details of the text message.

"We have evidence to show that the message was sent to my personal number from a pre-paid mobile phone triangulated to within five hundred feet of your home. Can you explain that?"

"No comment."

"You see, the thing is, you're the only common link within that radius, Arthur. You're the only one who knows me personally and, believe me, we've interviewed all the other residents."

Ryan slapped a hand on a brown file which was filled with statements.

"What do you say to that?"

"No comment."

Ryan shrugged.

"Alright, Arthur, let's move on to the next piece of telephonic evidence. We have evidence to show that you telephoned the late Professor Jane Freeman from your mobile phone at one-seventeen on Tuesday 4th August, triangulated to your home address. That's the same day that your wife died. Do you remember that?"

"No comment."

Ryan cocked his head towards Phillips.

"I'm wondering, Phillips, why an innocent man who had just found his dead wife, would choose to call a woman he claims he hardly knew, instead of the police."

"I'm certainly drawing adverse inferences from his silence," Phillips replied, with another broad grin.

Ryan clasped his hands together and tapped his thumbs while he regarded Gregson with endless patience.

"We're tracing the money," he mused. "It's interesting, because during the process of unravelling your ill-gotten gains, a name popped up that we've heard before, didn't it, Frank?"

"It certainly did," Phillips said, leaning forward to pick up the rhythm. "A certain James Moffa, more commonly known as Jimmy 'the Manc.' D'you know him?"

"My client became aware of Mr Moffa during the course of his professional career, which has spanned over thirty years of dedicated service—"

"Blah blah blahdy blah," Ryan overrode the rehearsed speech. "You called him, didn't you?"

Gregson's eyes flickered and sweat began to pearl on his nose and forehead.

"You see, there's another call listed here as outgoing on your mobile, not long after your chat with Jane Freeman," Ryan continued, scanning the print out in front of him. "To an unregistered number."

"Why didn't you call the police, Arthur?" Phillips asked again. "That's two separate calls, neither of which were to the Control Room. If you were under threat, or if you'd found Cathy dead, why didn't you call the police?"

"My client wishes to make a statement," the lawyer said smoothly, drawing out a pre-prepared speech.

"Come on, then, I'd like a good laugh," Phillips said, giving her the 'come forward' gesture with his hand.

Gregson took the piece of paper and began to read the story he had cobbled together during his time back inside the Royal Victoria Infirmary.

"After receiving three text messages from my wife, Catherine Gregson, on the aforementioned date, I proceeded to drive home with all speed, understanding her to have been locked out of the family home. Upon my arrival, I was set upon by two aggressors and whilst fleeing the house via the patio doors, I was attacked by one of them from behind. I cannot account for any telephone calls made from my personal telephone during the time I was unconscious, but I presume they were made by either or both of my attackers. It is also my understanding that evidence has come to light suggesting that my beloved wife, Cathy, may have died at their hands without my knowledge. I can offer no insight except to mourn her loss and hope that the true culprits are brought to justice."

There was a short pause, then Ryan began to clap slowly.

"That was very moving, wasn't it, Phillips?"

"Oh, aye, fair brought a tear to my eye."

"Now, cutting through all that crap, what we neglected to tell you was that we had a very cosy chat with a few of your old comrades inside the Circle. And guess what?"

Ryan wriggled his eyebrows.

"It was very illuminating," he said icily, all of the cajolery gone. "They rolled on you, Arthur. They sang like fucking canaries, a sweet tune about all the things you've been up to over the years. All about how Freeman threw you to the wolves, as soon as she became the new leader."

Gregson's face drained of colour and Ryan's lips twisted.

"You called Freeman, who refused to help you, didn't she?" he continued. "So you called your old mate, Jimmy, to come and give you a hand."

Gregson's eyes watered, but he said nothing.

"Is that why you killed Freeman? We know that you sent her that package, Arthur, and we know it was poisoned. Why did you do it? Because she cut you out? It isn't nice to be out in the cold, is it, Arthur?"

"This evidence is purely circumstantial", the lawyer interjected. "No jury is going to accept the hearsay evidence of your alleged criminal informants set against the unblemished career—"

"Well, I guess this might help to convince the jury otherwise," Ryan tapped a finger on his pile of paperwork, which was a fraction of the paper trail generated so far. "Copies of which are already in your possession," he reminded her.

"Setting aside the money stuff," Phillips moved the conversation on, "I'm really interested to know how you managed to get your hands on that botulinum."

"My client has no knowledge—"

"Let your client speak for himself," Phillips said mildly. "Jane Freeman licked the glue along an envelope you had sent to her that had been laced with a fatal cocktail of cyanide and a noxious protein called botulinum."

"I don't know anything about that," Gregson muttered.

"Sorry?" Ryan held his hand to his ear. "You'll have to speak up for the recorder, Arthur, because that sounded like a load of bullshit."

"I didn't fucking do it!" Gregson shouted, then subsided at a horrified glance from his counsel.

"We've got documentary evidence from the couriers to say otherwise," Ryan averred.

"It wasn't me."

"What about Steven Walker? There's a nurse at Rampton Hospital who swears that the lives of her children were under threat if she didn't leave Steven Walker a fatal dose of pills, arranged into the shape of an inverted pentagram. What do you make of that?"

Gregson's eyes closed and he shook his head.

"You don't know what you're talking about," he said dully.

"So, tell us!" Ryan exclaimed. "Tell us why you ran from the hospital, Arthur."

Gregson surveyed the two men who had served under his command and felt his life slipping away from him. For a while, hope had bloomed again that he might yet walk away from this nightmare. The Circle was finished; he knew that much. First, the junior members amongst its ranks had succumbed to the threat of imprisonment and, once one person deviated, the rest followed. Soon, Ryan's team had uncovered the underground tunnels, the old papers stashed at Freeman's home and they were starting to understand the breadth of the Circle's reach in terms of financing. They had barely scratched the surface there.

And yet, he could tell from the speculative lines of questioning that they still did not understand who had really killed the Circle's most recent leaders; who had toppled the dominoes until everything they had built together lay wasted in front of them.

Gregson huffed out a laugh. It was all so devastatingly simple.

"I didn't kill any of them," he repeated.

* * *

During a break, Ryan sipped at a can of *Diet Coke* while he surveyed Gregson and his lawyer through the viewing panel next door.

"He's obstinate," Morrison commented.

Ryan nodded.

"It's surprising," he was forced to admit. "I pressed him on his behaviour at Bamburgh and the admissions he made up there but he's completely clammed up. It's like he's accepted his fate and isn't bothering to argue any longer. The information we have so far suggests that the murders of Walker and Mathieson were ordered by Freeman rather than Gregson. The same probably applies to Cathy Gregson too but I wanted to see his reaction to the accusation all the same. We already have more than enough evidence to secure convictions based on his involvement in numerous historic crimes, all helpfully recorded in the old papers we have uncovered."

"A jury is bound to find him guilty of some, if not all, of those charges," Morrison stated. "He's going to spend the rest of his life behind bars whether or not he admits any involvement in the more recent killings." She looked through the glass partition and watched a man she had known for years about to be stripped of his identity and felt no qualms about it. Like Ryan, she believed in justice for the dead.

"I'd like to know where Donovan buried the bodies of those girls," MacKenzie said, from across the room. "They're still missing."

"We can ask, but he's unlikely to tell us even if he knows," Phillips said, sadly.

There was another pause, while they collectively grieved for the loss of eleven young women who had hardly lived at all.

"It's frustrating that he keeps denying any involvement in the deaths of Bowers and Freeman," said Ryan. "Despite the information we've received from other former members of the Circle, we haven't been able to find anything solid to link him or anyone else to their deaths."

"They ended up prosecuting Al Capone for tax evasion, didn't they?" commented Lowerson. "Maybe we just have to accept that all we can do is put him away on the basis of all these combined smaller charges."

"Unless—"

Heads swivelled to look at Ryan as he thought aloud.

"What if Gregson is telling us the truth, at least partly? Phillips? Hand me the file with the artist's impression, will you?"

He accepted the file containing the sketch of the person Anna had seen during her evening at Heavenfield Church. MacKenzie moved quickly to look over his shoulder.

"This isn't Gregson," Ryan said, matter-of-factly. "Anna would surely have recognised him. Who is it, and what can they tell us?"

CHAPTER 30

Heavenfield Church gleamed brightly in the early afternoon sunshine as Ryan and his team walked the gentle incline towards its doors, which stood open to a small gathering of foreign visitors who enjoyed the peace that such a restful spot could bring. Wild flowers bloomed over the fertile soil and there was hardly a breath of wind to spoil the easy atmosphere.

Inside the church, they found Keith Thorbridge scrubbing away after the CSI team had given him the green light to tidy up the interior and return things to normal. While the others waited at the rear, Ryan stepped forward with MacKenzie in tow. A flagstone creaked as he approached and Ryan noticed that a woven cloth had been draped over the altar, presumably to hide the remaining blood stains.

Thorbridge turned at the sound of the stone creaking and rose to his feet, holding a bottle of detergent and a soapy cloth in each hand like a mitre and crosier.

"You again?"

MacKenzie ignored the animosity and held out her warrant card.

"You remember me, Keith? I'm DI MacKenzie and this is DCI Ryan."

"Oh, aye, the one who's in all the papers," he mocked.

Ryan found himself warming to the short, prickly man with an obsessive love of cleaning.

"They do love a pretty face," he agreed, and thought he saw an answering twinkle in Thorbridge's beady eyes.

MacKenzie gestured around the small church. "The place is looking good, Keith," she said with a smile which didn't quite reach her eyes. "I'll bet you're glad to have all those devil-worshippers out of the way, eh?"

"Don't know what you mean."

"The thing is, Keith, we went ahead and got a warrant to look around your house while you were gone," Ryan said. "We found your box of secrets."

Thorbridge turned a hitherto undiscovered shade of red and Ryan stared at him in fascination.

"Got no *right* to poke around a man's personal things!"

"I didn't read the letter from Sheila," Ryan held his hands up. "Promise."

"We did notice your notes on the Circle," MacKenzie said swiftly, then waited for the old man to speak up.

Sun beamed through the stained glass windows, casting rainbow hues over the flagstones and Thorbridge lifted his face to the light, basking in the rays.

"Aye, I'm glad they're gone," he said softly. "Heard all about it on the news."

"How did you know their names, Keith?"

"Put it together after watching the news, like I said."

"Did you snoop on them, Keith? Did you see Patrick Donovan killing those women?"

"Never saw no killing," Thorbridge muttered angrily. "Knew something was amiss, though, and saw him leaving afterwards."

"Why didn't you say something? Why didn't you report it?"

Thorbridge shuffled his feet.

"Didn't know what they might do," he admitted, fear shining in his wrinkled brown eyes. "I didn't want much. I only wanted to be able to look after this place," he looked around him and Ryan felt compassion stir in his chest. Love was shining from Thorbridge's leathery face. "Didn't know what to do. Then that one—Bowers—died, and they started dropping like flies."

"Did you kill Mark Bowers?" MacKenzie had to ask.

Thorbridge looked hurt.

"I done lots of things in my time, not all of them good. But I never killed no-one."

"You saw Anna though, didn't you?" Ryan threw the question at him, to catch him off guard, and Thorbridge shifted his attention to him.

"Don't know anyone called Anna."

"The woman you scared half to death that night up here in the church," Ryan added, helpfully, and noticed Thorbridge's eyes fritter away, somewhere in the distance.

"Feel badly about that," he admitted.

"What were you looking for, Keith? What was on the wall?" Ryan pointed a finger towards the wall directly facing the altar.

Thorbridge said nothing but his eyes strayed tellingly towards a large chip on the surface of the limestone. Ryan followed his gaze and turned to trace a finger over the chipped stonework, which looked fresh.

"Was this what you were looking at?"

"The wall is damaged!" Thorbridge complained. "It's one thing to bleed all over the place, that can be mopped up, but chipping the old stonework—"

Ryan's dark brows dipped and MacKenzie gave him a questioning nudge as she came to stand beside him and stare at the chip, hoping that it would give her the answers.

"What is it? What am I missing?"

Ryan pushed his hands in his pockets and smiled to himself, appreciating the game, the forethought, the planning. He may not have liked the man for the harm he had caused, but he could appreciate a good mystery.

"We've been missing something right under our noses," he said, then dipped down to the floor, indicating that MacKenzie should step back a couple of paces.

He felt around for the loose flagstone and lifted it upwards to reveal a hollow space beneath, like a roughly hewn well, several feet deep. He reached for his phone and turned it to the torch setting, shining it inside. Intrigued, Phillips and Lowerson abandoned their football chat and moved to join them.

There, deep in the darkness, lay an antique duelling pistol. A clear plastic bag was attached to the grip, to prevent powder residue transferring onto the hand of the man who discharged it. A thin rope was tied firmly around the butt of the weapon, and a heavy weight was attached to the other end of the rope. Beside them, they could just make out the other half of the wooden ice lolly stick.

“I don’t understand,” Phillips said. “How did the pistol get down there? Did somebody dispose of it?”

Ryan let the flagstone fall back into place for the moment and stood up again, rubbing an absent hand against his healing stitches, which were starting to itch.

“Bowers took care of everything,” Ryan explained. “Down to the finest detail. He set up his own suicide to look like murder, implicating me in the first instance because—well, he hated my guts.”

Four faces nodded awkwardly.

“My guess is that Bowers sent me that text message from somewhere near Gregson’s house using an unregistered phone. That was his first pointer towards Gregson but he also wanted me to suffer for a while, probably because of Anna. I got the girl, you see.”

“Standard motive,” Phillips pronounced.

“He had a tumour, so he knew he didn’t have long for the world and he wanted to leave a legacy—as the High Priest who brought down his own Circle from beyond the grave. He collected that weapon from the auction house, posing as Daniel Mathieson, and used it to put a hole in his own head.”

“If Bowers killed himself, how did the pistol find its way under that flagstone?” Lowerson asked, with a suspicious glance in Thorbridge’s direction.

“Clever trick using a weighted rope,” Ryan provided. He thought of their shared love of Conan-Doyle and smiled at the man’s audacity. “He made sure the pistol was weighted down and the rope was pulled taut, so that when his hand fell away after discharge, it would ping away from him as the weight fell. He used a wooden ice lolly stick to prop open this flagstone where he’d found or dug a hole fairly deep underneath. When the pistol sprang out of his hand, it smacked against the wall and chipped the stonework before it was pulled underneath the flagstone. The lolly stick was knocked aside as the pistol was pulled down and it snapped in half under the weight of the falling flagstone, as we know.”

“Conceited of him to think it would work,” MacKenzie snorted, but had to admit she was mildly impressed that it had. “How did he know there was a dug-out hole, under there?”

Ryan cast his eyes downward, his own version of prayer.

"It's been there a while, I think." There were other things down there, mixing with the scent of decay. "I could be wrong, but I think we haven't just found Donovan's kill site, we've also found what remains of his victims."

They fell silent, a mark of respect.

"I think it's awfully convenient that we haven't been able to come up with any CCTV evidence whatsoever, throughout our investigations," Ryan went on, after a minute. "Not at the post office where Gregson was supposed to have sent that package, not at 17 Haslemere Gardens and not at the auction house. The administrators told us that the cameras were working just fine until recently."

"Freeman made sure that Bowers' tracks were covered?" Lowerson suggested.

"Precisely," Ryan agreed. "I think we might find that Bowers picked botulinum as his poison of choice as an ironic two fingers to his former flame, Jane Freeman. It's the protein used in tiny quantities to make up the Botox compound. I expect he added the cyanide just to make sure she got a lethal dose."

"They normally mix a very small quantity of the powdered botulinum with another solution. Freeman's beauty salon reported the loss of a sachet of powdered botulinum to the authorities less than a month ago," MacKenzie had done her homework.

"Twisted sense of humour," Phillips muttered.

"We can't prove it yet, but I strongly suspect Bowers sent that package to Freeman by courier with a postponed delivery date and registered Gregson as the sender, to set him up. He stole the botulinum and prepared the envelope. The pathologist said he found glue residue on Bowers' hands, didn't he?"

MacKenzie and Lowerson nodded.

"But he couldn't have managed the rest—what about Gregson's wife, Walker and Mathieson?"

"Freeman must have arranged that," Ryan shrugged. "We know that she tried to have Gregson killed in hospital and that she ordered the attack on me." They had already heard the confessions of several young police constables and a junior doctor who had turned up the other day seeking police protection from the Circle.

"Perhaps Freeman and Bowers made a deal of some kind on the basis that Gregson would be removed, with me as the bonus prize. Freeman could never have anticipated what Bowers already had in store for her or that he double-crossed her."

"Whoever heard of a man killing people from beyond the grave?" asked MacKenzie. "It's a fantastic notion."

"Some might say, folk like Freeman and Gregson, they had it coming to them," Phillips scratched his ear uncomfortably.

"No good wastes of space," Thorbridge agreed soundly and they all turned startled eyes in his direction, having forgotten he was still there.

They stood for a long moment, considering the ramifications of what they had discovered under the flagstones of Heavenfield. They thought of the ones who had died and the families who lived on; of the people who had been terrorized for generations by a band of men and women who had risen above the law.

Ryan jiggled his car keys.

"It'll take weeks to tie up all the loose ends but it looks like we're finally going to be able to close these files."

He looked around the simple church and thought of its history.

"It's funny," he murmured. "Men died here fighting for what they thought was right. The Circle tried to sully it, to claim back the land. But, you know what?"

He shook his head in wonder.

"The land doesn't belong to anybody. It's seen good and bad times, light and darkness. It'll still be here long after we're gone," he said softly, then shook himself. "But, until then, Phillips has got paperwork to fill out and I need to find something sparkly and expensive."

Phillips scowled.

"Paperwork?"

Ryan grinned, then turned and walked back outside into the light.

AUTHOR'S NOTE

The landscape of Northumberland is truly unique and has attracted many thousands of visitors over the years. In writing the DCI Ryan series of mysteries, I have always tried to remain authentic in my descriptive passages of some of the best loved parts of the region. This is equally true of *Heavenfield*, where I have endeavoured to stay loyal to the character of St. Oswald's Church and Bamburgh Castle, that mighty fortress by the sea.

From time-to-time it has been necessary to embellish the layout of the castle or the church to fit the fictional story and enhance the reader's experience. However, for the most part, readers choosing to visit any of the sites mentioned in this book should find them very similar to the descriptions herein and well worth seeing for yourself.

As a final point to note, the inclusion of a cult 'Circle' is entirely a work of fiction. To my knowledge, there is no such circle in existence and visitors needn't worry that they will receive anything other than a very warm welcome from the people of the North-East.

LJ ROSS

25th February 2016

ABOUT THE AUTHOR

Born in Newcastle-upon-Tyne, LJ Ross moved to London where she graduated from King's College London with undergraduate and postgraduate degrees in Law. After working in the City as a regulatory lawyer for a number of years, she realised it was high time for a change. The catalyst was the birth of her son, which forced her to take a break from the legal world and find time for some of the detective stories which had been percolating for a while and finally demanded to be written.

She lives with her husband and young son in the south of England, but will always be a northern girl at heart.

If you enjoyed *Heavenfield*, please consider leaving a review online.

The next book in the DCI Ryan series is due to be released in late 2016. If you would like to be kept up to date with new releases from LJ Ross, please complete a contact form on her Facebook page or website, www.ljrossauthor.com.

ACKNOWLEDGMENTS

Writing the DCI Ryan series has been both a pleasure and a revelation. When I left a legal career, I never imagined that writing could bring so much joy, or that I could come to care so much about the characters I have created. I am even more humbled to know that there are so many readers out there who have enjoyed the series so far, many of whom have taken the trouble to send me an e-mail, drop me a line on Facebook or leave a kind review on Amazon. I am so grateful to them for their unstinting support and for understanding my kooky sense of humour.

The process of writing a story, even one that you enjoy, can have its ups and downs and I am thankful to my family and friends for putting up with my 'creative mood swings'! How mortifying to think that I have conformed to the writer's stereotype! Special thanks go to my husband, James, and my son, Ethan. Two blue-eyed darlings who keep me smiling even through the writer's block. Special thanks also to my mum, my dad and my sister, whose support and confidence in LJ Ross has been amazing.

A number of other individuals have offered their expertise and assistance with particular elements of the story so that it remains authentic, albeit a work of fiction. In no particular order, many thanks to: George Pask for his forensic insights; to Roger Clegg for his image of Heavenfield Church which graces the cover of the book; to the curators of Bamburgh Castle; to Liz Hands; to Jon Elek and Millie Hoskins; to the team at Audible; to Jonathan Keeble for his wonderful narration of the previous two books and his forthcoming voice talents in *Heavenfield*; and as always, to the wonderful Geordie girls.

Finally, most particular thanks go to Jim Kitson—my dad—for his location scouting and evocative description of *Heavenfield* which provided the inspiration for this book.

Made in the USA
Middletown, DE
06 November 2019

78053145R00158